
LOVE TEST

Love doesn't test, but people do.

HOLLY MANNO

D1603417

fraud(pr)ess
hollymanno.com

ISBN: 978-1-7337869-2-8 Paperback
ISBN: 978-1-7337869-3-5 Ebook

This is a work of fiction. Names, characters, businesses, places, events, locales, and incidents are either the products of the author's imagination or used in a fictitious manner. Any resemblance to actual persons, living or dead, or actual events is purely coincidental.

fraud(pr)ess
All rights reserved.
©2019 Holly Manno
www.hollymanno.com

for Boo, Lil, Mo & Mi,
The kids who jumped on the train and the brightest part of their love.
xo
Mamo

1

Chaos

Lanie sat at the kitchen table, starring out the large bay window that over looked a well-maintained back yard. The roses were in bloom, reaching to their full height. Their colorful heads stretched tall, extending toward the few remaining days of hot summer sun. It was the middle of August, and in a matter of weeks the sunshine would be replaced by the haze and smattering of showers that Portland, Oregon, was most known for. Today, however, overcast skies seemed light years away.

Half in a trance, she became aware of a screeching sound. A not so distant car desperately needed a brake job. Kids music blasted from the TV and the banging of pots and pans against wooden floors was impossible to miss. Hearing Audrey's voice brought her out of her reverie and into the moment.

"Lanie, are you listening to me? Lanie?" Audrey's voice was becoming shrill.

She looked up at her best friend. Audrey's brown hair was disheveled from raking her hands through it. Her bright blue eyes were a little dark underneath from the lack of sleep. She thought the person before her was quite a different version from the Audrey of a few years ago. That was before marriage and babies. She marveled that even in oversized sweat pants and a messy pony tail, her friend still looked beautiful. When they were younger and single, men would flock to her. Often it felt like a curse having such a man magnet as a friend, but Lanie could never be jealous. She loved Audrey like a sister.

"Sorry Aud, I guess I zoned out for a minute."

With a snort of sarcasm, Audrey replied, "You're just like Ron, blocking everything out. Seems to me you're ready to get married." Lanie observed a slant at the corners of her mouth as she continued, "You've already got your man ears."

Chuckling, Lanie apologized. "Sorry, I was listening, well I meant to. I guess I am in my head today. I have to admit; this scene scares me a little."

Audrey surveyed the room. There were stuffed animals strewn about and a diaper bag on the floor. Its contents had been pulled out one by one, thanks to little Lee. In the corner, a baby swing moved to and fro as infant Lily dozed.

"What are you trying to say? Is my life not glamorous enough for you?" Her tone was joking, yet with the slightest hint of hurt feelings.

"No, that's not it. I'm really putting my foot in my mouth. I don't know what's gotten into me lately."

Unable to stop herself, she continued in a soft tone, "Do you ever miss it?" Lanie's green eyes drilled into hers. "Working, I mean. You were on your way to being a corporate big shot when you and Ron got married. I know Lee arrived a little sooner than you expected, and then Lily a year and a half later; do you ever miss the life you had before all this?"

2

Audrey turned her coffee mug around and around. Her delicate hands circled the base of the cup. She stopped to examine her wedding band and her eyes met Lanie's.

"There are days when I romanticize my former life. I loved getting dressed up for work, and I do miss wearing my signature MAC red. It was such a rush, preparing for important meetings, and flying in to land the deal—don't get me started on the travel perks. But then I remember the other side of it. The work was challenging, and the paychecks were sweet, but there was something anti-climactic about it. I'd make a big sale, and before the ink even dried I'd start wondering how I would do it again next month. There was a lot of pressure."

"You're happy with your life changes, then"—Lanie paused—"even with all the diapers and the crying?"

She finished her sentence and as if on cue, two-year-old Lee took a spill. He landed on hands and knees, and began wailing. The ruckus caused Lily to jerk in the swing; her eyes opened, but she settled back down, thank goodness.

Audrey stood and scooped little Lee into her arms. Placing him back on his feet, she kissed his chubby little hands and comforted him. "Now pick yourself up and dust yourself off 'cause life is going to send you worse, little man." She tapped his perfect nose and smiled into those big blue eyes.

Only moments ago his eyes were swimming with unspent tears, now they were beaming back at his mother. "Okay, Mamma," said Lee in his deliberate baby voice, and off he went to sit in front of the TV.

Lanie had witnessed this little ritual and quote a dozen times before. It always amazed her that it worked, causing Lee's tears to dry up.

Resuming her seat, Audrey continued to talk. "I

wouldn't change anything. Ron and these cuties are my world. Sure, there are times when I feel like a nag, or a dairy cow"—she was still nursing Lily who was only five months old—"but this life is more fulfilling than my career ever was."

Audrey studied her best friend, whose full lips were set in a straight line and her eyes downcast. Lanie looked even tinier than usual, like a little ballerina with very big hair. She waited a beat then ventured, "What's bothering you?"

Lanie took a deep breath, her eyes resting on the salt and pepper shakers before her. She noticed grains of salt littering the shiny dark wood and contemplated aloud, "I guess I'm a little afraid of losing myself. I mean, look at you—one day you were jet-setting to Dallas, New York, or California, closing deals and smiling all the way. Now I see you with the babies, dying to get adult time, and cursing Ron for his career."

"You know I don't mean it. Sometimes I need to vent. You forget that I had plenty to bitch about when I had my big career. I had a love-hate relationship with the travel. Worse was the pressure to produce or be fired, all while tiptoeing around the 'men's teepee.' This may not appear to be an ambitious role"—Audrey waved her hand around the messy room—"but for me, nothing is more important."

Lanie smiled, but her eyes remained distant. Audrey took the silence as an opportunity to continue.

"You know you don't have to change to be James' wife. Once you have kids things will change, but you'll have time to adjust. Trust me, when it happens, nothing will be more important or make you happier."

Lanie took a deep breath before responding, "I know you're right. My mom has said the same, only . . ."

"Only what?" Audrey pressed.

"Only, look at my mom. I've watched her over the

years. We were always her priority and, in a sense, she lost herself. She's only recently regained her identity after thirty years of serving her family."

Lanie's expression went from serious to nearly blank. The transformation was interesting, as if something in her had resigned.

"Breathe." Audrey touched her hand. "It's going to be great. James is a good guy. He is different from your father. You won't need to serve him. He knows how to take care of himself. You love him and he adores you. Relax and enjoy this time, even the uncertainty."

Lanie sighed. "I'm sorry for moping and carrying on about this. Maybe I am having cold feet . . ." her voice trailed off. "After all, I'm not the best at making permanent commitments. I guess James isn't either. It isn't meaningless that, I'm thirty-four and he's thirty-seven and neither of us has even lived with a significant other."

Audrey exhaled before speaking. "Lanie, I've known you a dozen years and in all that time, I've noticed two things about you. Are you ready to hear them?"

Her smile let Lanie know she was in for it. "I am."

"Number one, you are the most analytical and risk-averse artist I've ever known."

Lanie snorted. "Great, can't wait for number two."

Undeterred, Audrey continued, "And number two, you have the power to manifest whatever you want. Since I've known you, you've had the ability of creating exactly what you envision. If you want your super power to work, you've got to let go of the fear and focus on the dream.

"Think about your situation for a minute. The gallery is doing fabulous. Your work is sought after, and you've got artists desperate to have their work displayed at your studio. James encourages your independence. He's not going to take anything from you. The choice to lose yourself is yours. If you think I lost myself, you're wrong. It took Ron and these two little monsters to show me who I was."

Audrey lowered her voice, "Try not to worry so much and don't feel it's not right because you're having these thoughts. It's normal to look behind you when a major change is ahead. You have been taking your sweet time, but remember what I always say—"

Lanie lifted her gaze and interrupted, "I know, I know, beautiful things never hurry."

Audrey always knew what to say. Her words resonated and gave Lanie the kick in the ass she needed. "Will you forgive me, Audrey? I'm sorry if anything I said offended you. Ron is amazing. Lee and Lily are so precious. Of course, you're happy beyond words. I am an idiot."

Audrey rose and put her arms around her dearest friend. To lighten the mood, she teased, "I think the remedy to this whole thing is a wild bachelorette party. What do you say?"

The two laughed, causing Lily to wake and announce her presence with a balls-out scream.

2

Confucius Says... Take the Test

After leaving Audrey's house, Lanie took the MAX and got off at the NW Glisan exit. From there the walk home was just over a mile. It was five thirty and James would be at her place by seven, so she had the time.

The evening was warm and she wanted to soak up as much sunshine as possible. As she strolled through the Alphabet District, her skin was dappled by the brilliant rays that filtered through the already changing leaves.

She thought about the seasons. They were like recurring bookmarks defining chapters of time. This gave her pause, and she contemplated everything else that was changing. Her life was about to shift. Within three weeks' time she would become James Roberts' wife. What a strange idea that was. In the old days it would have meant she officially belonged to him, like property.

She shook her head and admonished herself in a silent rant. Determined to snap out of the mind-numbing thought process that dominated her every waking moment, she opened the door to her favorite Chinese restaurant.

The brass chime announced her arrival and she was greeted by the owner, Charlie.

"Ah, Lanie, where you been, girl? I haven't seen you in weeks. Must be cheating on me with that Thai Palace, aye?"

Though Charlie had been in the U.S. for more than twenty years, his accent was still discernible. With a soft chuckle, she replied, "Yep, Charlie, you busted me. I've been eating fresh rolls instead of your delicious fish soup."

Charlie, never without a good retort, said, "I knew it. I'm going call inspection department on them. Then we see how much business he take."

They both laughed.

As her order was being boxed, he kept the conversation going. "So, how the wedding plans? I did not received my bachelor party invitation. Did James somehow forgot to include ol' Charlie?"

Lanie gave a half-hearted snort and Charlie noticed. "Whatsa matter, Lanie? Everything's okay with the wedding?"

Upset with herself, she realized she'd been transparent with her thoughts. Quick to rebound, she said, "No, everything is fine; great, actually. We are coming down to the last weeks, and it is all falling into place."

As she finished speaking, Nancy, Charlie's wife who handled the finances for the business, entered the room. She commanded, "Charlie, go check on the egg rolls. That new boy is having hard time with fryer."

He grumbled under his breath, something undecipherable. With his eyes to the ground, he marched back to the kitchen.

"Lanie, I see in your eyes. You have the cold feet, yeah?"

Lanie tried for a smile but with Nancy there was no

point. She was like a bloodhound when she got on a trail—a bloodhound with beautiful black hair. Sniffing out even the slightest hint of trouble, Lanie was met by her most observant stare. "It's really great, Nancy." She flinched. "I guess I am a little . . . um . . ." She couldn't find the words.

"Very normal, Lanie. Before I marry Charlie, I was awake three whole nights thinking if it was right."

Waving her hands for emphasis she continued, "He not the most handsome man, and he have thin lips, but he brought me flowers every week when we were courting. Does James bring you flowers?"

Lanie found herself comforted by the simplicity of her words. "Yes, he does bring me flowers."

"Good, good, then nothing to worry about. Unless Charlie gets invite to that bachelor party, then you can go to Thai Palace for now on."

Lanie and Nancy laughed in time for Charlie's return with her complete takeout order.

———

SHE INPUT the code and opened the door to the 1920s red brick building and moved through the lobby. After taking the stairs to her fourth-floor unit, Lanie went inside. It wasn't large, but the twelve-foot ceilings and wall of glass made the condo feel spacious. The windows—though not energy efficient, something that troubled James—were her favorite feature. Not only was the treetop view fantastic, but the space was flooded with natural light, even during the grey months.

The furniture combined modern and well-worn vintage. Each room had its own style, with the priority of art as the major focus. The walls were white, to serve that purpose.

Being an artist herself, she had a difficult time choosing any specific medium. Above the sofa was a mixed media piece. The artist had incorporated branches, jewels, and of all things, a hammer. The rest of her collection included smaller pieces, some political in nature.

Her favorite was a sketch she bought from a local street artist. The picture was a head shot of a brunette woman, done in black charcoal against an ivory backdrop. The dramatic color exception was a large red scarf that covered the subject's mouth, making the message overt.

Inside the doorway stood a carved wooden coat rack. She hung her purse and moved past the dining area toward the kitchen. She had enough time to change and pour a glass of wine before James arrived.

Pausing in the dining room, she straightened a few magazines on the 1950s Formica table, and pushed the similar-era chairs into line. The sun reflected through a crystal vase, lighting the myriad of glass beads it held. The result cast a rainbow of sparkles that danced around the room.

A low, honey-colored buffet sat against the wall. Inside was an assortment of dishware that Lanie had collected over the years. She enjoyed buying individual pieces and preferred the unique to matching sets. This was a point of discussion with James as they planned their reception. Well, not so much with him, but his parents weighed in on the topic. They preferred uniformity while Lanie gravi-tated toward unexpected combinations.

With the dining area in shape, she continued into the modern kitchen. Setting the bag of food on the counter, she removed the boxes and placed them into the oven on warm mode. Taking a bottle from the rack, she selected a local pinot noir for the night. After opening the bottle so it could breathe, she went to the bedroom to change.

As she made her way down the hall, Lanie stopped at the doorway of the second bedroom. The room's purpose had not been a bedroom since she moved in; instead it was her sanctuary. She would often settle into the burnt-orange Papasan chair to read, and sometimes she would paint in this room. The light didn't compare to the dining room since this side of the building was west facing, but the afternoon sun was vibrant here, if only for a while.

Lanie knew she would miss her home once she and James moved into his house in the Southeast side of town and rented out the condo. Though she hadn't found a tenant yet, she was certain it wouldn't be a problem. With the wedding plans, and work being so busy, she'd not put a lot of effort into advertising it. The first few people who were interested didn't seem right. She told herself that once the dust settled, she would resume marketing.

Realizing she'd paused long enough, she continued down the hall to her bedroom. This room was unlike the others. It was spacious and dim. The walls were done in a soothing beige grey with bed linens to match. She walked to the windows and straightened the velvet curtains, adjusting the bottoms until they pooled neatly on the floor. Next, she smoothed the silk duvet and pulled her robe from the corner of the creamy headboard.

She made a sharp right into her spa-like bathroom and hung the robe behind the door. For this space she'd gone with a monochromatic feel. The floors and counters were travertine and the cabinets a pewter color. Several small windows and a large skylight flooded the room with natural light.

Continuing past the shower, she entered the large walk-in closet. Lanie scanned the options before choosing her favorite navy-blue jersey dress. It hung to the ground and was one of her most comfortable articles of clothing. After changing, she tugged her hair into a lazy bun and finished with a spritz of her signature vanilla perfume.

HE CAME through the door with a relaxed smile on his face. His dark, wavy hair was a mess, as were the khakis and the blue Oxford he wore. Hanging over his shoulder was the messenger bag Lanie gave him on his last birthday, number 37.

She had to suppress a look of panic when she noticed he held a lovely summer bouquet. The flowers made her flash back to her conversation with Nancy at the restaurant. *He does bring me flowers*, she thought.

James couldn't contain himself a second longer. In one step, he closed the distance between them. Wrapping his arms around her, he squashed her arms to her sides. Stooping down to reach he took her lips with repeated pecks. Between each kiss, he whispered, "Hi." Finally, he pulled himself back, and held eye contact. A fiendish smirk was on his face. One last "hi" and his mouth consumed hers.

Lanie melted into his green eyes and wondered what on earth her problem was. He could be a model or an actor, he was so good-looking. His frame was lean and he was the perfect amount of tall, six foot on the dot. When he and Lanie were out together they were often noticed. People stopped to watch the tall, dark, and handsome man and his fairy-size lady. He looked like the panther while she could be perceived as a doe.

James released his grip and stepped back. He looked her up and down with a sly smirk on his face. "Three more weeks, woman"—he paused for dramatic effect—"three more weeks until you are mine."

As if to emphasize, he shoved the bouquet toward her. Lanie reached for the flowers, automatically raising them to her nose. They smelled sweet and clean.

"They're beautiful, James. Thank you." For a flash, she considered telling him about her conversation with Nancy, but realized it would be hard to explain. She refrained. Reaching for normalcy, instead asked, "How was your day?"

Lanie went to the kitchen while James dropped his messenger bag on the floor. "It was great. We heard back on the City of Portland project. Guess who won the solar contract for the next ten years?"

Lanie ran from the kitchen, with two glasses of pinot noir in hand. She handed one to James then raised her glass in toast. "Here's to all your hard work and wanting to do the right thing. Congratulations, honey, I'm so happy for you." Their glasses clinked. After a sip, Lanie could feel the soft notes of pepper and earth tickling her taste buds.

James settled himself into the deep linen sofa. "Yes, and this win is not only great on its own but it puts O-NRG on the map for future projects of this scale. I'm sure it will strengthen our position for the MAZE contract that's coming."

"James, I really am proud of you. This project has taken you years to win. You must be on top of the world! Have you told your parents yet? What about Dave Junior? Does he know?"

James' parents, David and Susan Roberts, lived in Marin County. Ironically, David Roberts Sr. was an attorney who made his fortune representing the interests of oil companies. Here, the apple did fall far from the tree. James, the younger of the two Roberts boys, drove a Nissan Leaf and worked in alternative energy, much to the family's confusion. His brother, David Jr., worked with their dad at the firm. As a result, the family rarely spoke of their professional lives.

"Ha, ha, ha." James snorted with an obvious amount of sarcasm. "I'm not sure how excited Dad or David will be to learn of my success, but Mom will have something nice to say— that is until she segues into something wedding related. I could use a little breather from that today."

It was Friday and for once, the two had no wedding errands to run or decisions to make. It had been such a challenge attending to the details, but they were finally closing in on the big day.

James reached his arms around Lanie's waist, pulling her off of her feet and onto his lap. The second she landed, James' mouth sought hers. Lanie was definitely not as demonstrative as he, but in this moment, she liked the comfort of his advances. She could always count on him to close any gaps between them. Their kiss was interrupted by the stove buzzing. Lanie pulled herself up and walked toward the kitchen. Though reluctant to let her go, to substitute James grabbed his glass of wine and settled back into the couch to watch her exit.

"Are you hungry?" she called from behind the partitioned wall.

"Um-hum," he said in a slow drawl, "but I may need to have a long, leisurely dessert after dinner." Lanie poked her head around the corner in time to see James grab the TV remote. The sound of CNN reporting live, from this place or that, could be heard in the background.

"I guess you'd like to make it a TV dinner night?" There was no reply from James, which she half expected. Lanie put their plates together and carried them into the living room. James perked at her return, and they ate dinner as Anderson Cooper filled them in the on the day's events.

At the first commercial break, James said, "So, you haven't told me much about your day. I know you had Jay handle the gallery this afternoon so you and Audrey could talk about the bachelorette party." He sounded miffed as he asked, "How did that go?"

Lanie had to chuckle. He was worried about the bachelorette party, and she was worried about getting married. Oh god, did she just admit that to herself?

Pulling it together, she smiled and tried to soothe James. "We spent very little time discussing the bachelorette party. You know how visiting her is, the kids as usual were awake and completely needy so we didn't have a lot of time to talk. It was great to see them though. Audrey seems happy."

———

HE NOTICED something in Lanie's tone and turned to look, but she was focused on the TV commercial. She appeared to be entranced by one of those lovetest.love advertisements. It was another internet dating site promising the perfect match.

"Ahem." James tried for Lanie's attention. When that didn't shake her from the screen he spoke up. "Excuse me, but I have to shield your eyes from that commercial. You are nearly a married woman."

He crossed the room and stood in front of the TV. This brought her eyes to meet his. That's when he realized something might really be wrong. He made his way to her seat in the chair and kneeled in front of her. "Lanie, is everything all right?"

RUNNING her fingers through his soft, dark locks, she replied, "Of course it is, but did you see that commercial? What a neat idea."

James shook his head as Lanie stood up. "What idea are you talking about?"

"Well, that wasn't the typical lovetest.love commercial. They now have events where pre-selected groups meet socially."

James rose from the floor, a pained expression on his face. "What's so neat about that? I thought the point was to see someone you like, talk to them, and then ask them out, one-on-one. Is it a friendship site or a dating one?"

"They've got some new way of matchmaking. You answer an in-depth questionnaire, like a personality profile. The computer groups people who have high compatibility scores, and assigns them to local mixer events. Everyone meets at a restaurant, or bar, and you see if you're drawn to anyone. They're pairing technology with destiny. Interesting, right?"

James looked at her oddly. "Yeah, it sounds great. Maybe they can start a reality show around the concept." He was having a difficult time understanding her fascination with this idea. "Okay, so what about this is good? You've always said you hate the idea of internet dating. In fact, isn't it you who has said there is nothing romantic about looking at resumes? I can see why people do it, but it's not for me. Am I missing something here?"

Lanie replied, "It's true. I have said that, but this is a little different. First of all, you're not doing the picking, the computer is, and second, you're not going on a date with one person. You're going to a party where there could be dozens of people who you'd get along with." But in that moment, Lanie didn't know why this was so important to her.

It was dawning on James what Lanie wasn't saying. "Hey, you've got cold feet."

"No, it's not that. Well, maybe a little but not in a serious way. Hear me out for a second. We met at a bar, and though no computer designed our encounter, two very good friends may have. If we hadn't both known Audrey and Nick, we wouldn't have met. I spent a long time single back then. People always used to tell me to get online, but I could never bring myself to do it."

"And that's a good thing"—James' eyes pleaded—"because now we have each other."

"That's true, and as for cold feet, I guess our wedding does have me thinking. It is exciting, but also a little scary, don't you think?"

He hesitated. "Sure, Lanie, but I am so much more excited than scared. I'll save my cold sweats until after the bachelor party." He grinned and dodged a glare from his intended. Instead, he pulled her into his arms and turned the visual attack into a bear hug. CNN returned from commercial break, and not a moment too soon. "Good girl." He kissed Lanie on the forehead, and resumed his position on the sofa.

Taking her seat, she asked, "James, do you think we'd be compatible if we filled out the profile test?"

Pursing his lips, he appeared to contemplate. "But of course, my angel. You aren't really concerned, are you?"

Her eyes implored. "No. You're sure, right?"

James always knew what to say. "We are a perfect pair."

Lanie's focus was back on the news, but James couldn't take his eyes off her. She was so beautiful with that full mouth, dark brows and halo of blonde hair. She looked like a doll.

"I have an idea," he announced. Lanie didn't look up. "Why not try it?"

This got her attention. "Try what?"

"Why don't we create profiles to see if we're matched by the system?"

Her expression was incredulous. "After six years of dating, and our wedding three weeks away, you want to set up dating accounts to see if we're compatible?"

"Sure." His reply was a little too matter-of-fact for Lanie to trust.

"You want to do that?"

This time his eyes were affixed to the screen. "Sure, why not? Let's be honest, you belong to me. I have no fear that a computer could change that."

Now it was her turn to smirk. Sometimes James had the same smug confidence she'd witnessed in his father. "You're certain the system will match us?"

"Yep, and I want us to go for it. I think it will be fun, romantic even. Can you imagine the story we'll have to tell our kids and grandkids one day?"

"What? You're flooring me here." Lanie was genuinely surprised.

James' voice was sweet now. "I know that you are my person. You're the one I'm meant to spend my life with. It has taken me a long time to say, and I'm sorry for that. No matter, I know deep down that you belong to me. If creating an online profile and going to a party will allow you to sow one last oat, by all means, let's go for it."

His smile was contagious, and a little overconfident. He egged her on, knowing she wasn't one to walk away from a challenge. "Okay, fine, I'm in." Matching his confidence, Lanie thought logistics. "One thing though"—James' eyebrows shot up at her request—"let's bring Audrey and Nick."

Nick had been James' best friend since junior high school. He appeared confused. "Huh? I don't understand."

"So we don't have to walk into the place alone. You know how much I hate that."

"Sure, but we'll have a hard time explaining to those two the reason we're doing it."

James had a good point. Her wheels were spinning. "It's simple; Nick has obvious commitment issues since he's never kept a girl around longer than a few months. He'll understand wanting to take one last chance."

James thought Lanie was making sense, with one exception. "And what about Audrey?"

Lanie was quick to reply, "I'll tell her you bet me. She knows that I can never walk away from a dare, and that nothing but the truth would ever work between us."

"All righty then." James felt anything but sure. A foreboding tickle ran down his spine, the physical manifestation of his concern. His voice didn't waiver. "I guess this is a challenge?"

From her vantage point, James looked ready to take it on. They met in the middle of the room. James extended his hand and Lanie hers. They shook on it, and the deed was done.

⸺

SUDDENLY, James scooped Lanie over his shoulder and carried her to the bedroom. The windows were open, bringing a glow of light as a gentle breeze tickled the edge of the curtain. He set her to stand, and kneeled at her feet. Clutching the bottom of her dress he moved up the length of her body. His nose grazed her thighs, hips, and belly as he raised the hem. When he reached his full height, he tugged the slinky dress over her head, and it became a puddle on the floor.

Her OCD for matching panties and bras was a quirk James adored. Today she was wearing a blush set. Lacy pink bottoms framed her perfect little V, and her full breasts were caged in a flirty demi cup. Hungry for her, he wanted nothing between them. In one expert snap, her bra joined the dress on the floor. No matter how many times he'd seen her, each time it took his breath away.

Pulling her close, he tantalized her lips with his, and she surrendered. Their soft tongues teased, and touched. Lanie felt a rush of heat for him. Before she got her bearings, he swept her off her feet, and tossed her onto the bed. Running his finger from her throat to her navel, he stepped back to look at her indecent figure.

His expression was savage as he unbuttoned his shirt, revealing toned abdominals. The show continued as he unbuckled his belt and dropped his pants. Uninhibited by his nakedness, he pounced onto the bed.

Capturing Lanie beneath him, he suckled her bottom lip until she moaned. Liking the control, and her submission, he began a slow, tortuous descent down her body. He teased her ear lobe, kissed her neck, and moved to the ticklish flesh of her collarbone. When he reached the pink flesh of her taut nipples, he got close but only blew, moving from breast to breast. This caused Lanie to wiggle. She could feel her panties getting wet.

"Stay still, angel," James cooed. Pinning her shoulders, he administered repeated soft flicks with his tongue. Her breasts rose toward the source of this exquisite assault. Using his thumb and index finger, James pinched her nipples. Then ever so gingerly, he used his teeth to torture her more. She moaned and pressed her pubic bone toward him. He cracked a devilish smile; the waterboarding was nowhere near over. Hooking his thumbs into the sides of her panties, he slid them off. Holding them to his nose, he inhaled before tossing them aside.

Beginning his ascent at her toes, soft kisses littered her instep, ankles, calves, and inner thighs. This sweet agony caused Lanie's back to arch as she thrust her spot forward. James landed kisses all around but held his tongue in reserve.

Her voice was a rasp. "James, please."

At her urging, he blew near her clitoris, causing Lanie to shiver involuntarily. Her juices glistened and he could wait no longer. Finding the perfect entry point, he used his finger to press inside. Aroused by her pliancy, he had to taste her. He removed his finger and buried his face, using every centimeter of his tongue. Her voice was uncontained, and her body stiffened, letting him know he was on the right track.

"James, I want you inside of me."

Her plea was all he needed. In one move, he slid himself up the length of her body and into her. His hands cupped her bottom. Her legs encircled his torso as they pressed forward trying to get even closer. Lanie's nails bit into his shoulders. Their eyes met as they combined rhythm toward one final thrust and both were spinning out of control. They convulsed into euphoria. Gratifying sex sounds filled the air, and a last all-consuming kiss swallowed them into oblivion.

3

Let the games begin.

Saturday mornings at the gallery were usually slow, and today was no exception. Morning light diffused through the floor-to-ceiling windows, illuminating the space. Matte white walls and concrete floors set the tone for the unobscured exploration of art. The exhibit included valuable paintings, two life-size sculptures, and even a couple of jeweled crowns.

Opening the gallery was Lanie's dream. Her parents were less than comfortable with the idea and told her so at every turn. There were times when Lanie herself doubted it would work out. Sheer determination, a love for what she was doing, and three years later, she was turning a nice profit.

As she entered the building she saw her assistant clicking away on his laptop. Until she arrived he was the lone inhabitant of the space. "Good morning, Lanie," announced Jay as he jumped to his feet. "How's the little bride-to-be today?" He walked toward the barista-caliber coffee machine, a beautiful and useful fixture at the back of the gallery. After tapping a couple of buttons on the console, the aroma of freshly brewed espresso filled the air.

"Good morning, Jay. I'm fine." She could hardly wait to tell him about their game of Russian roulette—NOT. Lanie knew how excitable he could be.

He looked gorgeous as usual. His long, lean body moved gracefully as he added the frothed milk to her drink. Pressed Levis paired nicely with the navy and tan oxford he chose for today. Jay was six-two with sandy blonde hair that leaned red. He had the most piercing blue eyes, but the icing on the cake was his wide and beautiful mouth.

Choosing a safe topic, she asked, "Has it been slow since you opened?"

He snorted. "What do you think? It's Saturday. Things will start picking up this afternoon." Jay closed the distance between them and handed her a latte.

"Thank you, kind sir." She smiled and sucked in her first swig of the frothy pick me up.

"I did get a call from Mrs. Anderson, though." Jay let that comment hang in the air. "Mr. Anderson agreed that they must possess the Luc Triane's piece, *Luna*."

Lanie thought her eyes might roll out of her head. The transaction would be the most significant since she opened. "Oh my goodness, Jay!"

Lanie jumped, slopping latte over the edge of the cup and onto the floor.

Jay smiled and went to get a cloth. "I thought you'd like hearing that news."

"Like hearing that news? This is incredible, and I don't mind saying, this was your baby. The way you've worked with Mrs. Anderson for months—you've been so patient each time she's visited the piece. You sealed the deal, and a very fine celebration dinner is in order."

Lanie hugged Jay ferociously and took the towel from his hand. She continued to smile as she mopped up the frothy milk. This transaction would send shock waves through the art world. Now was as good a time as any to address the other shock wave that was about to go out into the universe.

"Well Jay, you aren't the only one who has a surprise today."

He perked up at this statement. "What surprise are you talking about, Lanie?"

She stood, and walking toward the sink, spoke over her shoulder. "The funniest thing happened last night, and now James and I are in a challenge."

Jay wasn't sure what to think so he pressed, "And?"

Lanie smirked and wondered how she would explain. She figured she may as well get it over with. "James and I were watching TV and one of those lovetest.love commercials came on."

Jay's expression was perplexed. "Where is the surprise in that? Those commercials are incessant."

"Surprise is probably not the right word." Her gaze moved to the storefront, and to traffic outside.

Concern raised his voice an octave. "Lanie, what is going on?"

"There was a commercial for a new thing they're doing. You take a profile test, and based on your responses, the algorithm groups you with likely matches. Then, lovetest.love holds a mixer where people with the highest compatibility scores meet. I don't know what I was thinking, but I mentioned to James that I thought it was an interesting idea."

Jay gasped. "Wait a minute; you thought this was a good idea, you who doesn't believe in online dating? What is it you compare it to? Oh yes, studying resumes."

She stiffened. "Yes, I know, but this was a little different."

Lanie grew quiet realizing her explanation would not work with Jay.

"Honey, you've got a case of seriously cold feet." Touching her elbow, he guided her toward a white concrete bench at the center of the space. They sat, and he asked, "What is going on in that head of yours?"

She had expected all kinds of comments from Jay but not the concern he was displaying. "It isn't a big deal, but I'll admit—as I was watching the commercial, I wondered if James and I would be matched. I said as much to him. I know it's silly, but . . ."

Jay knew she was in an unclear space, so wondered aloud, "So, how did James feel about your query?"

She looked up from her shoes. "He was a little concerned at first then he took it in stride. In fact, brace yourself," she warned, "he said we should create profiles to prove we're a match. He was so certain we'd be paired, he couldn't wait to confirm it."

Jay looked panicked. "Lanie, I know you can't back down from a dare, but are you sure you want to take this kind of risk? Your wedding is a few weeks away."

Lanie adjusted her thoughts and face to match. "It's just an experiment, and look at it this way—we will have quite a tale to tell afterwards."

Seeing her determined expression, he knew any further protests were pointless. Resigned, and now very interested in the game, not to mention the outcome, Jay perked up. Taking Lanie's hand he pulled her to stand. "Okay, if you're going to do this, I am getting front row seats."

Now this was the reaction she was expecting. He led her to the computer where they worked up her dating profile. Jay rubbed his hands together like a mouse before picking up a crumb of cheese. His fingers moved effortlessly across the keyboard.

"Okay—lovetest.love . . . set up new profile . . . select algorithm mixer option."

Lanie piped up, "What? It doesn't actually say that, does it?"

A broad smile cracked on Jay's face. "Yes, it actually does." He turned the monitor her direction, and received silence in reply. His eyes were squinted like a sharpshooter about to take his shot. "To be certain the computer does the matching, and not your sexy fiancé, you'll want to be anonymous."

The moment was surreal, and she was having reservations. "Agreed."

"Then you must use an alias. Good thing this site doesn't show a profile picture once you select the mixer option."

Mouth agape, Lanie stared through Jay.

Taking her quiet as a license to carry on, he said, "I am going to pick the perfect profile name for you." He was silent for a fraction of a second then tapped on the keyboard. He proclaimed, "Your name will be Natalie Shane!"

Lanie felt the blood rush from her head.

Jay taunted, "Natalie . . . oh, Natalie . . . earth to Natalie." The man could not contain his excitement. He practically squealed. "Now it's time for the fun stuff, answering the questionnaire."

At that comment, Lanie stood and circled the desk. Shooing Jay away, she commandeered the computer. "This will only be a real experiment if I answer the questions."

A slightly miffed Jay walked to the front door to say hello to a couple of well-timed visitors while Lanie settled in to complete the profile.

IT WAS MONDAY MORNING. The elevator buzzed and the doors opened, but James didn't exit until his co-worker, Luce, snapped him out of his reverie.

"James, you coming in today?" Luce had a questioning look on her face.

Her words woke James from his internal trance and prompted him to exit the car. "Thanks, Luce, guess I'm just a bit distracted."

She smiled and soothed. "It happens to the best of us. Last week you closed the biggest deal in company history and are now at the end of wedding planning. You must be completely overwhelmed."

James offered a half smile in response as the two walked. "Yeah, I am a bit stretched."

"Don't worry," she replied. "It'll be over before you know it. All that work for one day, and it passes in a flash. Well, have a good day."

"You too," he said, and they parted ways, heading for their respective work spaces.

James shared an office with his best friend and co-worker Nick Hawke. The two had known one another since before middle school, when Nick's family moved to Marin, purchasing the house next door. That summer and ever since, the boys were almost inseparable. Navigating the last few paces to the office, he wondered how Nick would react to the strange test he'd gotten himself into.

Rounding the corner, he came face to face with Nick, who was on the other side of the glass wall. He was talking on his headset while practicing his putt. As James entered the office, Nick's deep voice filled the room.

"Yes, James and I will have the value engineering assessment to you by the end of the week as planned.

That's right. I've got to run into a meeting now. You have a good day too." Nick clicked the button at his ear to disconnect, and landed the putt from a good 15′. Smirking and chewing on a tooth pick, he shot a stare in James' direction.

"What's happening, little buddy?"

Though James was no shrimp, his ginger-haired, blue-eyed pal had him by a good 3″and at least 50lbs. The nickname started when they were sixteen and Nick had an ill-timed growth spurt, leaving James temporarily in his dust. The name stuck ever since. James thought it as irksome then as it was today, more than twenty years later.

He looked at his friend and responded, "Not much, dumbass. Was that Guy Chapman on the phone?" James could quickly slip in and out of business mode with his oldest friend.

"Yep, I let him know we are on track. I met with engineering early this morning and confirmed. They'll have the re-design complete by Thursday. The presentation will happen on Friday before we leave town. After that, it's party time."

Nick's face lit up with that last comment. Saturday was the start of bachelor weekend, and he was the best man. This also left him in charge of the bachelor party, a fact that both thrilled and concerned James.

"Good deal. Do they need anything else from me to complete it?" James had been working on the opportunity for nearly a year.

"Nope, I relayed your notes and the redlines from our sessions. Engineering is working on the calculations and new drawings as we speak. I'll meet with the team again on Wednesday for a last review before they finalize, and get us the revision."

"Great work, Nick."

That James complimented without jibe did not escape him. "Hey, is everything ok? You're not getting a hard time from Lanie about the bachelor party, are you? Please don't tell me you are already completely whipped?"

James shrugged and walked toward the windows, taking in the view of downtown Portland. "No, nothing like that."

Nick could feel the mood in the room change when James arrived. He'd known him too long to miss those vibes. "What then?"

James took a deep breath, and turned toward his friend. Leaning both hands on the desk, he shared the events of the previous evening. "This is going to be hard to explain."

For once, Nick was silent.

"On Friday night Lanie and I were having dinner when one of those lovetest.love commercials came on TV and . . ."

Nick tilted his head to one side and waited for James to share the balance of the story.

"Well I'm not sure how it happened, but by the end of the commercial I was challenging Lanie to . . ."

This had Nick's attention. "To what?"

"To see if we'd be matched by the computer."

The comment was as loud as a fart in yoga class. After a moment of silence Nick regained his voice. "Okay, I'm obviously missing something here, or this is a practical joke. You and Lanie are supposed to be getting married in, like, three weeks. The bachelor party is this weekend. You'd better not mess that up." He studied James' face for any signs of levity but found none. "What the hell is going on?"

James sat and Nick did the same, settling into the chair across from him. Nick studied his friend. With the backlight from the windows he was a silhouette. Overpowering the morning light, his black hair and glowing green eyes beamed through.

Unable to remain still, James stood and paced as he tried to reconstruct Friday night's scene. "They have a new approach to dating. It's a computer-generated program that uses an algorithm to pair people based on their responses to a survey. The highest potential matches are invited to mixer events. It's science and 'destiny' combined."

Nick listened and said, "This is just the type of thing you hate doing. Why are you telling me all of this?"

James huffed and resigned to spit it out. "Nick, Lanie and I are going to create profiles to see if the computer matches us."

Silence filled the space between them. One one-thousand, two one-thousand, three one-thousand. It started as a rasp, then a chuckle, until Nick was full-throat laughing. "Ahh ha ha—good one, friend. You got me that time." Nick stood and crossed the room toward his desk. "You had me going, little buddy."

James wasn't in the mood for his verbal weggie. "Nick," he snapped, "I'm serious. It is happening."

James' sharp tone got Nick's response. "What is happening, James?" His expression was doubtful.

Raking his hands through his hair, he started again. "I don't know. We're in a contest, I guess. Lanie was watching the commercial, and said the concept sounded interesting. She wondered if the system would match us. It started as a joke and somehow became a test."

Nick was having a hard time reconciling this information. "You threw down the gauntlet three weeks before your wedding, to see if a computer program finds you compatible? You've been with the girl for five years."

James corrected, "Six. We've been together for six years."

Nick's eyes bulged at his correction. "Even worse, you've been together for six years, and you need a computer to validate the union?"

James was silent so Nick continued. He found himself in unfamiliar territory. "This doesn't sound right. You guys have had your ups and downs, but to tell you the truth, I sort of count on you. If you and she can't pull the trigger, there is no hope for me. Not that I'm interested in that particular noose. What's really going on?"

James thought for a moment, the two had always been transparent with one another. "I don't know, from my standpoint I'm as ready as I'll ever be. I have to say I do wonder how things will change between us. Now, we have our own places. We spend a lot of time together, but we also have the room to do our own thing. I wonder what it will be like accommodating another person full time, and how it might be for her."

He continued, "To be honest I think more about it from her perspective than my own. Lanie has always been more reluctant than me about getting married. She admits it is an issue with her parents. She and I have had many conversations about the way her mother is like an assistant to her dad. She's gun shy because of it. I guess I thought if we did the profile, and we were a match, it would ease her mind once and for all."

Nick had to know. "How will it affect you? If the woman you've asked to marry you requires computerized confirmation, doesn't that concern you? Shouldn't she know deep down in her heart? I mean, she is a chick after all."

James had considered this and told Nick as much. "The truth is, Lanie is worth it. I love her, but I'm not sure that I alone can convince her. I kind of feel like once she sees we are matched, well, everything will be ok."

Nick hated playing the devil's advocate, but it was the elephant in the room. "What if you two aren't matched?"

James hadn't even considered that as an option. After a beat he filled his lungs with false bravado. "Not a chance, friend. With your help, she and I will be confirmed! Will you help me set up the profile?"

Finally, the Eddie Haskell version of his friend showed up. Nick's straight white teeth were framed by a mischievous smile. "Okay, little buddy, if that's what you want, let's land you a wifey."

They put their heads together, completing the profile, and created the pseudo-name Chris Slate.

4

Thoughtful Errands

Between setting up that ridiculous profile and the impromptu meeting with engineering, it had been a hectic morning. James was glad to get out of the office for a while. As he walked the city streets, he was oblivious to the ding of the MAX train and the ladies in the cafe who all but fell from their chairs after seeing him pass. The paint-can drummer's rhythmic beating was a distant backdrop as he contemplated the situation he found himself in.

Thinking back on "the test," and how he handled it, James wondered if he should have done something differently. Instead of suggesting the duel, he should have put his foot down, and told her how jealous the idea made him. It was too late now to second guess his decision.

Normally, he was confident, but relationships were the chink in his armor. Before Lanie, he put little effort into dating. Sure, there were women, and some were around for a while, but his career came first. Eventually, even the light-spirited companions he found grew tired of being a distant second.

Driven by nature and forced by his upbringing, James

knew how crucial it was to have success in life. His father ruled the home, instilling that accomplishment and appearances were everything. Often, he and his older brother were pit against each other, challenged to compete, though there were two years between them. This made him stronger, and it pushed him away.

Growing up he had no choice but to follow "Roberts Law." Once James became an adult he was compelled to forge his own path in life, and career. He could see how his choices were perceived as rebellious. It was his way of breaking free.

As a child, he saw his dad come to the defense of major oil companies, when their spills devastated habitat, and the economies of fishermen. He'd see news reports with images of black liquid suffocating the ocean and marine life, then overhear his father establishing legal strategies to protect the corporations responsible. It was hard for an impressionable child to reconcile.

Though Susan Roberts always displayed a united front, honoring her husband's family leadership, she and James had a special bond. Knowing he was interested, she would take him for hikes and talk to him about the birds and plants. When they went on their adventures, James saw his mom in a different light. She gave him the encyclopedia of animals for his 7th birthday. To this day he still had the book and would read the inscription when he needed a little pep talk. Inside his mother wrote, "James, you can be anything you dream. Soar with the birds and always come home." He adored her, and the feeling was mutual.

His thoughts shifted to Lanie, and how he reacted when they met six years ago. She and a friend walked into the bar, and it was like the movies when all at once everything slows down, and the camera zooms in. His pulse quickened as he remembered the night—an errant curl fell at her cheek, and every man in the place stopped to watch her pass, mesmerized by her petite frame. He was smitten at first sight.

It was a good thing Nick was there. Without him, he might have remained still, as if his legs were filled with cement. True to form, his over-confident friend marched up to the women using his best one liner. He admonished, "It took you two long enough to get here." The women looked at him as though he were an alien.

This snapped James out of his trance and as usual, he came to the rescue. Shaking his head, he placed a hand on his buddy's shoulder. "You'll have to forgive my friend here. He just got out of the psych ward, and still has delusions of grandeur."

This got a chuckle out of the girls, and even Nick.

From that night on, James and Lanie were often found together. They had a relaxed chemistry, sharing a lot of the same ideas about the environment, and the arts. After a while, they met one another's family, and though they were very different, there was an ease between them. James adored everything about Lanie. He wanted her, and he wanted to keep her just as she was. It gave him pause and all at once, a sense of urgency.

He thought again about the root of his angst. Maybe his childhood and Lanie's independent personality made him gun shy? He couldn't imagine taking her light, and had concerns that marriage and motherhood would change her, even make her unhappy. Reservations aside, he couldn't fathom a life without her. His strong traditional upbringing drove him to finally make their commitment official.

He opened the door to the vintage jewelry store, and was greeted by the sing-song voice of the clerk. "Good Afternoon."

James smiled in response. "Hello."

The attractive young woman behind the counter inquired, "What can I help you with today?"

"Well, I'm looking for something special, a wedding gift for my fiancé."

The woman's smile practically expanded onto the walls. Her voice seemed even higher as she began, "How wonderful! When is the big day?"

He answered, "It's just under three weeks away."

The clerk studied James. He was handsome and nervous. With a knowing expression she asked, "Do you have anything in particular in mind?"

James thought about it, but fell short beyond knowing that he wanted to select a vintage jewelry item, and one that included emerald to match her eyes. After sharing this with his host, she nearly exploded out of her skin.

"That is a wonderful idea. I may have just the thing for you." Excusing herself to the back, she returned a moment later with a black velvet box. "I'm Evelyn, by the way."

He smiled in response, extending his hand. "James. Nice to meet you."

He watched as she opened the latch. Her eyes were aglow as she turned the box his direction. Though no expert in gems, even he could see the beauty of the piece. The case contained the most delicate bracelet he had ever seen. The cuff was comprised of Asscher-cut emeralds, surrounded by white gold. The clasp was delicate and blended artistically into the bracelet.

The clerk told the story of how they'd procured the piece. "We received this from a dear older woman. She and her husband have patronized the store for a long time. Before she left it, she made me promise that whoever purchased it would cherish it for all it symbolized. Her intended gave it to her on the eve of their wedding, and it was important that the person receiving it know some of the history. Annette is quite the romantic, and believes there's magic in the stones. What do you think?"

James liked the story and the way the delicate facets shone on the narrow bracelet. His silence urged her to carry on.

"There are five carats of high-quality emeralds. The piece was fabricated in 1920 and has no signs of repair."

Touching the stones with tentative fingers, he thought it was perfect in every way. His green eyes met Evelyn's, who flushed at his gaze. "I can't think of anything more fitting. I'll take it."

IT WAS a beautiful day as Lanie drove the short distance from work to Vancouver, Washington. Morning sun shot spears of light through the heavy steel bridge, and the river sparkled below. She approached the center of the structure and looked up in time to read the sign, "Welcome to Washington." She felt a strange symbiosis with the water that was divided between two states.

She thought of her husband-to-be. From the first time they met there was a relaxed connection between them. He had follow through, a twist from the type she'd found previously. In the past, she may have been drawn to less than "real" men, deliberately. Though it was nice to have companionship, she was so independent. There were things she wanted to accomplish, and if she married too soon, they wouldn't happen. Until she met James, she'd dated no one for longer than six months.

As they got to know each other, she was slow to get serious. This was an issue between them because James was all in. He told her he never wanted this with anyone before. She took a while to tell James she loved him back, although she had strong feelings for him months earlier. Somehow, she thought she might lose the upper hand if she admitted her feelings.

It boiled down to an argument her parents had when she was small. Lanie could hear they were fighting about money, which was often the case. Her dad came home with a flashy new car, and her mom was furious.

Rani pleaded, "Drew, how could you make this decision without even consulting me? You know I'm the one who manages the budget. We're still trying to pay off the restaurant remodel you insisted on last summer."

Drew could be dismissive. He sharply replied, "Rani, when are you going to realize that I earn the money around here, and I'll buy what I like."

From her bedroom, Lanie felt enraged by her mother's oppression. Though she didn't understand her feelings, she vowed no man would ever make her feel that helpless.

The navigation system interrupted her memory. Lanie redirected her attention, following the GPS to the address of a well-known vintage watch dealer. She hoped to find the perfect Tissot as a wedding gift for James. Pulling to the front, she saw the storefront gleaming with treasures.

She entered and was greeted by the man she had spoken with on the phone. "Hello, how may I help you?"

"Hi, I'm Lanie. Are you Eric?"

"Yes, yes," he agreed. "We spoke on the phone last week, right?"

"That's right," she confirmed. "I'm looking for a watch for my fiancé."

"I'm so glad you made it in. We procured another beauty since you and I last spoke. I have a few for you to choose from, but when I heard the story of our newest acquisition, I thought it was the one for you. Excuse me a moment." He disappeared into the back.

Before Lanie could peruse the cases, Eric returned from behind the counter with a worn leather box in hand. He indicated she come over. "Take a look at this." He snapped the lid open, and with a broad smile turned the box around.

Cushioned in black velvet, she found an unassuming white-faced watch with gold hands, finished with a black leather band. As she studied the piece, Eric shared the history. "It is called a Mathey and was fabricated in the 1950s. Though the watch looks simple, a Tissot fan would love to have this piece in their collection."

He continued, "That is not what makes it special. I was friends with a couple who visited my shop for many years. This watch was a gift that the woman gave to her fiancé before they were to be married. When he gave it to me, he made me promise that whoever purchased the watch know a little of its history. He wanted them to cherish its power and hopefully it would continue the love they found."

Lanie removed the watch from its case. It looked like a well-made watch, but without the story, she wouldn't have understood the meaning it carried. "I'm confused by this, wouldn't the couple have wanted their children to inherit such an important keepsake?"

Eric sighed. "Unfortunately, there was a heartbreak. This was their way of carrying on the legacy of their romance."

The front door chimed and Eric excused himself to greet the latest patrons. Lanie flipped the watch over. There was an inscription. It read, "Thank you for your patience."

Her eyes pooled, and she knew this had to be the gift.

When Eric returned she told him as much, then asked, "What happened to them? Did they pass?"

Eric's expression was downcast. He'd made a promise, and was not one to break his word. "I'm sorry. I'm not at liberty to say. I assured them that I would not relay their current status. You understand, don't you?"

Intrigued and certain this was the gift, she wanted the watch. "I'll take it."

5

The Undercurrent

The next morning, as Lanie arrived at the gallery she was greeted by a very ecstatic Jay who leapt out of his chair. He jumped with such force that the chair rolled, smacking into the wall behind him. Ignoring the effect, he rushed from behind the desk to greet her.

"Good morning, Ms. Popular."

She responded with a hesitant expression, "Good morning."

"You will not believe what I've been up to."

Taking the bait, she asked, "Okay, I give. What have you been up to?"

Nearly bursting out of his skin, Jay skipped in place, "Well, I've been working on your lovetest.love persona."

Rolling her eyes with disinterest, Lanie managed an indecipherable grunt.

Jay went on, "Since yesterday your profile has amassed fifty hearts and at least thirty messages. I've been weeding through the bunch and have replied to only the A list."

Unimpressed she walked past Jay to the barista station and selected a tea for herself.

Not the slightest bit deterred, Jay pursued, "There are a few highly qualified bachelors writing us, I mean you."

With a sniff, she retorted, "You mean you, Jay. They are writing you."

He dismissed her, "That's just semantics."

She laughed, "The semantics is that they're reading a profile written by me but they are talking to you. How can you not see the truth in that?"

He accepted, "Okay, so they may be corresponding with me, but they wouldn't have if it weren't for your profile."

Shaking her head Lanie tried to dismiss the topic. "We don't have time for this today. There is still so much to do before our showing and open house party tomorrow night. Can we please focus?"

Like a freight train that needs to make a sudden stop, Jay can't. "Yes, but first, I want to let you know that your mixer is scheduled for this Friday night. It's at six o'clock at Hotel Monaco."

Suddenly queasy and filled with dread, Lanie felt her heartrate increase. "Uh, I don't know about this Jay."

His eyes narrowed, and met hers. "Lanie, you were the one who cooked this idea up. There was a reason. Don't you owe it to yourself, and James, to see it through?"

She paused for a moment, not sure how to address the conflicted emotions she was experiencing.

Jay took her silence as license to carry on. "Lanie, it is just a mixer. Approach it like another gallery function. Have a last fling and get yourself some clarity. Marriage is meant to be forever. Don't go into it with even a shred of doubt."

Needing to flee the dialog, Lanie refocused Jay. "Okay, I'll go to the mixer if you agree to drop this subject for the rest of the day. We have to confirm the caterer, the music, and exhibitors. It's crunch time. Let's get this done."

Conceding, Jay closed the topic with one final detail. "Of course, Lanie, but know that I have entered the information into your calendar, and I'm holding you to your word. You will get this out of your system once and for all."

A sinking feeling washed over her, but she dismissed it. Grabbing the event binder, she began to address the check list with Jay.

———

JAMES GOT off the elevator mentally reviewing the day's tasks. He was in the final stages of completing the proposal for an extensive "green" rollout, for the logistics giant, MAZE. The project included all 70 of their U.S. distribution facilities, outfitting the sites with solar systems, green roofs, and electric vehicle charging stations. The contract would be worth half a billion dollars over the next five years. It was an incredible opportunity, but due to the complexity, non-conforming sites, and the varying tax laws in each state, it was a massive undertaking. James and Nick were tackling it along with a broad internal team. The coordination effort would be daunting. Thriving where others drown, James was thrilled for the challenge.

Taking his usual route to the break room, James filled his mug with coffee, added cream, and rounded the corner to their office. As he entered Nick was engrossed in the screen before him. Not surprised, James knew how much work there was to do. He was glad to see him already at it.

Nick looked up as he entered. "Hey, good morning, stud." Nick snorted.

James' face half squished by the weird greeting.

"What's up? Did we get the site drawings for the Blue Rabbit building yet?"

"All business, as usual. Yes, they just came in, and I sent the link to design. They will deliver the prints to us shortly."

"Good." James said as he booted up his computer.

Nick cleared his throat, like a tap on the shoulder, which elicited the response he was looking for—James' attention. "Guess who is getting a lot of action today."

James couldn't figure out what Nick was referring to, and his expression said as much. Nick continued, "Turns out you are quite popular with the ladies."

Still at a loss, James stared at Nick, "Huh?"

"lovetest.love, your profile." Nick shared, "Dude, you got over twenty smiles and seven hearts since we set it up yesterday."

James reset his attention to the log in screen, "I couldn't care less Nick. With only forty of the seventy MAZE sites reviewed, and two weeks until our deadline, a looming wedding, and bachelor party, that," he emphasized, "is not my priority."

Undaunted, Nick walked over to James' computer and pushed the shutdown key. James snapped, "What the hell?"

Nick taunted, "Do you want to get back to work?" James took a full deep breath, his eyes huge and lips set, "Fuck, yes, I do."

Unafraid, Nick forced, "Well, then get your ass over here. I have something for you to see."

Resigned and eager to get to work, James crossed the room to Nick's desk. Smiling at his win, Nick pulled the chair out for James. As he sat, he jammed the chair forward smashing James' stomach into the desk. "Hey, asshole," James stood.

With a big smirk on his face, Nick soothed, "Aww poor

baby, he has to read the profiles from what I imagine to be stunning babes, all of whom are chomping at the bit to become his sex slave."

"You have a vivid imagination." Disgusted, and over the entire thing, James sat back down. He knew his friend well enough to realize that no work would be done until he acquiesced to his whim.

Nick stood beside him and gave him a quick navigation tour. "Here are the messages, and if you click here, it drives you to their profile. My personal favorite is Vanessa. She has a couple of quotes that would definitely make my playlist."

James shook his head as he skimmed through the profiles. He had to admit, they were a clever selection, but reading a narrative never did it for him. Besides, he was certain none held a candle to Lanie's stunning looks. Concluding his review, he looked up at his friend. "Are you satisfied? Can we focus on the $500 Million-dollar proposal now or should we braid each other's hair, and day dream some more?"

Almost satisfied, Nick agreed, "Sure but one last thing, your mixer is this Friday night. It's at the Imperial Hotel. I took the liberty of adding it to your schedule."

James heart skipped a beat hearing this and he had a wary feeling. Nick noticed the cross his oldest friend's face and said, "Look, your fiancé has some reservations, right?" James nodded almost imperceptibly. "This was her idea and you did nothing to stop it. In fact, it sounds to me like you egged her on. If you want her doubts to disappear, and maybe a few lingering ones of your own, you need to follow through."

AFTER A LONG MORNING OF DETAILS, Lanie needed some fresh air. She walked the ten blocks to the dress shop where she had purchased her wedding gown. It was her final fitting before the wedding, and Audrey was meeting her to try her dress too. They agreed to go to happy hour after, a rarity these days.

As she moved along the city streets, Lanie soaked up the sunshine, and tried to be present. Unfortunately, her thoughts kept going back to the lovetest.love challenge she and James agreed to. She knew she would tell Audrey about it over drinks, and wondered how her friend would take it. She also wondered how it came to this, and what it might mean that they both agreed to such an eleventh-hour test.

She arrived at the store almost too soon. When she entered, Audrey was already inside with a glass of champagne in hand. She rushed over to her friend.

With an easy smile on her lips, she said, "Well hello, little bride. How are you today?"

Lanie hugged her, a little too tight, which was all the indication she needed to know that something was up. "I'm good, busy morning at the gallery with the open house tomorrow night."

Within seconds, Jan, the store owner, arrived with a flute of pink champagne and handed it to Lanie. As she did, her assistant carried the gown into a nearby fitting room. "Hello, Lanie, you are glowing today."

Accepting the wine, she replied, "I walked from the gallery. It must be from the heat outside."

"Tsk-tsk, Lanie—you are too humble and unaware of your allure."

Lanie sniffed. "You know Jan, I've already purchased the dress, there's no need to kiss up at this stage."

Shaking her head, she shooed the ladies to their respective dressing rooms. Audrey's gown was a silken, blush-colored number with a lovely cowl neck. It was fitted below the breast but flowed smoothly otherwise. Perfect for the mother of two who was working toward her pre-birth physique.

Lanie's dress was magic. She chose pure white with a halter neckline, and plunging back. The dress was smooth satin with beading around the edges and neck. At the center was an enticing cutout that showed a peek of her decollate. The front of the gown was short enough to graze the top of her shoes. At the back, a glimmering four-foot train was edged in the same lovely beads. Instead of a traditional veil, Lanie had a jeweled crown made by one of her close friends. It was encrusted with pearls, crystals, and even a few sapphires to cover her "something blue" base.

They stepped into the main floor simultaneously. Lanie gained her vocal cords first and said, "Audrey, it is absolutely perfect on you. You look like a model. Ron is going to lose his mind when he sees you."

Audrey tried for the right words. "That is the most perfect dress in the world. Look at your tiny waist and how your perfect boobs pop. Holy crap!" She turned her to the mirror and whistled at the open back and peek of her tailbone. "I don't think James will be able to wait until after the reception to take you, wearing that little number." Her eyes shone with happiness and not a shred of envy for her best friend.

Jan smiled and exclaimed, "You both look breathtaking! With a few minor tweaks, everything will be divine." She and her assistant made quick work pinning a few spots on each dress and they were done. "Please be careful as you remove them, I don't want any blood pricks on those masterpieces."

AUDREY RAISED her glass in toast. "Here's to my best friend, may your wedding and life with James be as wonderful as you are." Tears shone in her eyes, causing a ripple effect as Lanie's glistened too. At once they both said, "Cheers." Their first sips were a delight. The warm weather and smiling passersby set the tone for a girls chat.

Audrey studied her friend from across the table. Today she wore a simple grey boat neck tank, and an above knee flowing skirt in taupe. Setting down her glass she asked, "So, tell me how you're feeling?"

Lanie looked at Audrey. The sun streamed from behind, highlighting her high cheek bones. The ivory shift dress she wore was made when she paired it with a classic blue choker. The woman across from her looked nothing like the harried mommy of two, instead, an even more spectacular version of her former self.

Evading the question, Lanie said, "You look stunning by the way."

For a beat, Audrey took the bait. "Lately I feel anything but stunning. Most of the time when I get dressed, I'm holding Lily on my hip while keeping an eye peeled to see what baby Lee is getting into. If my clothes match when I walk out the door it is no small miracle. The days of accessorizing ended once Lee found it a thrill to rip the earrings right out of my lobes, and started using any necklace as a choke collar." Audrey taunted, "Nice redirect by the way. How are you feeling?"

"I'm doing well. I mean there is a lot going on. We have the show tomorrow night and so many details to attend to before the wedding, but I'm hanging in there."

"Lanie"—Audrey had to level with her closest friend —"it's me you're talking to. I remember how I was before

Ron and I got married and so do you. Why don't you stop talking like I'm a stranger, and give it straight?"

Realizing that the bomb she was about to drop would raise an enormous red flag, Lanie felt a jolt of anxiety. "I do have something to tell you but before I do you have to promise not to read too much into it."

She hesitated and Audrey knew her friend well enough to keep quiet.

Her silence only heightened the intensity of emotions swirling through Lanie's mind. "You're not going to believe this, but James and I are doing something kind of crazy. I'm not sure how it happened, but we sort of got into a test."

Audrey looked at her friend with a confused expression. "Okay, what is the test?"

"You've seen those commercials for lovetest.love, right?"

"Of course, they are on every day. How could you miss them? What does that have to do with anything?"

"The other night James was over and the commercial came on for their new mixer events."

Shaking her head, Audrey confirmed, "Yeah, I've seen that one. Pretty cool idea if you're into online dating."

"Well, for some reason I thought so too and told James as much. Actually, I told him that if I were single, I would consider doing it."

Audrey's head tilted to one side but she remained quiet, prompting Lanie to carry on.

"The conversation turned and I asked James if he thought we would be a match if we were on that site."

"Sounds like someone has the pre-wedding jitters to me," Audrey said with a smile.

"Well, maybe."

Lanie was still and this time Audrey did press. "Lanie, what is going on?"

After a big intake of breath, she came out with it. "James and I decided to set up online profiles to see if we were a match. We agreed to go to one of the events."

"What!" Audrey's shriek caused the people at the next table to perk up.

"I know, after we shook on it and every moment since I have been wondering what we were thinking."

"And James agreed to this? This does not sound like him at all. You, nervous Nellie, I kind of understand, but you've always hated the idea of online dating."

Prepared for this, Lanie agreed. "I know but I guess I was feeling a little unsure at the moment, and that commercial was so compelling. I thought it was a better idea than trying to pick someone yourself from a few pictures. The marketing was good, and uh, I don't know, I was at a weak point."

"Okay, you have to rewind and tell me exactly how this happened."

Lanie went over the test in full detail. When she finished, Audrey was quiet for a beat then said, "You know, this isn't that bad of an idea. My guess is the computer will pick you and James as a match. Maybe this is the final confirmation you need."

Lanie smiled at her friend, she was always such a comfort. "Does that mean you'll go with me to the mixer on Friday night?"

Now Audrey's face was aglow; a beaming grin in place, she picked up her glass in toast. "Wild horses couldn't drag me away! Here's to your last chance."

6

About last night...

It was Wednesday and the day of the gallery open house. Lanie and Jay had been at it since 7 a.m. and the place was abuzz with energy. Jay was frantically wringing his hands while ordering the workers to be careful. Everything was in flux as they shifted pieces to accommodate the sculptures that would be on display for the next month, starting today. After sending a few final emails Lanie decided it was time for lunch, and perhaps an adult beverage for Jay.

Collecting her handbag, she walked to him and not so gently cupped his elbow, calling behind them as she dragged him toward the front door, "Robin and Hector, we are heading to lunch. You have the floor plans. I know we are in good hands."

Her special events coordinators smiled. "You two have a great lunch," Robin replied. She and Hector exchanged relieved glances as their shoulders come out of their ears.

Lanie responded, "Thank you, guys. Charlie should be bringing the crew's order any time now. Take a break and enjoy my favorite Chinese food."

Jay can't help but put in a last word, "Don't touch anything before cleaning your hands."

Lanie shoved Jay through the door. "You are like an anxious father awaiting the arrival of his firstborn."

Jay snorted and asked, "Oh yeah, and how would you know?"

"Touché." She smirked and changed the subject. "I do know just the place for lunch today." They walked a few blocks to Andina, a Spanish tapas style restaurant.

They went inside and were greeted by a young, blonde hostess wearing a tight black T-shirt. Her arms were adorned by graphic tattoos, in contrast to her innocent-looking face.

She politely inquired, "Will you be joining us in the dining room or bar today?"

Lanie was decisive, "The bar please."

They followed the girl a short distance and were seated at a table overlooking the street. The bar was cast under an orange glow, thanks to the lighting and carved wooden walls. Colorful figurines sat on shelves, giving the impression they were eating with an audience.

Within seconds of our arrival an attractive man with dark hair and eyes greeted us. "Ello, my name is Serge, and I will be your server today. May I offer you a beverage while you are looking over the menu?"

Lanie replied, "Iced tea for me and a very strong beverage for my friend." She looked at Jay who was drooling over Serge. She kicked him under the table to bring him back to earth.

He startled, then brought out his best smile. "Double Angel's Envy on the rock, please."

Serge's smile lingered. "I'll return with your libations."

Lanie couldn't let the opportunity pass. "Looks like it's on between you and sexy Serge."

He smiled but his eyes couldn't help but follow Serge through the space. Once he was out of sight Jay turned back to his companion.

"To what do I owe this impromptu lunch?"

Lanie's face squished. "Jay, if I didn't get you out of there Robin and Hector were going to walk out on us. You, my friend, need a chill pill."

Miffed by her answer, Jay retorted, "Well, somebody has to make sure nothing is broken. My goodness, did you see how they were man handling that fountain?"

She loved Jay and all of his many quirks. Thankfully, Serge returned with their drinks. "Are you ready to order or would you like more time?"

Lanie responded since Jay had once again lost his voice, "Please give us a few minutes. We are taking our time this afternoon."

Serge left them. Jay now had two reasons to squirm in his chair. "Lanie, you are going to drive me nuts. We need to oversee the installation of the—"

"Stop." Lanie raised her glass. "Here's to the promise of another successful opening. I am so excited about our emerging artist, Hans Martl. His whimsical portraits are out of this world. I know the show will give him the visibility he needs and our clients will adore him."

Jay clinked his glass to hers and drank deeply. The sweet taste of burnt orange and spice stung all the way to his belly. "Ahh," he breathed.

"Better?" Lanie solicited, knowing he needed the reprieve. It would be a long day and Jay could get so worked up.

"Yes." Jay perked up as if he just remembered something. "Hey, what happened when you told Audrey about your little test? How did she react?"

Lanie wondered how long it would take for the subject

to surface. "How do you think she reacted? She was shocked, of course, but she knows me and my tendency to run."

"And," Jay prodded.

"By the end of the conversation she thought it was going to be a good exercise for us."

"Well, you've certainly had a lot of interested people." Now it was Jay's turn to raise his glass. "Here's to the test, and a successful show tonight."

THE GALLERY WAS abuzz with energy, and more bodies than they'd anticipated. Lanie's cheeks ached from the constant smiling. Surveying her domain, she was overjoyed with the outcome.

Looking across the room she saw Jay was in his element. A consummate host and professor, he captivated the guests with details about the artists, and their work. At present, he and Hans Martl were joined at the hip.

Hans had quite the following. He was in his late 50s, and only began his art career at 40 when he lost his wife in a fatal car accident. He fell into a deep depression after her death, and lived in relative seclusion; during that time, he painted. It was the start of his career, and his second chance at life.

She noticed the Flemings were absorbed by his *Mystical Fairy* piece. Mrs. Fleming seemed smitten. Mr. Fleming had long since acknowledged his wife's infatuation with the arts, and sometimes artists. He even found it cute. Before Lanie could intervene, Jay's keen instincts raised his eyes to meet hers, a silent indication he had it under control. Observing their easy conversation, she sensed a nice sale coming.

She turned her attention away as Audrey and Rob entered. They met in the middle and hugged one at a time. "Hey, you two. I'm so glad you were able to make it tonight."

Rob rocked on his heels, out of his element in the artsy world. With a disingenuous tone he replied, "Yes, we are too."

At that Audrey snorted. "Sure, he was so excited to come tonight. I hardly had to convince him at all. You won't believe the promise I made to get him here. Let's just say," she continued in a hushed tone, "I'll be testing out this eighteen-hour lipstick later."

Lanie laughed and aimed a hawk-like stare at Rob. "Uh, I think I'll make the rounds, check out the new display." He smiled and made haste for the bar.

Turning back to her Audrey, she joked, "Thanks for taking one for the team, friend."

Audrey asked, "Where is James?"

Lanie realized that he wasn't there yet and it was already 8:30 p.m. "I'm not sure. My guess is that he's working on the MAZE proposal that is due just before the wedding. You know how he is when there is a big deal at stake, extremely focused." The question made Lanie squirm.

"Hmm," Audrey managed. The cocktail server approached with tall glasses of champagne. The girls each took one. "Well, here is to another smashing success, my friend. You deserve all of this and more."

"Cheers." They clinked glasses in unison.

Just then Jay approached with the Flemings in tow. "Ladies, I'm sorry to interrupt, but the Flemings would like to discuss procuring the *Whimsical Fairy* piece."

Audrey excused herself to join her husband.

WHEN THE LAST patron said goodbye, Lanie locked the front door and joined Jay on the bench.

He had a bottle of bubbles in hand, and poured two glasses. Lanie sat and kicked off her black suede stilettos. He handed her a glass then said, "Here's to another incredibly successful show and to the best boss in the world." They tapped glasses and drank deeply. Jay continued, "I mean it Lane, you really are the best. I can't imagine working with anyone as terrific as you. Thank you."

This brought tears to her eyes. "Aww Jay, I feel exactly the same about you, which is why I am going to give you a five percent bonus on all profits moving forward. I've already spoken to the attorney, and he is drafting the new employment contract as we speak."

"Oh my god, Lanie! Thank you so much." Jay could not believe her generosity nor his luck at finding this true friend; this was why he had to verbalize the thought nagging at him all evening. "What happened to James tonight?"

Remembering she'd been without her phone, Lanie jumped to her feet and walked to the desk to get it. "Good question, I'm sure he sent me a message but I haven't had my phone with me." She gestured to the strappy black dress she was wearing and said, "Go figure, no pockets in this little number."

When she unlocked the device, she noticed no missed calls or messages from James. The downcast expression that flashed across her face did not go unnoticed.

He pressed, "What did he say?"

Her silent response was telling. "Lanie, are you really okay with everything? The dating test is in a couple of days, and your fiancé is MIA on one of the biggest nights of your year; how are you feeling?"

Lanie knew it was pointless to evade his questions—Jay was too persistent. "I'm feeling fine. You know how James gets when he's in the mode. I'm sure he lost track of time, and is still pouring over the details for his big presentation." Jay was silent for a beat, causing Lanie to defend him further. "I know it isn't ideal when he gets immersed, but in a way, I don't always mind. I need space to focus on my work too. With James I have the leeway."

"I know you, Lanie. I agree, but I also see you're disappointed. You are about to marry this man. It took a long time for you guys to commit, and I wonder if there might be some red flags for both of you. You deserve to be first sometimes."

Lanie's eyes glassed up. "Don't worry, Jay. He puts me first when it matters most. The timing of our wedding, the show, and his big presentation just"—she paused, searching for the right word—"compressed. I'm sure he'll make it up to me."

Jay knew enough to stop pushing. His strong, independent friend could sometimes get sensitive, and he didn't want to take away from the glory of their evening.

There was a soft tap at the front door, and who was waiting outside? The attentive server from lunch this afternoon.

Lanie smiled wide, and elbowed Jay. "I guess it's for you. On that note, I'm heading home for a long sleep. Don't forget, you are opening tomorrow."

Looking toward the front door, Jay barely acknowledged her.

LANIE STOOD at the edge of the long pier. The calm water began to boil around her. The pier shook, boards buckled beneath her. She didn't know if it was safe to turn back, but knew she couldn't remain in place. The water formed into waves. A big one was coming in her direction. She had to run, but as she did there was a deafening sound of cracking wood, and then she was free falling. She gasped for air and awakened to the sound of her phone ringing.

Disheveled and shaking she reached for it. Running a hand through her tangled hair, she answered. It was James.

"Good morning, angel." He sounded so calm. Her heart was racing, and still foggy, between sleep and reality.

She rasped a short, "Hey," while catching her breath.

"Are you ok?"

"Sure, sure. I just woke up. Actually, your call saved me from falling into boiling water."

"What?" a confused James replied.

"Yeah, it was a dream, one that felt very real."

His voice softened and he said, "Tell me about it."

"Oh, it was no big deal." She struggled to brush the residual emotion off.

"You sure you don't want to get it off your chest?"

"Yeah, I'm fine. I guess I was a little overtired or something."

"Hey, I'm sorry about last night." His tone was conciliatory.

"What happened?" she inquired, already knowing the answer before she asked.

"We were so busy working on the final details before submitting the first pass to MAZE that I completely lost track of time."

She gave him a reprieve, "I understand. How do you feel about things? Are you guys ready?"

Always happy to share every nuance of his work, though most of it was over her head, he went into the nooks and crannies. After a few minutes, Lanie cleared her throat bringing James to a halt.

"I'm going down the rabbit hole again, aren't I?" he acknowledged.

"A little," she agreed.

"I'm sorry, babe, and that I disappointed you last night. I should have been there."

"It's okay; you've got plenty of time to make it up to me." she responded, with a pouty quality in her voice.

"Oh yeah, wish I could get away, and start making it up to you right now." He matched her tone.

"Is that how you think this works, you blow me off last night, and then you think you can walk in and seduce me the day after?"

He laughed but she could hear the clicking on his laptop in the background. "Hey honey, I'm sorry to do this, but I have to cut this short. I am due for a review meeting with the execs and I still have some stuff to pull together before hand. I was thinking we should wait to see each other until our inevitable match on Friday night. What do you think?"

Lanie laughed. "Sure, I've got a lot to deal with after the show last night. We have several pieces to ship and install."

"Good, it went well then?"

"Yeah, Hans was a hit." Lanie heard the intercom on his desk phone interrupt their chat.

He responded to the caller, "Give me a moment," then returning to Lanie, he said, "Honey, I want to hear all about it. Will you fill me in on Friday?"

"Sure, Friday it is," she agreed.

"Love you, angel." Before she could respond Lanie

heard the click at the other end signaling the conclusion of their call.

Timed perfectly, a text from Jay buzzed through. It was a picture of two dozen long-stemmed white roses in a bright blue milk vase. The text read, "From James to my angel. Forgive me and let me make it up to you on Friday."

She smiled and set about her day. Time for a cup of coffee.

7

Missed Connections

James looked up from his screen and cracked his neck. Glancing around the office, he could see from the empty cubicles that most of the staff had vacated for the weekend. Just then Nick returned from his last meeting of the day.

"Hey, princess," he taunted, "you look like you just woke up from a nap."

James stood and twisted his torso then rolled his shoulders. "Yeah, I'm beat. This was a long week but a productive one. Did we get the design on building nine complete? Will they have the drawings for us on Monday?"

"Yep. We are all good. Why don't you go freshen up so we can get started on your last night out?"

James had put the whole thing out of his mind until then. "Uh, I forgot about that."

Nick snorted. "I don't know another guy on the planet who would forget issuing a last-minute dating test to his fiancé. Coming from you, I am not surprised. It's a good thing you have such a brain for business, otherwise you'd be sunk my friend."

Ushering James along, he said, "Go on, take a few minutes to freshen your makeup. It's show time."

Dragging his feet, James headed to the restroom. He took a moment to splash cold water on his face and studied himself in the mirror. He had to laugh; in a few minutes he would be seeing Lanie, and this test would be behind them. Who knew what the night would bring. Maybe it would end with a game of role play. That idea renewed his energy.

———

NICK MET James at the elevator and they agreed to go to have a drink at Bacchus Bar before the event. Walking the few blocks from their office, James was uncommunicative. His silence was something Nick had long since gotten used to. His friend always had a lot going on upstairs, and some of his greatest epiphanies came from his quiet. The silence tonight was different. It made him pick up the pace, in anticipation of a cocktail.

Though Nick was an idiot where relationships were concerned, he had to admit this "test" worried him. If James and Lanie—the two most organized people he knew —were having doubts, what prospect could there be for him? Arriving at the bar, he swung the door wide. With a smartass smile plastered on his face, he gestured for James to enter first. "Please, my lord, go ahead."

James narrowed his eyes and bumped Nick in the gut as he crossed the threshold.

They walked past the hostess after stating they were just in for a drink, and went to the bar. Nick ordered. "Barkeep," Nick called. A stocky blond bartender arrived.

"What can I get you guys tonight?" His voice was deep and face unsmiling.

"We'll have two shots of Patron." Nick tossed down a hundred-dollar bill. "Bring a second round in a few."

This seemed to perk up stone face. "You've got it." Seconds later he returned with two shot glasses and filled them to the brim.

Nick raised his glass, James followed. "Here's to a night we won't forget no matter how many shots we take."

They raised their glasses before swallowing the tequila.

Nick made eye contact with the bartender once again, with a finger at his glass he gestured for a refill. After the second round, Nick thought it time to get his friend into conversation mode. What good would he be if he lumbered around as the strong silent type all night?

"Hey, earth to Gilligan."

James faced Nick and for once didn't look like he was about to tackle him, hearing the worn-out term of endearment.

"Yep," was all he managed.

"What's up dude? You ok?"

———

JAMES LOOKED TOWARD THE BAR, studying the shelves of colorful bottles. He considered how he was feeling. Though Nick could be a complete moron, he was also his closest friend. He knew deep down, sometimes very deep down, he was a good guy and decided to level. "I guess I am a little weirded out that Lanie and I are doing this. I mean, why would she agree to something this crazy two weeks from our wedding?"

Nick asked the question he had been wanting to all week, "Why did you?"

James snapped his head and looked at his buddy. "I don't know. Maybe I wanted to be sure myself. I don't want

63

us to end up like my parents. I don't want to turn into my dad. It's hard to admit but I know that I have some of his traits."

Time to chime in. "Dude, the fact that you are thinking about it means you won't." James' gaze was downcast.

Nick went on, "Look, I know that you can get uber focused, and that causes you to forget things around you. You let your passion for the environment take over at times, but there are worse things. Lanie has known you for years, and she loves you. You're not hiding yourself from her. She knows what she is getting into, and let's be honest bro, she's pretty independent. You didn't pick a woman like your mom."

James knew he was right. Maybe this was a case of cold feet. He'd always seen the stereotypical stories in movies, but couldn't believe it was happening to him. He planned for everything, and liked certainty. This very new feeling was foreign to him. He was out of sorts, and knew his friend was right in what he was saying.

Slapping Nick on the back, he raised his eyes and caught the bartender's attention. "Another round, please. This one is on me."

THE GALLERY CLOSED AN HOUR BEFORE, but Lanie couldn't bring herself to dismiss the woman visiting the Shamsia Hassani painting. Patience was the cornerstone of art dealing, and she could tell when someone was on the verge of making an acquisition.

The piece was of a raven-haired woman wearing a hijab and playing piano atop a skyscraper. The street below was active, but the subject introspective, giving the viewer the sense of her isolation. It was a remarkable piece and one she was proud to display.

Looking at the time on his computer, Jay realized it was nearly 7 p.m. Panicked and frustrated, he made a bee line from behind the desk to the place where Lanie stood.

Whispering sharply, he exclaimed, "You are late for Prince Charming! If I didn't know better I would think you were trying to avoid this whole thing. Not good since your fiancé may be standing at the altar."

Hissing back, she said, "Jay, Ms. Franc is close to pulling the trigger on—"

"Exactly why is it you gave me that big bump recently? You do remember that I am here, and more invested than ever. I am giving the woman space. Now, get the hell out of here. Audrey was going to meet you by seven. Don't leave that poor married woman standing around with all those single vultures."

He was a little too righteous for his own good and hers. Huffing slightly, she took her purse from Jay's forceful hands and turned on her heel.

"Wait." He stopped her and, walking a few paces to her side, took her hand and slid the engagement ring from her finger. "You can't exactly walk into a dating event wearing this rock. I'll put it in the safe."

Fine, she thought. "Good evening, Ms. Franc. Jay will be here to answer any questions."

On that note, Jay walked to Ms. Franc's side. In a conspiring tone he inquired, "Now that the boss is gone, I was thinking of opening a nice bottle of bubbly. Care to join me?"

A smile crossed Liv Franc's face and Lanie knew she was a goner.

RUSHING TO PARK, Lanie was in a frenzy when she arrived at Hotel Monaco. When she entered the lobby, she was greeted by the hotel mascot, a mature male golden Labrador. Tail wagging, he pressed his full weight against Lanie's bare legs, blocking her path until she acknowledged him with a pat.

"Hello, mister. Are you my date this evening?" She stroked the dog's head. This seemed to satisfy him and he sauntered off toward another guest.

Lanie suddenly remembered she forgot to call Audrey. Seeing the signs for the lovetest.love event, she began walking and dug for her phone in her oversized bag. Before she knew it, she was hit by a strong jolt. Registering shock, she realized she had walked smack into the chest of . . . Adonis?

The man in front of her was tall, maybe 6'1". His sandy blond hair had a touch of grey at the temples, and he had the most piercing blue eyes she had ever seen. Flustered and trying to regain her composure, she cleared her throat and stammered, "I'm sorry. I wasn't looking and am in a rush."

The man looked down, and a teasing smile played at his mouth. "No problem. Bump into me anytime."

Oh my god, Lanie realized, he was flirting with her. Now more than ever she needed to find out where Audrey was. "Excuse me." She took a few steps away, and stopped near the wall to find her phone. It was in the side pocket where it belonged but rarely was.

When she unlocked the screen, there were several notifications including a missed call from Audrey. Deciding for speed, Lanie dialed her number.

"Hello." Audrey's voice a reassurance through the wire.

"Hey, where are you?" Lanie urged.

"I guess you didn't get my message," she replied.

"No, sorry. I got tied up at work and made it as fast as I could. Are you here?"

"Nope, Ron threw a fit and now I am in hot water for even suggesting it. He thinks you and I are crazy, not to mention James."

Feeling a combination of awkward and remorse Lanie replied, "Oh shit, I thought he would be okay with it. Sorry for the trouble."

"Yeah, tell me about it. I didn't get to play, and I still have to pay. Sorry to leave you hanging but I have to go. We are in the final stretch of getting the kids down, and then my real job begins. Ron is going to take some serious soothing."

Lanie could hear Ron's voice in the distance. "That's right woman, you are my slave tonight. I'll teach you a lesson after that bullshit you and your little friend were trying to pull."

A squeal came out of her friend's mouth and screeched through the phone. Lanie knew they would be fine. Before she could say goodbye, the call was disconnected.

Shaking her head, she tossed the phone back into her bag and took the few steps forward to enter the room. Walking into a party alone was daunting, but she knew it wouldn't be good to keep James waiting any longer.

Standing just inside the doorway, she took in the beauty of the space. Bright pink floral rugs and polished wooden walls set the tone. The focal point of the room was a beautiful wood-burning fire place. The façade and mantle were marble, creating a light contrast to the rest of the décor. Brocade chairs and settees were placed in strategic locations creating intimate conversation areas. It was lovely, but she didn't see James, nor did she notice the man she'd bumped into earlier observing her.

CURIOSITY GOT the best of him, and he had to know why this lovely nymph would use a dating site to meet a companion. Ryan was immediately taken by her dazzling green eyes and blonde locks. She was wearing a simple tank dress in navy blue and a pale pink pair of heels. It was impossible to miss her tiny waist and round backside. She was quite a sight to behold.

He knew they had to meet. Walking to stand behind her, he deliberately cleared his throat. "Ahem."

Relieved at the sound, she turned, expecting to find James. Her expression matched her tone as she replied, "Oh, hello."

"Don't look so happy to see me, you might give me a big head or something," he teased.

At a loss, Lanie struggled for something to say. "I'm sorry, I was expecting someone."

"Well, their loss is my gain."

"Uh, no, I mean . . ." Lanie was once again tongue tied as she looked at the handsome man in front of her. His shirt was crisp, and the lightest shade of grey. He wore designer jeans, and a beige belt that matched his well-made leather shoes.

"Since it would appear as though you've been stood up, why don't you let me buy you a drink?"

Worried that James would appear any minute, Lanie knew she had to decline. "No, I can't, thank you."

"Listen little lady, you owe me one." A sly look played across his face.

"Owe you?" She appeared confused. "For what exactly?"

"For bruising my chest when you bumped into me." He

smiled. "I'll have to make it two if you bruise my ego, by turning me down."

"Thank you, but . . ."

"Look, you're here and so am I. Join me for one drink. What could it hurt?" Lanie hesitated which was all the room he needed. Extending his right hand, he introduced himself, "Ryan Glass."

She politely shook his hand, and introduced herself, stopping shy of using her real name. "I'm Natalie Shane."

"Now that the pleasantries are behind us, what can I get you to drink?"

Resigned and actually wanting a glass of wine, she caved. "I'll have a pinot noir."

———

HE MADE his way toward the bar and Lanie couldn't help but notice his physique as he strode away. Snapping to, she admonished herself then gave it a break. She was after all a patron of the arts, and who could avoid seeing the beauty in that man?

———

FEELING HER ATTENTION, Ryan turned around in time to catch her looking. An embarrassed smile crossed her lips, making her all the more intoxicating. Maybe the night wouldn't be a loss.

Returning to Natalie, he placed his hand on her back, directing her to a cocktail table with tall chairs. There was a candle lit at the center, setting the scene for a romantic night. He knew the event planners went all out, attending to every last detail to ensure the night's success. People paid hefty membership fees to be on lovetest.love, and they expected to be wowed.

To say he was a reluctant attendee was an understatement. He had no choice after promising his editor he'd write a story about the newest innovation in online dating. Candlelight sparkled against Natalie's perfect bone structure, and he gave silent thanks for the assignment.

A moment later their cocktail waitress arrived, tray in hand. She placed a glass of wine in front of Lanie, and a short glass of scotch in front of him. Thanking her, Ryan raised his glass; Lanie followed. "Here's to chance."

Lanie replied politely, "To chance." Nearly gulping the first taste of wine, she knew the liquid couldn't get into her system fast enough.

"So, Natalie, what brings you here this evening?"

Think fast, she thought. "I was meeting a friend who asked me to come for moral support."

Interesting; he sensed the slightest hesitation, but could not care less. "Is this the friend who stood you up?"

"Um, yes, she got cold feet." Uttering that statement made the hairs on Lanie's neck prick. She scanned the room. Luckily, she could see the entry and most of the room from their table. What would she do if James walked in?

"So, Natalie," bringing her back to the moment, Ryan continued the conversation, "what do you do?"

Oh god, she hadn't thought this far ahead. What the fuck was she doing? "I am an artist." She responded with a half-truth.

Intrigued now and more confused than ever, Ryan thought she looked like a model, sans the tiny stature. She was expensively dressed for an artist. His investigative instincts were at full attention now. "What is your medium?"

"I paint predominantly—abstract— but I also make jewelry from time to time."

"You're quite talented. Do you show your work anywhere I might know?"

Wow, this was going to get tricky, "Most of what I do these days is on a commission basis. I haven't shown my work in years."

For self-preservation purposes, it was time to turn the tables. Lanie asked, "What about you, Ryan. What do you do?"

Now it was his turn in the hot seat. Always honest because it made life that much simpler, he admitted, "I am a journalist." Leaning forward as if the two were conspiring, he said, "I'm on assignment as we speak."

She looked interested and alarmed. "What do you mean, assignment?"

"One of my co-workers is out sick. She handles the relationships section of our site and paper. You're probably familiar with 'Ask Jane' from the *Oregonian*, right?"

Lanie's eyes opened wide; Jay was an addict and she had to admit, she liked hearing some of the stories too. "Of course."

"Well, I promised my editor I'd fill in for her tonight. I cover the political column."

It dawned on Lanie why his name sounded familiar. James was a big-time follower of his. After checking email each morning, the second ritual he had was reading Ryan's column.

"Wow." Realizing that he was there to write a story gave her a new reason for discomfort. "You're not going to write about me, are you?"

It didn't go unnoticed that she looked worried. "No, I'm covering the event from more of a PR standpoint. My boss is friends, and alumni, with the woman who started lovetest.love. Since this is the launch, I'm writing about the program and their cutting-edge approach to matchmaking. I've already interviewed the event coordinators and a couple of the participants. I was about to leave when you assaulted me."

He was good, she had to admit. Clearly Ryan was comfortable in his own skin. She felt herself relaxing in response. The combination of the wine and their easy banter was to blame. Intrigued, she wanted to know about his work. "You've written some pretty terrific features. Aren't you an author as well? Didn't you write that book on prescription drug abuse in teens?"

A flush came across his face. "I've been fortunate. I found my passion early in life, and have had strong mentors along the way. Our nation is in crisis, and I couldn't get enough of the macabre topic. My fascination naturally resulted in a book."

Impressed, Lanie raised her hand in toast, but saw her glass was empty. "So much for my toast," she said with a laugh.

Their server noticed the exchange as she couldn't keep her eyes off Ryan. She hurried to their table. "Would you like another round?"

Before Lanie could protest, he confirmed, "Yes, please."

Three drinks, and as many hours later, she realized the time. "I can't believe what time it is."

"Me either. You're easy talk to. I especially enjoyed hearing about your family."

Those details Lanie couldn't fabricate. "Yes, me too. I can only imagine what it was like growing up in a family with three brothers. You painted a pretty funny picture."

Ryan reached for his wallet, and grabbed the check. She gestured for her purse, "Let me help." Ryan held up a hand and feigned insult. "Absolutely not. Besides I want you indebted to me because I have to see you again."

Warning bells were ringing in Lanie's ears. She hadn't thought this far ahead. He took his cell phone from the table and began typing. Looking up he asked, "What is your number?"

She gave him the digits but misspoke the last number. How could she have anticipated he'd call her on the spot?

The phone rang and a strange person's voicemail answered. Pinning her with his eyes he pressed, "Natalie, have I entered something incorrectly?"

She recounted the digits, this time giving him the right number. He dialed and her purse buzzed. "Now you'll know it's me when I call you tomorrow."

Taking a breath, she stood and collected her bag. Ryan stood as well and before she could protest, he pulled her into a warm hug. His chest was as firm this time as when she walked into him earlier. His cologne lingered between them. Checking herself, she pulled back. "Thank you for a great conversation, Ryan."

His eyes were affixed to her lips. Her stomach dropped. Taking her hand, he pulled it toward his lips and kissed ever so gently. "No, thank you, Natalie. Until tomorrow."

<hr>

JAMES AND NICK entered the Imperial Hotel through the adjoining restaurant. Before following the signs to the lovetest.love event they decided a quick stop at the bar was in order. Though they'd already sucked down four shots apiece, something happened when the two got together, forcing their livers to get a work out.

"Barkeep," Nick called in a tone too loud for the surroundings, and time of night. It was only 7:15 after all.

A thin hipster-looking dude headed their way. His dark hair was slicked off to the side in a fashion that made the crisp checkered bow tie fit. Hesitant, he asked, "What can I get you guys?"

James chimed in, "May as well stick with it. How about a couple of shots of Patron?"

The bartender reached for the bottle behind him and filled two glasses. "That'll be forty dollars even. Do you want to start a tab?"

James pulled cash out of his pocket, placing three twenties on the counter.

"I'll get you some change," said the bartender.

Downing his shot, James raised his hand in protest. "No, keep it."

Not totally grounded, he rose to his feet and bumped the barstool. It scraped against the floor. Following his lead, Nick stood, making a similar ruckus. They walked toward the main lobby then followed the signs toward the lovetest.love event. As they entered the room, they could see the place was packed. True to form, Nick pointed out the bar, so they started there. The bartender was a little cutie and Nick would not let the chance to order from her pass him by.

"Hi, guys." Her sweet voice matched the ginger hair and creamy complexion.

Nick was in a daze so James piped up. Realizing it was time for a switch, he ordered for both. "Hi, we'll have a couple of gin and tonics and two waters, please."

Nick leaned on the counter to create the illusion of stability, and to get a closer look at her apple-shaped ass.

Turning around, James scanned the room for Lanie. The area was thick with bodies. People were standing at cocktail tables, sitting in sleek leather chairs, and mingling near the jazzy fireplace. At first pass he didn't see her or Audrey anywhere.

The bartender returned with their drinks and water. Nick pulled his credit card out; speaking in a syrupy tone, he asked, "What's your name, sweetie?"

Immune to guys of his kind, the woman leaned forward and said, "Bob." Nick was confused as he extended his credit card. "Should I keep it open?"

Regaining his voice, and wanting to rebound from the not so subtle brush-off, he smiled broadly. "Yes, please, Bob. And thank you."

She turned on her heel and began inputting something into the console.

His attention span short as ever, Nick turned toward the main floor and scanned the crowds. He noticed several good-looking women and was mentally grappling. Speaking his less than ideal thoughts aloud, he asked, "I wonder how many numbers I can get tonight?" With a smirk on his face, he tried to rap. "Some of these ladies should be having my babies, babies."

Though intoxicated, James had never been the most aggressive. Annoyed by Nick, he also marveled at his friend's unrelenting over-confidence.

Taking his drink in hand, Nick turned to James. "Ok little buddy, I'm out to find my Mary Ann."

Resigned, James accepted that they may be tossed out at any moment. "You go. I'm going to sit here a minute. Good luck," he called back toward the already disappearing Nick.

Turning his chair, James scanned the room once again for any sign of Lanie. She was nowhere to be found. He wondered what happened. They did get there late since the mixer started at six. Fuzzy from the shots, he tried to remember what time he and Nick arrived. It was almost eight now. What if she and Audrey came and left? He was so deep in thought he didn't notice the woman who took the seat to his right.

When "Bob" arrived to take her order, he knew someone was there, causing him to glance over. Woah, he thought. Was it the alcohol giving him beer goggles or was that woman for real?

After taking her order, Bob redirected to James. "Can I get you a refill?"

Noting his drink was nearly drained, James nodded in agreement. "Yeah, thank you."

A moment later she returned with a Cadillac margarita, placing it in front of the babe beside him, then set James' gin and tonic down.

The brunette raised her glass, cleared her throat and said, "Here's to Friday night."

He looked over and followed her lead. Raising his glass, he repeated, "To Friday."

Together, they said, "Cheers."

After a sip, James set his glass down. In his peripheral vision he could see that the woman turned her seat to face him.

"I'm Rebecca."

He faced her, but stayed silent.

"Rebecca Cahn." She extended her hand for a shake.

He took it and introduced himself, "James Roberts."

"Good to meet you James. What brings you here tonight?"

The liquor was coursing through his veins now, and he hadn't thought this thing out. "Funny story, actually. I'm sure you don't want to hear it. I'm not really on the market."

Intrigued now, she had to know his story. "Ahh, a mystery. I love a good puzzle. Do tell."

James was wowed by her smooth complexion and piercing blue eyes; both were enhanced by her long, dark hair. Rebecca was a knockout. He mentally cautioned himself to be careful. "Trust me, it isn't all that great."

Sensing a sadness in the guy, she pressed, "Look, I don't know you and you don't know me. Seems like you need to get something off your chest."

He turned his chair again and after another review of the room, he somehow knew Lanie would not show. He was crestfallen, which was dumb. Maybe it would help to share his story. "It's a long story. I'm actually engaged."

Rebecca leaned back a little. "Then what are you doing at a lovetest.love event?"

He stared down at his glass. "It's stupid. Somehow I got into a test with my fiancé and we decided to set up profiles to see if the computer would match us."

"What the hell? Hold on. You are actually engaged and she agreed to this?"

Lifting his brows, he replied, "In a way, she sort of suggested it. Well, not really. It's a long story."

Taking a sip of her drink, Rebecca sat back in her chair. "I've got the time and it seems like you need to work this out."

With six drinks under his belt, he told the story of their test. When he was done, he looked over at Rebecca. Her feline expression made his stomach flip.

"How long have you guys been together?" she asked.

"Just over six years now."

She was starting to see the picture. "When did you get engaged?"

"About six months ago."

"And when is the wedding?"

James' jaw was set; his extraordinary green eyes didn't light up as he replied, "The wedding is two weeks from tomorrow."

Unable to contain her shock, she said, "That's a pretty bold move for two people to make."

James nodded. "Yeah."

"Well you know how this works, right? Maybe the computer didn't match you."

His expression was bleak. "I was so sure we would be a match. I even pushed the envelope to do it."

"Listen, James, I don't know you, or your fiancé, but no one agrees to a test like that if they aren't willing to walk away. You must have made peace with that idea or why would you be here?"

"I never thought that far ahead. I've been so busy at work and have been trying to get things done before the wedding that I've barely looked up."

Not convinced, she tried another tack. "So why did it take you six years to get engaged?"

Wow, James thought, this woman was relentless and stunning. He couldn't miss the pink gloss on her full lips, or the come-hither look that her body seemed to communicate. "I don't know. I guess we both had a lot of things we wanted to accomplish before getting married."

"How long have you lived together?" she pressed.

Shit, this would not solidify his case. "We don't yet. She has a place she loves, and so do I. We thought we'd figure it out after the wedding."

Her sultry voice purred, "This isn't my place, and how could I advise you after talking for only an hour, but James"—she placed her manicured hand on his shoulder —"I'm an outsider, a neutral observer, right?"

Meeting her gaze, he was taken aback by the pull he felt toward her. His silence gave her room to continue.

"Something isn't right. It took you six years to decide to get married. You haven't lived together, and two weeks before your wedding you're on a dating site? It doesn't take Freud to figure this one out." Leaning even closer, her long leg brushed against his. "I don't think marriage is what either of you wants."

Her scent lured him. Lost in her eyes, and wondering things he shouldn't, he needed to get away before he fucked up. Backpedaling, he said, "You know, I'm not feeling that great. I'd better get going."

Standing, Rebecca asked, "Why don't I join you?" Leaning close, her full breasts brushed his arm. She whispered, "I bet we fit. Let's find out."

A half chub filled his jeans. Uncomfortable in more ways than one, he stood abruptly. "Rebecca, you are unbelievable, and I can't tell you how much I want to take you up on that, but I can't cheat on Lanie. Tempting as you are, and believe me, you are smoking hot"—he shifted, trying without success to adjust his manhood—"I'm not going to blow it tonight."

Undaunted, she reached into the side of her purse, removed her card and slid it into his shirt pocket. "Call me when you're ready, James."

Backing away was almost painful. He went for the exit, and was grateful for the rush of air as he made his way outside.

8

Don't forget you are mine.

James took a few steps outside of the hotel and knew what he had to do. He saw a cab at the curb then got in, and slurred the address to Lanie's place. It was after 10 p.m., and hopefully she'd be home. Once they arrived, he paid the driver and walked to the intercom entry. Finding her unit, he pressed the button to ring her apartment then heard something behind him. He turned to find it was Lanie.

"Hey you." His voice sounded a little higher than normal, indicating he was drunk.

"Hey yourself." She was overwhelmed by an instant sense of remorse.

Without a word, she entered the code, releasing the door. Silently, they walked the four flights up to her unit. After they crossed the threshold, Lanie hung her bag on the hook. The room was lit by only the filtered moonlight that spilled in through the tall windows. The grainy lighting matched his mood.

From behind, James placed his hands on Lanie's shoulders and pulled her toward his chest. His hands gravitated to her breasts and pinched through the smooth blue fabric of her dress. Pushing her forward to grasp the zipper, he tugged until it reached the hem. Standing, he shrugged the dress off of her shoulders. It fell to the floor. She stood, wearing a sheer black thong and bra.

He would not wait, couldn't wait. Prodding her toward the kitchen table, he pressed at the back of her neck, motioning for her to bend over.

———

HOW COULD she deny him after what she had done? Willingly she did what his hands instructed.

A beat later he hooked his thumbs at her panties and pulled them to the ground. Not even allowing her to step out of them, they remained tangled around her ankles. Unbuckling his belt and dropping his pants, it took no foreplay for James to get hard. Fortunately, her high heels brought their bodies closer to the correct height. Stooping slightly, he entered her in one strong thrust.

It took her breath away.

Pressing his pelvis forward, he pinned her to him. Unsnapping her bra, he tugged it off and pulled her upright, toward his chest. He pinched her nipples while thrusting himself deeper. Accepting pain and ecstasy, Lanie gave him what he wanted. His hands on her nipples were anything but gentle. Once again, he pushed her head toward the table, then outstretched her arms.

That perfectly toned ass was calling to him. Wetting his thumb, he placed it on the rim of her anus. She squirmed but James placed his left hand at her tailbone. When he spoke, his voice was hoarse and foreign. "Open up, Lanie."

Keeping her hands affixed to the table, she arched her back to meet him. Everything was a blur—Lanie couldn't tell where her throbbing ended or where his began. This was a side of James she rarely experienced. Everything about the night had been unexpected. She was overwhelmed by sensations. His thumb tip was inside her while his cock pressed deep. Pain intertwined with euphoria. Her legs shook . Balancing on tiptoes, his thrusts caused Lanie to ricochet off of the table. Tomorrow there may be bruises. He growled as she reached behind to cup his balls. This caused James to slam into her even harder. The glass beads in the vase collided. The table jerked. Another stroke and he exploded. Feeling his throbbing, and the effects of his prodding thumb, Lanie joined him with a scream that even the neighbors could hear.

AFTER A HOT SHOWER TOGETHER, they snuggled in bed. Lanie could sense that James was sobering up. He stroked her side while his other hand cupped her left breast. The silence between them should have been strange. They'd barely spoken all night. So far, the non-verbal communication was what they needed.

Breaking the silence, James murmured, "Lanie"—pulling her even closer—"you belong to me." His soft words and warm breath tickled her ear; the faint hint of alcohol lingered between them.

Saying nothing at first, she nuzzled closer. Not sure if the words should be spoken—for that may give them life—yet unable to stop herself, she asked, "Do you think it's a bad thing that the computer didn't match us?"

Trying to dismiss the truth that had been nagging him too, false bravado and indignation intact, he responded, "I don't give a fuck what a computer says. It doesn't know us, our history or lives. There is no way we could possibly let that matter." He felt something wet on his arm where her face rested. Tears. Rising to his elbow and softly turning her face upward, he soothed, "You are my angel. I cannot imagine life without you in it. So what if we aren't a perfect match, according to an algorithm that was invented by a bunch of computer geeks? We know how far we've come together. That's all that matters."

Tears were streaming down her face now. As tenderly as a breeze, he touched his lips to hers. Tasting the salt and feeling her relax, he knew what he needed to do. He had so much to make up for. Opening his mouth, his soft tongue found hers. Meeting his pace, she tentatively responded, touching his with soft taps. She felt his heartbeat, like warm sunshine breaking through the dark clouds. All that mattered was now. This was her man.

His gentle hands caressed her collarbone, leisurely moving to her swollen nipples. His touch a whisper against her skin. He raised his lips and face from hers then studied her incredible body. She looked glorious, unabashed. His fingers resumed their lazy descent down her sternum. In an excruciatingly slow pace James traced the center of her body. Giving soft, wet kisses to her mouth, his tongue danced with hers. Finally, his hand met her spot. Knowing she would be tender, he put his finger into his mouth. Wetting it, he replaced it at her opening and slid it inside of her.

Her breath caught, which he silenced with a more insistent kiss. Her tongue teased them into an even greater urgency. She needed him again. Moving effortlessly, he rolled between her legs. Not breaking eye contact he entered her.

Lanie's eyes closed and she wondered how he did this to her. There was something about him, the way he moved and his persistence. It gave her a rush to submit to his demands.

"Lanie," his voice was a rasp.

Meeting his gaze, she managed, "Yes."

"Don't leave me."

Their bodies intertwined, and with pleading thrusts, they came together.

A BEAM of light reflected off of the mirror, as Amos Lee crooned in the background, jostling Lanie from her sleep. The intoxicating scent of bacon and fresh brewed coffee wafted from the kitchen. Propping herself up, she saw the bed looked like a tornado hit it. Noting the tenderness between her legs, and at her hips, she couldn't help but replay last night's homecoming.

She walked into the bathroom and studied her reflection in the mirror. A pang of excitement, followed by acute remorse, came over her as she remembered her time with Ryan Glass. Shaking it off, she took a band from the drawer and wound her hair into a bun. Pulling the kimono from behind the door, she slipped it on and ventured toward the delicious aroma.

As she entered the dining room, the table was set. The French press was full and waiting. James stood at the stove and was making a feeble attempt to sing along to the song, *Careless*. A fresh twinge of guilt overtook her. Walking toward him, she came from behind and wrapped her arms around his trim waist. He turned and matched her embrace.

Looking down, he smiled sweetly, "Good morning, angel."

He pecked, then pulled her bottom lip into his mouth.

She could feel a rise in his boxers, and so could he. "I'd better stop this before I burn the crepes."

"Oh crepes, such a treat. To what do I owe the honor?" she joked, and headed for the coffee.

He turned to watch and when she returned his look, he said, "I might have been a little rough on you last night."

Lanie couldn't quite place the expression. "Ahh, so your guilt has motivated you to make my favorite?"

His face was serious. "Something like that."

Pouring the coffee, she decided it best they navigate past last night's events, and steered the conversation. "What time are you meeting Nick today?"

"We are supposed to hit the road at one. Now sit down and eat your breakfast or else."

She smirked. "Are you ready for your bachelor party getaway?"

"Honestly, I'm concerned. We still have a ton of work to get through before presenting to MAZE's leadership, and our wedding, of course." Taking her hand, he kissed it devilishly.

This caused Lanie to flash back on her encounter with Ryan. Noting the expression change, James mistakenly reassured her. "Don't worry, I will get everything done so we can have an uninterrupted wedding and honeymoon. I can't wait to explore Italy with you at my side. We're bringing our computers so we can work on the details during the trip."

Nick was joining James and so was his boss, along with a few of his friends from the engineering group. It would be a party with some work in the mix. Only James would want a bachelor party that included the boss and a Power Point presentation.

"What are you going to do to keep yourself busy while I'm away these next days?" he asked.

"Jay and I have some work at the gallery after the show. We sold a few pieces so we need to oversee the logistics of the deliveries."

"Good for you, angel." A soft expression crossed his face; his eyes shone as he said, "I'm so proud of all you've accomplished."

Knowing he meant it, Lanie thought again how stupid her cold feet were. "Thanks, babe."

As breakfast wound down, he rose and cleared the plates. She stood to help but he put a hand on her shoulder. "Nope, I've got this. It's the least I can do after last night. Besides, you look like you need to lie down again." His mischievous expression could not be mistaken. "Why don't you get back into bed and wait for me? I won't be long."

Lanie did as told and headed back to bed. As she made the short commute, she couldn't help but berate herself for ever giving Ryan Glass the time of day. She had the best man imaginable. Women would kill for a kind, driven man with his looks and finesse in the bedroom.

———

SHE ARRIVED at the gallery just before noon and, as usual, Jay was already there. Finishing a phone call, he glanced her way and waved. Stowing her bag, Lanie went to the mini fridge and pulled out a sparkling water. Popping the top, she sipped before heading to her desk to check on the impending shipments.

As Jay's call ended he said, "Good morning, boss."

"Afternoon, sir," she taunted.

The man had no patience when waiting for gossip and he rushed her. Sitting at the edge of the desk, he looked like an eagle studying its prey. "And?"

"And what?" She feigned naïveté.

"You know exactly what—don't give me that. Spill!"

This would be painful but Lanie knew she wouldn't get a thing done until she told him. Jay was one of her closest confidants and there was no way to evade him.

"I went but Audrey stood me up. I didn't realize she couldn't make it until I was already there."

"You went on your own and let me guess—stood around like a wallflower? What did James say when he got there?"

Lanie was silent for a beat, but knowing she had no choice, she admitted the truth. "He wasn't there. We weren't a match."

Jay screeched in response, "What? Oh no. Tell me what happened?"

Lanie was silent a moment. Taking a gulp, she knew the only way to put this whole thing behind her was to get it all out. "When I got there, I needed to call Audrey but before I got my phone out, I accidentally bumped into this guy. It was super awkward. Anyway, when I called she told me she couldn't make it. I wasn't sure yet if James was there so I needed to take a look. Somehow, the guy I ran into saw me and . . ."

Panting now, Jay had to know. "And what Lanie? What happened?"

"We wound up having a drink, several actually."

Somehow Jay didn't look surprised. "How was it?" He asked so calmly that Lanie almost thought it a trick.

Considering her next words carefully and trying to minimize it, she said, "It was fine. He was easy to talk to and that's that."

Jay knew there was a hell of a lot more to the story but he could also see that Lanie was struggling. "Lanie"—her gaze met his—"it's okay. You're allowed to speak to other people."

She agreed in theory, but remembered the way Ryan kissed her hand . . . "I know. It was a strange night all around."

Knowing enough to give her space, Jay walked toward his computer. Sitting down he entered his credentials. "Who was the guy anyway?"

This would create a stir. "His name was Ryan Glass."

Whatever composure Jay had earlier exited the building. Jumping to his feet as though someone had left hot coal in his chair, he squealed, "Ryan Glass from the *Oregonian*? The one who wrote that book; oh, what was it about?" He pondered for a moment.

He couldn't recall so she prompted, "The prescription drug crisis in America. None other."

His jaw hit the floor. This wasn't a casual chat. That guy didn't do casual. He was a serious reporter and if memory served, seriously fine. Logging on to his computer, he typed. Yes, there he was. Jay clicked on images and saw the handsome, blue-eyed devil poised on a director's chair. Turning his screen toward Lanie, he asked, "Is this the man you talked to last night?"

Lanie was met with the same piercing blue eyes that had monopolized her evening. She had just gotten that image out of her mind and here Jay was, once again reminding her. "That's the one."

"Oh my god. You and James were not a match, and you ended up spending the night with Ryan Glass. This is unbelievable." He was unraveled.

"I did not spend the night with him. We were just two people sharing a table and some conversation. It was perfectly innocent."

Something didn't sit right with Jay. "I'm confused, why

would Ryan Glass need to go to a lovetest.love mixer?" Lanie's expression was insulted; Jay's tone acknowledged, "Lanie, you had to wonder yourself."

"He was there on business, reporting for the paper. His good friend Jane, from the 'Ask Jane' column, was sick. His editor asked him to fill in."

That made more sense. "Oh, I love her. Funny how the stars can align, don't you think?" Jay was testing the waters.

"No, Jay, it was a coincidence that we met. Nothing else."

In the strangest twist of timing ever, Lanie's cell phone rang saving her from a continued brow beating.

"Hello," she answered. The caller at the other end of the wire was none other than Ryan Glass. Instantly flushed, she couldn't stop an anxious smile from forming on her lips.

"Yes, I enjoyed talking with you too."

Running to her side, Jay pulled the phone away from her ear so he could listen in.

His voice was as warm as she remembered. "I can't stop thinking about Salty's after that story you told me about crabbing with your family. They have the best Sunday brunch in town. Will you join me tomorrow?"

Lanie was silent for a moment, then Jay motioned for her to put him on hold. "Ryan, can you hold a minute please?"

"Sure," he answered.

Tapping the mute button, Jay insisted, "Lanie, you did this experiment for a reason. Brunch is not a crime and who knows, maybe he is in the market for a new piece of art."

Holding up her hand she said, "Nice try, Jay. If you

recall, I met him under an alias. He doesn't know about the gallery. Natalie Shane here, remember?"

"That is of no importance. What matters now is that you see this thing through. You have to—if not for you, for me. I want to live vicariously through you."

Shooing him away, Lanie turned and walked toward the window. Unmuting the line, she said, "Ryan, sorry about that. I don't think..."

He persisted, "What time should I pick you up and where?"

He wasn't going to take no for an answer, so she improvised. "I have something to do first. Why don't I meet you there?"

Ryan thought his face would fall off from smiling so wide, "Great, how is 11 a.m. for you?"

After a sharp intake of breath, Lanie accepted. "Okay, I'll see you tomorrow then, eleven o'clock."

When she hung up she turned to find Jay pacing the floor. "Wow, you met Ryan Glass and you have a date with him on a Sunday. That's huge. Engaged to one babe and another one a courtin'. My little girl has grown up."

"Shut up, Jay." Annoyed with herself and him, it was time to put this whole thing down and bury herself in work. That was the only way she could procrastinate facing the gravity of what she'd agreed to.

She made the mental pact to focus on work, when her phone rang again. James' name and a funny picture of him from the Halloween when he dressed up like a punk rock star showed on the display. With a pounding heart— flashback Edgar Allen Poe's "The Tell-Tale Heart"—she accepted.

"Hello."

James' guy voice came through the line. This was the

tone reserved for when his buddies were in range. It was a deeper and more clipped version of his normal diction.

"Hi, angel." In the background she could hear the group taunting him. Nick's loud mouth, true to form, raised higher than the others.

"Shut the hell up," he hissed at his bros. "Sorry Lanie. A bunch of animals escaped from the zoo and climbed into the car."

Disarmed now, she chuckled. "It sounds like you guys are on the road."

"Yep and heading toward Mt. Hood. I wanted to call you before we lost signal." Unabashed by his friends, James said, "I miss you already and can't stop thinking about last night."

Lanie felt the same way, but for different reasons, haunted by the evening in more ways than one. Trying to concentrate on her fiancé, she said, "Thank you for breakfast this morning. It was such a treat."

"My pleasure," his annunciation underlined the word pleasure. She could hear static now. "Listen, I'm about to lose you. Love you. I'll call again when we get signal."

Before she could respond the phone cut out.

———

FROM ACROSS THE room Jay watched Lanie. He knew her well enough to understand this was a mess bigger than she'd ever experienced or intended. He also knew there was nothing for him to do but be there for her.

9

Don't Jump

Sunday morning arrived far too early for Lanie's comfort. She arose needlessly, before 6 a.m. After a feeble attempt at going back to sleep, she knew it was useless so she got up and made coffee. Filling the bottom of the stove-top espresso maker with water, she placed the filter inside, and poured Italian roast to the brim. Screwing the pot together, she put the device on the stove top. Click, click, click and the gas burner came to life. Blue flames licked the sides of the unit. Turning to the refrigerator, she removed the milk and filled the automatic frother.

While she waited, she walked to the windows and pulled back the curtains. The dining room was flooded by morning light. On the rare occasions when she was awake this early, she enjoyed the quiet before the world kicked in. Only a few tentative calls from the earliest rising birds sang in the background. Finding her phone, she activated the Wi-Fi and turned on the music. Selecting the shuffle mode, she decided the plants needed watering. Filling the decanter, she made it to each of her house plants before the aroma of fresh coffee filled the house.

She learned from a barista the importance of removing the coffee from the heat as soon as it's percolated, or you'll ruin the taste. She quickly removed it from the burner. Selecting her biggest mug, she filled it with the frothy milk then poured the dark liquid on top. Now for the final touch, a few drops of cream and her breakfast was complete.

She used the time to work on a new piece she had been kicking around. Taking the tall mug into her pseudo-studio, she looked at the blank canvas sitting on the easel. She set the mug on the window sill and contemplated the paints in front her. In the background she could hear Billie Holiday singing "My Man." A bit ominous, she thought, and immediately put it out of her mind. To make something of this blank slate, she would need one mentally as well.

Selecting a sharp charcoal pencil, she let her hands guide her to a basic shape. This would be the outline for her paints to follow. Replacing the pencil with a wider piece of chalk, she defined the shapes further. Building dimension and depth, she stood back to study her progress. This method of unplanned exploration allowed her hands to connect with her mind.

When she got out of the micro she saw the piece taking its basic form. It was a mountain. No, it was a sheer cliff with a tiny figure standing at the top. The parallel to this moment in her life was glaring. On the verge of making her biggest leap ever, she related to the figure at the foot of the bluff.

Setting down the charcoal, she took a rag and wiped her fingers before picking up her coffee. It had grown luke-warm, which she didn't mind—a fact that always baffled James. Taking a swig and rolling her shoulders she contemplated the next steps. Was this a metaphor for her life?

Dismissing the thought, she replaced the cup on the ledge and selected a palette of colors. Using a smaller brush, she filled in the background, blue skies with an ominous dark cloud looming in the distance. She followed this by outlining the mountain top and darkening the person at the edge. Finally, she built depth along the face of the rocks. The colors were faint blue, peach, and a range of greys and browns, bringing life and reality to the painting.

She looked at the clock behind her and saw it was after nine. She had been at it almost three hours. It was time to get ready to meet Ryan. The time painting was therapeutic because she worked out what she needed to do. Over brunch she would explain the whole sordid story. He would think she was an idiot which would solve the situation. Relief swept over her as she went to the bathroom to shower and get ready.

STEPPING out of the steamy enclosure, she wound a towel around her head and used a second to dry off. She applied her makeup and pushed past a wave of nerves. Satisfied with her face, it was time to do her hair. She added a liberal amount of straightener, and dried and styled it in sections. When she was done, she stood back and looked at the results. "Good," she uttered, though no one was there. "Just the look you were going for—all business."

She needed to select the right outfit. Since it would be warm, and she didn't know if they would be on the patio, she wanted something light. Choosing a simple sage skirt in linen and a white silk tank, she finished the ensemble with a pair of espadrilles. The look was casual, and not in the least bit sexy.

With only thirty minutes to get there and park, it was

time to go. Collecting her purse, she walked out the door and to her black Mercedes— the nicest vehicle she'd ever owned. Maybe she and her dad had more than their entrepreneurial spirit in common. She tapped the handle to release the lock and climbed inside.

As she drove, Lanie rehearsed what she would say to Ryan. Then she thought about the timing. Should she come right out with it, wait until they were seated, or tell him toward the end of the meal? The entire situation was nerve wracking. She could feel her body temperature increase as she neared the restaurant. Arriving at the portico, she removed her key and set it in the console. A young valet opened her door. His pearly whites gleamed as he handed her a claim ticket. Apprehensive, she started toward the entry.

As she got near the door, she heard someone's name being called behind her. Then it dawned on her, the person was repeating the name Natalie. *Oh God.* She twisted mentally, *He's here and I almost forgot my alias.* Turning around, she saw Ryan was wearing a pair of navy shorts and a light blue, short-sleeved button-up.

Her train wreck of a brain rambled, *Why did he have to look so cute? This is a curse.* As they met, he removed his aviator sunglasses and leaned in to kiss her cheek. She flushed at his touch.

"Don't you look pretty."

"Thank you," she replied.

Placing his arm around her, Ryan guided her past the crowd and ushered her into the restaurant. His touch felt foreign, inappropriate, and damn it, good. The hostess greeted him cheerfully. "Hi, Ryan. I've got your table ready."

Lanie was prepared to stand around waiting as she'd always done in the past when brunching at Salty's.

Apparently, Ryan had connections. They followed her to a table along the windows overlooking the Columbia River. The water was alive with sail boats, jet skiers and motor boats zipping along. "Thanks, Mazy. Say hi to Frank for me."

Before he could complete his sentence, a man arrived and greeted Ryan boisterously. "Do your own dirty work Mr. Glass." The two shook hands then moved to back slapping hugs.

Stepping back, Ryan made the introductions. "Frank, meet Natalie. Natalie, this is Frank, the GM here. We go way back and have known each other since college."

Still standing, Lanie extended her hand to shake. "It's so nice to meet you, Frank."

"Likewise. You let me know if you need anything while you're here or if you want the scoop on Ryan. I have some dirt." He winked and Lanie instantly liked him. His smile highlighted deep dimples and straight teeth.

"Thank you, but that won't be necessary." Lanie had the sinking suspicion she'd be a topic of conversation between them once her confession was made.

"Enjoy your lunch and bubbles." As he finished the statement, a server in formal attire arrived carrying bottle and an ice bucket. Lanie watched as he popped a bottle of Argyle sparkling rosé. Filling each of their flutes, the waiter, who introduced himself as Kirk, told them about the daily specials. They chose the buffet as that covered every imaginable food option one could dream up.

When he left them, Ryan raised his glass in toast. Lanie followed his lead. "Here's to a magnificent day with a bewitching companion."

Their glasses tapped and Lanie took a deeper than typical sip. The flavor was excellent, and tiny bubbles danced in her mouth and down to her belly. She thought of how incredible a first date this would be, if only she weren't already spoken for.

Ryan's eyes danced and he was obviously happy. This made Lanie feel even worse about what she'd come to say. Trying to muster the courage, and as she was about to tell him, Ryan asked, "Shall we fill our plates with crab and nothing but?"

His enthusiasm was contagious and there was no reason to ruin his meal. Lanie stood in agreement. "Can't wait."

As they navigated toward the buffet, people stopped what they were doing to watch them pass. Unbeknownst to them, the entire place could see their connection. Catching a group of guys ogling, Ryan clutched Lanie's elbow. He pulled her close, and in a suggestive tone whispered, "Do you have a plan of attack or do you subscribe to a buckshot approach?"

Feeling strange at his touch but wanting to relax, if only for the meal, she retorted, "Oh no, I am very systematic. I like to focus on crab, shrimp, and bacon first. After that, maybe some roasted veggies, salad, or fruit. I always save room for dessert. And you?"

"Sweetheart, we are on the same page." He raised his hand in a gesture of high five and she met his.

Acting like kids, they practically ran to the seafood station, topping it all off with mounds of bacon. He liked a woman who wasn't afraid to eat. You'd never be able to tell from her figure, but he was relieved to learn she wasn't the starving model type.

They settled back at their table and after the first few bites, Ryan opened the conversation. "Talk to me about your art, Natalie. You seemed a little reluctant the other night."

Was now the time? Lanie felt the effects of a slight day

buzz, as the taste of crab dipped in hot butter scandalized her taste buds. She grappled with herself but decided it could wait a little longer. "I mainly paint these days, but dabble in other mediums on occasion as the moods drive me."

Intrigued and sensing she was holding back, he pressed, "Are you working on anything currently?"

Thank goodness inspiration had struck today. This would be one truth she could share. "Actually, I am putting the finishing touches on a new piece."

"Describe it, would you?" He seemed genuinely interested.

"Well, it is a painting of a high bluff. There is a person at the top and above her the sky is mainly blue." Her eyes traveled to the river beside them, following the path of a graceful sail boat.

Sensing her withdraw, he pulled her back. "Mainly blue?"

Boy, this guy didn't miss a thing. "Yes, all except one very dark cloud in the distance."

"That sounds foreboding." He had so many questions, but rather than pepper her with them, he asked just one. "What gives you inspiration?"

Watching the bubbles race to the top of her glass, she ran her thumb along the stem. Making eye contact, she started, "Sometimes a beautiful moment has to be captured. Other times, I work out challenges through my art."

He was silent so she continued.

"When I was in school there was a lot of pressure to produce, and it did help with discipline. Looking back, I realize it wasn't my most inspired work."

Lanie wasn't used to this kind of attention. It was unusual and uncomfortable for her to talk about herself, but Ryan was interested. She realized this was part of the appeal when they met that first night. Needing to shift the subject from herself, she changed gears. "What about you? How did you decide to become a journalist?"

His expression flashed dark for an instant; after a sip from his glass he met Lanie's gaze. "When I was in high school, I lost my best friend to an overdose. I knew he'd been experimenting but had no idea the depths. After it happened, I researched what he'd been taking and how he got the drugs. I decided to write an article that was published in the school newspaper."

Lanie touched his wrist across the table. His lips set in a firm line, he continued, "It turns out, he found this local doctor who was willing to prescribe Oxycodone for a fee. I guess the guy had been doing it for years and my buddy wasn't the only kid who lost his life to the stuff. The local authorities got wind of the article and used it as a launching point for their investigation. He was indicted and served a hefty prison sentence. It was then that I realized the impact I could make as a reporter."

A powerful combination of empathy and admiration coursed through Lanie. "Ryan, thank you for sharing that story. Is that what motivated you to write the book, then?"

"It was definitely a factor."

Lanie had no idea what to say next. One thing was certain, telling him what she'd done wouldn't be easy after he was so open with her. Sensing her dismay, and wanting to lighten the mood, Ryan stood and reached for her hand. "Ready for dessert?"

It could wait. "Always."

"Okay, grab your purse."

Looking around, she wasn't concerned that a guest would take her bag but she picked it up anyway.

He led her to the side door and to the deck, which

confused Lanie since the buffet was inside. Coming to a gate, he unlatched the lock and told her to watch her step. Following his lead, she took the stairs to the pier below. At the end of the dock was a beautiful motor boat. The bottom was painted black and the interior was pure white leather. Lanie had admired the vessel from their vantage point at the table. Once they arrived in front of the ladder, Ryan turned to Lanie, "You don't get seasick, do you?"

What was happening? "This isn't the sea."

"Good point." He kneeled and untied her shoes. "No shoes on deck. It's a safety hazard."

"Wait a minute. We're going on this boat?" A fresh wave of nerves overtook her.

Smiling wide and tossing his shoes on board, Ryan said, "Yep, after you." He gestured for her to climb the stairs.

Once on board she noticed a cute table and two plastic wine glasses. There was an assortment of berries and petits fours. Ryan was still on the pier removing the rope from the anchor. He climbed the ladder himself, pulled it on board, and stowed it.

"You're not afraid of boats, right?"

Lanie felt like she was on a reality TV show, the kind where the producers created those over-the-top dating scenarios. How could she resist? "I'm not, as long as you know what you're doing."

He appeared to be in his element. Grinning like a boy, he walked toward the table, removed the cork from the bottle, and poured two glasses of the pink fizz.

"Well, what are you waiting for?" He gestured for her to join him.

Selecting an ornately decorated cake square, he raised the lovely confection to her lips. She took a tentative bite;

the flavors, so subtle yet haunting, overran her mouth. Orange, rosemary, and chocolate swirled on her tongue.

Handing her a wine glass, he instructed, "Quick, take a sip. It's all part of the experience, Ms. Shane."

Hearing her pseudonym brought Lanie back to earth. The flavors evaporated and she remembered this wasn't really a date. The wine was cathartic and she hoped it would be enough to get her through what she had to say.

He took her silence in stride. "Well, what's the verdict?"

"Oh Ryan, this is heavenly but . . ."

He stood, reached for her hand and pulled her to standing. For an instant their eyes locked. Panic took over as Lanie thought he might kiss her. He had another idea in mind. Guiding her toward the bow, he motioned for her to sit on the port side of the boat while he took the wheel.

He fired up the ignition. The vessel purred as they navigated away from the pier, entering the Columbia River. He advanced slowly at first, pointing out different landmarks along the way. A family of ducks floated near the shore. Mom and dad made sure their ducklings were tucked safely between them. Though it was a hot day, the movement created a gentle breeze and the awning provided shade from the insistent sun. Thousands of tiny waves sparkled while the boat skipped along the water.

She took a deep breath and tried to absorb it all. She had to tell Ryan the truth. She thought about James. Would she tell him about this and if she did, would he be able to forgive her? Lanie had never been in a situation like this. She'd never cheated on anyone nor kept secrets. She was so out of her element with Ryan, yet she had to admit, there was a strange sense of knowledge between them. She felt she already knew him. Dismissing the concept, she reminded herself that he was a reporter and a successful one. He was practiced at putting people at ease. Though she sensed he was sincere, and after what she learned about his schoolmate, she knew it wasn't just a job to him. He genuinely cared. Taking in a deep breath, she wanted to enjoy the moment. She convinced herself it could wait a little longer.

Unbeknownst to Lanie, Ryan was watching her. He sensed she was grappling with something but knew she would share when she was ready. Giving her a thrill, he said, "You up for a little fun?"

A tentative look crossed her face. "What more could there be?"

His white teeth gleamed as he spoke, "Hold on then!" Ryan floored it and her back was plastered to the chair.

She couldn't help but giggle as the spray hit her face, no doubt ruining her smooth hair style. Lanie's voice was gleeful as she cheered, "Faster, faster!"

He swerved, tossing them side to side, creating a lovely wake for the tubers along their path. It was such a thrill as they speed along the river. For a time, she could think of nothing but their excursion along the waterway. She felt such joy it brought tears to her eyes. After a while, he slowed the pace and pulled the boat to a nearby slip. Cutting the engine, he stood and set the anchor.

Lanie stood and stretched her arms overhead. Stifling a yawn induced by the early morning, tasty wine, and fresh air, she felt sleepy. As she surveyed their surroundings, she noticed it wasn't her stop. Above the pier was a row of floating homes she'd never noticed before. Ryan returned after setting the anchor.

Eyes toward one house, Ryan inquired, "Would you like to check out my house?"

Panicked and unable to hide it, Lanie didn't know what to do. "Umm, that may be a little fast for me."

Understanding and wanting to put her at ease, Ryan explained. "I didn't have anything crazy in mind. I thought we might sit on the deck for a while?"

Lanie's expression said it all. She was stunned and silent.

Ryan could tell he had made her uncomfortable and was mentally kicking himself. "I'm sorry Natalie. I should have asked you first before assuming you'd be okay with going to my home. I didn't mean to make you uncomfortable."

Was she being insane? She had no idea how to handle this situation. "No, it's okay. I'm not very versed at this stuff and well, you caught me off guard."

Ryan wondered if he might be reading it wrong. She seemed interested and her body language, though reserved, appeared favorable toward him. Clearly, she was not ready for this step. "I apologize. My intention wasn't to make you nervous. I don't want to move faster than you are ready for. Let's get you back." Shoulders slumped, he left her standing as he removed the anchor from the water.

Now she felt terrible for making things awkward. She couldn't fathom adding fuel to the fire by telling him what she had done. It was simple, they would part ways this afternoon and she would forget they ever shared this day.

After he stowed the ladder, he walked toward the bow; Lanie touched his arm, hoping her words would salve the wound she'd created. "Thank you for understanding and for such a beautiful afternoon, Ryan."

⸺

A MAN COULD ONLY SHOW SO much restraint. Her hand on his arm sent shivers up his spine. She was confusing and oh so enticing. He had to taste her lips.

Grabbing both arms above the elbow, he pulled her to him and devoured her mouth. At first, she resisted, but a beat later they were entangled in a time-stopping kiss.

⊏▭⊐

HER HEART WAS POUNDING in her ears. Ryan tasted foreign. His lips were firm and powerful. She didn't want it to stop. As that thought entered her mind, he pulled back. With inches between them, he studied her face for a beat, then continued toward the wheel to power up the engine.

The ride back was silent as they contemplated what the day meant. Almost too quickly they arrived at their original destination. Anchoring the boat, Ryan stood on the pier and helped Lanie down. Making their way in silence through the restaurant, she noticed it was much emptier now. At the valet station, she handed the attendant her ticket; they stood together waiting for his return. The valet pulled around and handed Ryan the key. He exchanged it with a crisp bill. He and Lanie walked the few remaining steps to the driver's side and stood awkwardly.

Breaking the silence, Lanie said, "This was so unexpected, a treat I couldn't have imagined. Thank you, Ryan." She kissed his cheek, fled into the vehicle and swiftly drove away.

⊏▭⊐

CONFOUNDED, Ryan stood there wondering if he would see her again. Something happened today. It both panicked him and gave him hope. She was a mystery and one he could hardly wait to unravel. He had the feeling he could spend a lifetime trying and still wouldn't have all the answers.

DRIVING ALONG THE ROAD, Lanie was in disbelief. What just happened? She went on a date. There was no other way to describe it. That was a date. She kissed a man. Worse, she enjoyed it. She didn't stop him from kissing her. She didn't tell him the truth about her engagement. She had officially cheated on James. Her intentions didn't matter. Facts were facts. She wanted him to kiss her. She kissed him back. She could never see that man again. What should she do about James? Should she tell him or pretend the whole thing never happened? Shit. Her mind was racing.

This was a nightmare. The thing is, the day had been perfect. Ryan was a gentleman. He was sincere and easy to talk to. It flowed so naturally but that didn't matter. She was marrying James in less than two weeks. She must never see Ryan again.

10

No Denying

As soon as she returned home, Lanie changed to her old standby outfit. Loose Levi cutoffs and James' T-shirt were her comfort clothes. Placing the skirt and blouse from today into the hamper, she heard her phone buzzing in the next room. She caught it by the third ring. It was him. Hesitating for a beat longer, but knowing she shouldn't hide, she accepted his call.

"Hello." She spoke tentatively.

His words were slurred. James had been drinking, as expected, and typical when he and Nick were together. "Angel. How are you?"

Unfairly miffed, she had to check herself. "I'm fine. How are you doing?"

"Me, um, I'm good. Just wish you were here. I need a nap and you would make that so much more fun."

Picturing his crooked smile, the one he wore whenever he overindulged, should have annoyed her. It typically did. Today, she had no right to feel anything remotely negative toward James. "It sounds like you may need an actual nap, mister."

Undeterred, he whined, "You know I need more than a nap."

Lanie was thankful for their distance. "I think you should get some rest. Are you having fun?"

"Yeah, fun." His voice was distant, as if he may actually doze off.

"James." She spoke but there was no response. Again, "James?" Dead silence greeted her. Raising her voice, she tried a third time. "James?" Still no response. "Okay, enjoy your nap. Be careful." She hung up.

As soon as she did, another call rang through. This time it was Jay. "Oh god," she cursed aloud, but since it could be gallery business, she answered. "Hi, Jay."

"Hi, yourself."

Now confident in his saucy tone that it was not gallery business, she regretted taking the call. "What's up?"

"Are you home?" he inquired.

"Yes," she replied.

"Alone?"

"Yes, Jay!"

"I'm coming over. See you in ten."

Before she could protest he hung up and Lanie knew there was no way around it. She took the last few moments of quiet to revisit her painting from earlier today. The colors were different now that the paint had dried. Studying the piece, she saw a glaring similarity to her own life. She was that figure standing at the precipice of the great unknown. The lone, looming cloud symbolized her confusion, or perhaps the decision she was about to make. Do I stand here with the life I know, or do I jump into the abyss?

Saving her from deeper consideration, the intercom buzzed signaling Jay's arrival. As she opened the door, she saw he carried a brown paper bag. All energy and life, Jay greeted Lanie with air kisses. "Hi, sweetie. I've brought sustenance."

Carrying the bag to the table, he unpacked the contents. There was a container of guacamole, fresh salsa, tortilla chips, reposado tequila, limes and cilantro. He was making his special margaritas. Lanie knew it was his way of getting her sauced up so she would talk.

Jay ordered, "Take a seat. I know where everything is. You sit there and relax."

Way too solicitous, Lanie thought. He would get the whole story out of her for sure. She watched as Jay transferred the dips into two pottery bowls, then the chips. He set those in front of her then turned back to the kitchen. Expertly slicing the fresh limes, he then found the agave on the shelf and mixed the tart concoction in a shaker. He filled two glasses with ice, and shook the mix one last time before adding it to the glasses. The finishing touch of minced cilantro was sprinkled liberally over each glass. He walked to the table and handed Lanie a glass. Raising his in toast, he said, "To girls' night gossip."

She sniffed and took a sip of the drink. The tart lime combined gracefully with just the right amount of sweet. Lanie loved this drink and Jay knew it. "You are an expert mixologist, kind sir."

"Yes, well my new friend Serge has been giving me some pointers. If you know what I mean."

She did.

Lanie picked up a chip and broke it into pieces. She tapped one corner into the salsa before trying it. Knowing she took some warming up when it came to serious conversation, Jay watched patiently.

"How is it going with Serge, by the way?" They both knew she was tap dancing.

"So far he's pretty great. I haven't seen the crazy side yet but it's only been a week."

Surprised that Jay and was even thinking this way, she was curious. "Will Serge be with us for a while?" Noting his expression change, she felt like a heel. "I'm sorry, but you know, you haven't exactly been the relationship type since I've known you."

His eyebrows rose in resignation. "You're right. I haven't. After losing Sebastian in 2008, I wasn't sure I would want another long-term partner again. He was so much more than I had ever hoped for. I still miss him every day."

She wasn't accustomed to Jay opening up about Seb. "Really? It's been ten years and you still think about him?" She was floored by this information.

"Lanie, he was the love of my life. In many ways I didn't realize it until he was sick. His health went downhill so quickly and our time became about the appointments and trying to prolong his life."

She studied her friend as he sipped his drink. "Do you know, I still argue with him mentally to this day? When I go to move something in the house, I wonder what his opinion would be."

Lanie snorted and responded. "I find it hard to believe you took his feedback to heart on the subject of placement."

He smiled but it didn't touch his eyes. "It's true, we fought like cats and dogs at times, but he was such a good friend to me. I loved him, faults and all."

This was the most serious Lanie had ever seen Jay. He was giving her a lot to think about.

Jay opened the subject they both knew was coming. "Lanie, what happened today?"

Turning the glass with her fingers, she studied the way

the sweat slid down the base. Her mouth was in a near frown as she looked up at Jay. He could see she was on the brink of tears.

"What happened today was a mistake."

Knowing her well enough to understand the gravity of her words, he tried to comfort her. "Lanie, there are no mistakes."

Lanie felt like climbing out of her skin. Maybe she could occupy another body or even become a plant? She'd do anything to avoid the truth of what she was experiencing.

He could see the war she was waging on herself and he also knew she couldn't win the battle alone. She had to open up. "Sometimes talking things through and giving life to the words inside your head is liberating."

How could she convey everything she'd experienced today? A thought occurred to her and she stood. "Grab your glass and follow me."

He did as told and followed her to the studio. She flipped on the light switch, irradiating her newest painting. His breath caught. For what seemed to be an eternity Jay studied the piece in silence.

She couldn't take it a second longer and asked, "Well?" Her insecurity was evident by her soft voice.

He finally looked away from the art and studied her for a beat. "Lanie, this may be your best work yet. The textures and depth are so dramatic and the message couldn't be more powerful. This person is looking at the future and running from the past. It's as if suicide is the only path."

She hadn't wanted to extract that perspective but that was the thing about art, it was subjective. She sat on the small overstuffed loveseat and Jay settled into the papasan chair. Kicking his sandals to the floor, he crossed his legs beneath him.

"What happened today?"

She studied the painting for a beat, then started. "It was beautiful. We had a great conversation. I learned why he became a journalist and saw a side of him that I couldn't help but admire. He's so accomplished and kind. We had lunch then he took me on his boat."

"Wait, what? He has a boat?" Jay leaned forward now.

"Yeah and it was thrilling. I felt good at his side. It was all so natural, except . . ."

"Except what?" he pressed.

"Except for the fact that I'm taken. I felt so many emotions. As good a date as it was, and yes, I've come to the realization that it was a date, I have no right to enjoy his company."

Her feelings were nothing to brush off but Jay wanted her to be okay. "Lanie, you and James entered into a pretty insane bet, right before your wedding. I don't mean to be blunt but facts are facts. James not only agreed, but from what you've told me, he wholeheartedly did."

She accepted his words. "I know and I'm a little pissed at him for that, but Jay, he kissed me. Not only did he kiss me but I fully participated in kissing him back."

Looking down, she tugged at the loose threads at the bottom of her shorts.

"I wanted it and I am so perplexed. I think I should tell James what happened."

Jay considered everything she had imparted. "Here's the thing, if you tell him, it could be the end. Are you ready for that consequence?"

Her silence gave him the opening to continue.

"Is it maybe what you want but can't admit?"

Too many thoughts were swimming in her head. Her

eyes began to tear up. "I don't know. I truly don't know. I wish the whole thing never happened. Life was so much simpler before this damn challenge."

"I can imagine feeling that way if I were in your shoes. Since I'm not you but I am someone who cares about your happiness, I'm going out on a limb. Don't hate me for what I'm about to say, promise?"

Nervously, she agreed. "I promise."

"Life is messy. Simple isn't going to bring the kind of love a passionate woman like you needs. This didn't happen to you. You made a conscious decision to raise the test and you accepted the date. I think you have to see it through."

Shaking her head in disbelief, but partially agreeing with Jay, she couldn't fathom living this double life for much longer. "How can I?" Her tone was desperate.

"By putting James aside for the next few days."

Her expression showed alarm as she replied, "What?"

"Hear me out. James and the boys will be gone through Wednesday night, correct?"

"Yes," she agreed.

"For the next few days, act like you are a single woman. Don't for a minute think that Nick isn't saying the same thing to James. That guy is a bad influence and you know it."

She sniffed but agreed. "He's a different kind of person, that's true."

"Let me share something about guys. Although I am not currently the macho, bro type, I had to pretend pretty hard in my formative years. I know that men tend to hang out with guys who have traits they wish they were brave enough to act on. James and Nick aren't that different, trust me."

Was he trying to push her? Miffed, she wasn't sure how to take his remarks. "What are you getting at, Jay?"

"All I'm saying is that boys will be boys. He's on a five-day bachelor retreat with Nick. They aren't angels and your kiss probably isn't as earth shattering as you think."

Literally saved by the bell, Lanie heard her phone chime in the next room. It was a text. "That's my phone. Let's see what the message is." Jay wouldn't have it any other way and followed her to the dining room. Snagging a chip, he scooped a mound of the guacamole, eating it in one bite.

Lanie unlocked her phone and Jay came to stand right behind her. It was a text from Ryan. "You took my breath away today. I don't know your schedule but it would be incredible to see you again tomorrow. Please say yes."

Jay was more excited than she was and he didn't hesitate to say, "Oh my goodness, Lanie. You see! This is a sign. He felt the same way you did. If you don't say yes, I will for you." She hesitated and he pounced. "Answer him and say yes for God's sake."

Before her senses returned, Lanie typed a simple response. "Yes."

An instant later he messaged. "Meet me at Union Station at 8:15 a.m. You may want to bring a sweater, just in case."

"In case of what?" She looked to Jay.

He shrugged his shoulders and smiled. "Beat's me."

What the hell was she doing listening to her lothario friend? Yet deep down she knew his heart had been taken long ago and that he only wanted what was best for her. She typed a response. "Okay, I'll see you in the morning."

"Good girl, Lanie." Jay's hand on her shoulder was anything but reassuring.

11

Orbit

She pulled into a parking spot across from Union Square. After cutting the ignition, she flipped down the visor and checked herself in the mirror. Her makeup hadn't changed since she applied it 30 minutes prior. Simple black eyeliner, mascara, pink blush and lipstick. Check. She wondered about her choice of clothes, but was reassured by the larger than normal bag she carried. Inside were a pair of strappy black sandals and a silken black halter. For her main outfit, she chose cropped jeans in dark blue, a fitted white T-shirt, and silvery pointed flats. In her ears were a pair of teardrop hematite earrings she made herself. They were simple and elegant, adding a feminine touch to the ensemble. Nervously, she opened the car door and walked toward the red brick building.

Deep breaths, she incanted silently. It had become a mental chant and her mantra for the morning. The train station was hectic. Business people moved purposefully as families with bags of luggage mixed in. The experience wouldn't be complete without the occasional transient asking for train fare. The surrounding hustle wasn't enough to squelch her anxiety.

Remembering last night's conversation with Jay, she was determined to move forward. There would be consequences, but she'd deal with that later. She had a plan she couldn't share with Jay because she didn't want him to be dissuaded. She would tell Ryan the truth. He deserved to know. She might be going through a crisis, and he didn't deserve to get caught up in it, at least not without his knowledge.

His voice rang into her thoughts. "Natalie?" She turned and watched him approach. He was wearing a black, snug-fitting V-neck T-shirt that outlined his toned physique. Dark jeans and stylish leather shoes finished his outfit, making her mouth water. Over his arm was a casual charcoal jacket. In his hands he carried two cups from Starbucks. "Good morning." He smiled as he handed her one. "Latte, right?"

Happy for the caffeine, and his recollection of her favorite morning beverage, she accepted the cup and a kiss on the cheek. "Thank you so much. This is just what I needed."

His gaze lingered and he said, "It's the least I can do after waking you so early. Are you ready for our adventure?"

Finally, her nerves were warranted. "I'm not sure what I'm getting myself into."

Noticing her oversized bag, he asked, "Do you have space in there for this?" He gestured to his coat.

"Sure, can you hold this a sec?" Handing him back the coffee, she took his jacket; folding it snuggly, she settled it beneath her blouse.

"All set." She smiled up at him.

Handing her back the cup, he put his arm around her shoulders and walked toward the entrance.

"If you haven't figured it out yet, we are taking a little trip. Do you like Seattle?"

"I do," she agreed, instantly remembering she was to utter those words to James in a matter of days.

Seeing her expression darken, he mistakenly reassured. "Don't worry, it is just a day excursion. I'll have you home before the carriage turns back into a pumpkin."

Put that out of your mind for today, she reminded herself. Be present. "Ok. Let's go."

They entered the historic building that was constructed in 1893. Polished white floors gleamed and were a stark contrast to the dark wooden pews. Her eyes could never get enough of the ornate arched ceilings. The building was a masterpiece of architecture.

Hearing an announcement overhead, he led them to their row in line. "I've already got the tickets. The trip will take just over three hours."

Excited now, Lanie said, "It's funny, but I haven't taken the train to Seattle in years."

Following the conductor's directions, they entered the car and found their seats. They sat side by side and Ryan deferred the window seat to her.

Once they were settled, he shared, "Whenever I have the time, I like to take the train. The views from the tracks are completely different from I-5 and it's a good way to get work done along the way. Besides, traffic can stretch what should be a three-hour drive into four or more."

"I agree. I love going to Seattle but getting there can be a deterrent."

He asked, "What do you do when you visit?"

"Well, I like to visit the Seattle and Frye Art Museums."

She gestured toward her cup. "I love the Starbuck's roastery, and who could forget Fisherman's Wharf?"

"What about the Space Needle and the Chihuly Garden and Glass exhibit?"

"I know this is hard to believe, but I haven't done either. I'm a little afraid of heights and haven't been able to bring myself to visit the Space Needle yet."

He smiled and Lanie suspected that was about to change.

The announcer asked everyone to take their seats, and the train eased forward making its slow trip north. There were several stops along the way, beginning with Vancouver, then Longview, Centralia, Olympia, and Tacoma. Lanie had forgotten how stunning the woods and waterways along the path were.

They chatted easily, covering a range of topics from the history of each train station, to the gold mining era, their families, and philosophies on faith. Both were spiritual, believed in a higher power but didn't practice religion. This was something very important to each of them. Ryan had seen firsthand what religious ideologies could do to a country. Lanie agreed.

Time passed quickly as they ambled along the track. Things were going so well that she didn't want to ruin the day with her truth, but what value would he see in any of it if she continued with the lie? For goodness' sake, he thought her name was Natalie.

Taking a deep breath, she knew it time to get it out in the open. "Ryan, I have something to tell you. You know the other night when we met?"

"Yes." His tone was oddly reassuring.

"Well, there's something you don't know. A few things, actually."

Placing his hand on her arm, he stopped her. "Lanie, you do know I'm an investigative journalist, right?"

Snapping her head back, she breathed the words. "You just called me . . ."

"Lanie? Your real name. Yes, I did. I know who you are, Ms. Blackwell, and I can understand why you used an alias. I can't imagine what it is like for women out there. Let alone you, who looks like this"—he poked her belly —"and have managed to build a thriving business. I'm sure you have to take extra precautions because of it."

Shit, he was good. He knew half of the truth, but not about James nor her pending nuptials. They had made no formal announcement in the paper and were trying to keep the ceremony intimate. Only family and close friends were invited.

Her panicked expression made Ryan want to reassure her. Leaning forward, he softly touched his lips to hers. They were feather light, a whisper against her skin. All the air left Lanie's lungs. It was as if his touch had awakened every hair follicle, blood vessel, and organ in her body.

Pulling back, his expression was tender. "You don't have anything to explain."

A muffled sound came from overhead. Lanie could decipher nothing. Fortunately, Ryan had his wits about him. Standing, he took Lanie's bag over his shoulder and pulled her to her feet. Going through the motions she stood and followed.

They had arrived at King Street Station and once they were at the curb, he hailed a cab. After they climbed in, he greeted the driver. "Hello, my friend."

"Yes sir, where to?" The driver had a thick Russian accent and clear blue eyes.

"Tilikum Place Café on Cedar, please."

"You got it."

The car navigated from the curb and headed south through the busy downtown streets. It was just after one in the afternoon and the sidewalks were filled with business people making their way to and from lunch.

Ryan looked over at Lanie who was watching the activity outside. "Have you tried the place before?"

Shaking her head and suddenly very hungry, she replied, "No, but I am ready for lunch."

"Good. I hope you'll like it. For a time, it was my home away from home while I was writing my book. I used to stay at a hotel not far from there in Queen Anne. The place has great views of the Space Needle. The best part though, was discovering this little restaurant. It's a gem for sure. I hope you'll like it."

The driver made several turns navigating the one-way streets and in no time, they were at their stop. As Ryan paid the driver, Lanie looked at their surroundings. The cobblestone walkway led to a few small businesses. Tucked in the middle, so discrete it would be easy to miss, Lanie saw the café. Placing his hand on the small of her back, he steered Lanie to the door. He held it open and motioned for her to enter.

The restaurant was bigger than she expected from her view outside. There were fifteen tables and a long marble bar with an unobstructed view of the kitchen. A flood of natural light filled the space, a result of the floor-to-ceiling glass frontage.

The hostess greeted Ryan warmly. "Ryan, so good to see you again."

Her dark hair was a stark contrast that offset her fair complexion. Round face aglow, she continued, "It's been a while."

"Too long, Annie." He leaned forward and pecked her cheek.

Gesturing toward Lanie, he introduced her. "This is my friend, Lanie. It's her first time dining here."

She smiled broadly. "Well hopefully it won't be your last."

Walking ahead, menus in hand, Annie gestured toward two bar stools near the kitchen. Settling her bag on the hook beneath the counter, Lanie took in the scene. Flames licked the bottom of a pan as a chef in a white coat tossed vegetables expertly. A sous chef was rapidly chopping herbs, his knife skill and concentration apparent. The aromas were tantalizing.

A moment later, a lovely blonde server greeted the two diners from behind the counter.

"Ryan, I heard you'd be in today," she said with a warm smile.

"So nice to see you, Amanda. How's that hubby of yours? Is he on the road or in town this month?"

"Thank you for asking, Ryan. He's actually in India. I leave next week to visit for two weeks. I'm so excited."

"It's good that you get to see so many places while he travels. Have you been to India before?"

"Nope. It'll be my first time. I'm a little nervous but so excited."

Ryan gestured toward Lanie. "This is Lanie. Lanie, meet Amanda."

The two shook hands and Lanie said, "It's nice to meet you, Amanda."

"Likewise. You must be pretty special for him to bring you here. He usually hides away in the corner tapping along on his laptop."

Surprised to hear this and feeling honored, Lanie

smiled in Ryan's direction. Turning her focus back to Amanda, Lanie spoke.

"I understand I'm in for a big treat."

"Yes, if you like great food, you've come to the right place. People think of us as a brunch spot but I never work those shifts. I think our lunch and dinner are amazing."

Looking toward Ryan, Amanda directed the next question at him. "Do you know what you'd like to drink today?"

"She's a pinot noir fan, so why don't you surprise us with your latest find?"

"You've got it." Amanda moved to the rack below and selected a vintage. Expertly, she uncorked the bottle and poured a smidge into the glass in front of Ryan.

"Thank you but I'm going to defer to my wine aficionado here."

Swirling the glass first, Ryan slid it in Lanie's direction.

"I'm no expert but I am happy to take the first sip." She picked up the glass, gave it a sniff, then took a tentative sip. Black pepper, cherries, and citrus flavors popped in her mouth. "Mmm, this is lovely."

"Glad you like it, Lanie." She poured a glass for Ryan then filled Lanie's. "I'll leave you two to your first tastes. Let me know if you have any questions after you've looked over the menu."

As Amanda walked to greet her other patrons, a young man brought over warm bread, olives, and butter.

"Thank you," Ryan said.

Turning his attention to Lanie, he raised his glass in toast. "Here's to a special day of new experiences."

Their glasses tapped and both drew in the decadent flavor.

"Ryan, thank you for arranging this. I can see you took the time to plan today."

He shook his head in dismissal.

She placed her hand on his arm. "Please let me finish."

He remained silent.

"I am honored that you chose to share this place with me. It's obvious that you're like family here. I also appreciate you taking the information you learned about me so well."

"Please, don't say another word about it. I'm happy to share this spot with you and glad you value it. Now, let's tackle the menu. I'm starving."

"Me too," she agreed.

"Do you like oysters?"

"Love them and all seafood. Actually, I eat almost everything as long as it is humanly treated. There are a few exceptions though, no duck, rabbit, frog legs or alligator. Maybe I should add snake, deer, and elk."

He laughed now. "Okay, that ruins the surprise. No rattle snake pudding for you."

As their two laughs combined, Amanda walked up. She couldn't help but notice how light Ryan looked by her side. They were a beautiful couple. She had the face of a doll and the body of a pin-up. His good looks were hard to miss. Tall, lean and well groomed, he didn't fit in with a lot of the Northwest guys.

"How are the first sips, you two?"

Ryan responded for them both. "Excellent; thank you, Amanda. Lanie, are you good with me ordering?"

Happy to delegate any decisions today, she agreed. "I'd love that."

Turning his attention back to Amanda, he ordered. "Let's start with a half-dozen of the Kumamoto oysters, the beet and anchovy salad, mussels, and last we'll share the pan roasted chicken."

"Perfect, I'll get those started." Amanda left them.

"Good lord, Ryan. Are we inviting others to join us? That sounds like a lot of food."

"Trust me," he said confidently, "we won't leave a morsel. Besides, you'll have time to burn it off after lunch. I thought we'd take a walk down to the wharf."

Lanie marveled at his selection. She would have chosen those dishes herself. She'd never expect to try all of them in one sitting, but today wasn't like any other day. While she was on the train, she decided to go with the flow and keep an open mind. Jay's words hit the mark on so many levels last night.

Interrupting her thoughts, the boy who served the bread returned. In his hand was a tray of freshly shucked oysters, accompanied by lemons and champagne mignonette.

The juices in Lanie's mouth were on overtime as they each selected one. After drizzling the sauce over the top, they loosened the little buggers from the shells and tilted their heads back to swallow. The freshness of the ocean, tang of vinegar and texture of minced garlic were to be savored.

"Yum . . ." Lanie's voice had an unintended seductive quality that Ryan couldn't overlook.

Beneath the bar, he moved his leg to touch hers. A sizzle was in the air between them. "Glad you like it, Natalie." He smiled torturously.

She choked, a reflex from his taunting. With a remorseful expression, she apologized again. "I really am sorry—"

He held up a hand. "Stop. To be honest, I kind of like you having an alter ego. It's pretty hot."

The tension between them was palatable. Fortunately, they were saved by their next course. A colorful salad of local greens, roasted beets, and minced anchovy was placed on the counter.

As they nibbled, Ryan wanted to hear more about her gallery. He couldn't believe he hadn't visited it prior to meeting Lanie. "Tell me about your gallery and how you got started."

It was her turn to tease now. "What, you weren't able to find that out by digging around, Mr. Investigator?"

"Touché. You have a point. I guess maybe I owe you an apology. Research is so second nature to me that I forget everyone doesn't do it. Sorry."

"No need. I was just ribbing you." She took another sip of the delicious wine and started.

"It was a dream of mine to open a gallery for as long as I could remember. I only hoped that some of the established artists I idolized would want to show their work in my space. As much as I enjoy producing, connecting with like-minded artisans has always been important to me. I love hearing about their process and learning from those around me."

"I couldn't agree more, Lanie. My writing has improved so much over the years by surrounding myself with other writers. I've been floored by the support and critique some amazing writers have given me."

She smiled and wondered again if this guy was for real.

He continued, "I call myself a student of life. There is always something to learn and I want to keep going."

She wholeheartedly agreed. Their eyes locked and Lanie felt a shift in the universe. Maybe it was the wine, she rationalized. Deep down she knew it had little to do with the burgundy liquid. She was falling for Ryan.

Saving her, Amanda arrived to check on them. She refilled their glasses as the runner removed their salad plates. Within seconds a mound of mussels in a pungent garlic broth was placed between them.

"How are you two getting on over here?" The double entendre was not missed by any of them.

Lanie flushed and Ryan responded chastely.

"We are doing well. As usual the meal is perfection. Tell Paul to keep up the good work."

"He'll be in tonight. I'll let him know you say hello."

"Thank you, Amanda."

Turning to Lanie, Ryan selected a shell from the pile. "Paul is the owner and a great guy. A little bit of an eternal child, but the birth of his daughter a couple of years back has settled the old dog a bit."

Knowing the type, she nodded in agreement.

They were quiet for a time each enjoying the tasty sea treats. Using the fresh bread, they soaked up the juices and ate happily.

Lanie could hardly believe there was more food coming after this but that was the wine talking. Their last course arrived with a flourish. Pan roasted chicken was braised to perfection, the skin artfully crisped. The fowl rested atop roasted potatoes and purple carrots. The meal, the service, and her companion made this the ultimate dining experience.

As lunch was winding down, Amanda's return was well timed.

"Well, what did you think, Lanie?"

How sweet of her to remember her name. "Two thumbs up. Now that I know this place, I'll come every time I visit Seattle. It was incredible."

"Glad to hear it. Are you two up for dessert?"

Ryan responded by handing Amanda his credit card. "I'm afraid we will explode if we eat another bite. Besides, we have some touristing to do."

Running the card, she smirked. "Is that a word? Touristing?"

He chuckled. "Nope. I made it up but you watch, Urban Dictionary will be adding it soon."

Returning the card and ticket to Ryan, she focused on Lanie.

"Take care of this one. He's pretty remarkable."

In that moment, Lanie wanted nothing more. "Thank you for everything, Amanda. You made me feel at home today. I can see why he loves this place."

Embarrassed, he shushed their sappiness. "Enough of the pleasantries, we have some waddling to do." Gesturing toward his trim midsection, Ryan walked Lanie to the door.

Calling over her shoulder, Lanie said, "Thank you."

The fresh air and busy street outside were a good transition. "Ryan, thank you for lunch and for sharing that place with me. It was delicious."

Liking the pink at her cheeks, he was glad to see she was so relaxed. "Don't mention it. I'm happy you enjoyed it. Shall we take a stroll now?"

"Please. I need to move, albeit slowly, after our huge lunch and tasty wine."

They walked close to the water, picking up the path between the tourist shops and restaurants. He took her hand as they moved in silence. They stopped to peer into storefront windows, and to watch the hungry seagulls steal food from nearby picnickers. It was like a scene out of a movie. The afternoon sun pricked her skin, and she couldn't miss the way his thumb caressed the underside of her hand. It was idyllic.

Coming up on a vacant bench, Ryan asked, "Would you like to sit for a minute?"

"Sure," she agreed.

He sat close to her; their legs touched and his arm snugged around her shoulder. The sea was calm as they watched a ferry launch, taking its course toward Bainbridge Island.

Pointing toward the Ferris wheel, he joked, "Since you mentioned you are afraid of heights, I guess I shouldn't suggest we take a spin?"

Genuinely panicked, she shook her head. "Not unless you want me to run."

Pulling her shoulder closer to him, he whispered in her ear, "I don't want you to run."

This felt too intense and Lanie needed a retreat. She decided for levity. "You probably won't believe this but I have been kicked off of several Ferris wheels in my life."

His face screwed up. "Kicked off? Explain yourself," he demanded.

"Well, one of the times it happened I was at Disneyland, actually California Adventure. There, they have these cars that slide around a smaller track as the wheel goes around. As if the heights weren't dizzying enough, the sensation of swinging and dropping was way too much for me. I seriously felt like I would fly out of my seat. Anyway, I panicked and grabbed the boy beside me. I told him not to move then started screaming, literally screaming."

Ryan had never heard of anyone being that afraid of a Ferris wheel before. He was having second thoughts about his evening plan. It was cute though, and he was trying not to laugh.

"I guess they have video cameras or something. The wheel went around only once and they stopped the whole ride so I could get off. It was embarrassing and I promised myself I would never try that again. To this day, I haven't."

"Woah, are you afraid of being in tall buildings or is your phobia specific to the slow-moving Ferris wheel?"

"There's something about an open car and heights. I can't do lifts either."

"Got it. No ski dates for you."

Faking indignation, she protested. "I'll have you know, I've adapted quite well on ski trips. I make the perfect lodge guest. I enjoy the view while sipping hot cocoa from the comfort of a cozy chair."

He thought again that Lanie was a most endearing person. Looking at his watch, he saw it was almost 4 p.m. "I have something else planned for today but I'm a little concerned now. Do you trust me?" he ventured.

I'd follow you to the end of the earth, she thought. Checking herself, she answered, "I think I do."

"Then we'd better get going." Noticing a cab on the path ahead, he motioned and the driver pulled up. "Hello, would you drop us at Chihuly?"

"Sure thing, mister."

Smiling and excited, Lanie was looking forward to their next stop. They arrived quickly, and after Ryan paid the driver they walked to the entrance with a couple of hours to spend inside before the museum closed. This would allow just enough time to see the unbelievable glass sculptures.

As they toured the museum, Lanie was floored by the incredible shapes and vibrant colors the collection offered. She couldn't believe how many captivating works were in one place. Colorful vines and incredible silken flowers surrounded them. The walls, ceilings, and display areas were abundant with the master's twisted and lifelike depictions. Lanie wondered why she had never visited before.

Turning to Ryan, fresh gratitude showed. "This is something else. Thank you for bringing me here."

He was glad the day was developing even better than he had hoped. "It's not over yet."

He steered her toward the door and into a lush garden. An explosion of natural plants intertwined with more of the unimaginable glass sculptures. The combination was breathtaking.

Ryan could resist no more. Turning her to face him, he paused, leaving no option but for her to make eye contact. A beat later, his mouth was on hers, sweetly at first then more aggressively as his tongue ventured. A sound escaped from the back of Lanie's throat and he knew she felt as he did. Their kiss was as gloriously twisted as the animated glass they were surrounded by.

He pulled back and her legs buckled slightly. Feeling her falter, he pulled her close. He, too, was shaky. What was happening? He hadn't reacted to another woman quite the same. Needing a moment himself, he released her. "Are you sure you trust me?"

Lanie wasn't sure of anything anymore and couldn't yet speak.

Taking her silence as permission, he said, "Come on. Let's go and conquer your fear."

Lanie wasn't sure what was more terrifying, the way she responded to his kiss, or rising 600′ above the earth in a glass elevator. They walked to the counter and she reached for her wallet.

"Let me get the tickets, Ryan."

Pushing her hand away, he stopped her. "Two please." He paid and took their tickets in hand.

"Thank you, again."

"Here's the deal," he began to strategize, "if you get scared, just close your eyes."

Using that philosophy, her eyes should have been closed for the past three days. "Okay," she agreed.

As they got to the front of the entrance, a young lady instructed them to look forward. A flash went off and

Lanie realized they'd been photographed. Ryan handed her their tickets and they were directed through the turn-stile, toward the elevator.

She could feel pricks of fear under her arms. What had she gotten herself into? The car's arrival was announced by a screaming beep, or at least that was how it sounded to Lanie. Her legs felt like lead.

Sensing her tension, he whispered in her ear. "You're going to like this and if you don't, just remember to close your eyes; I'll be right there."

His words worked and her legs slowly came to life.

The elevator was not remarkable. The face was glass, but from their floor everything was dark. When all of the passengers entered, the doors closed and a fresh wave of panic hit her. There's no way out now and the car was the only way down. The cab lurched skyward and Lanie stood frozen. She could sense Ryan behind her. They passed dark concrete walls and she realized she had been holding her breath. Suddenly, as if someone turned on a flood light, there was a flash, then the sparkling Pacific Ocean gleamed before them. As she stepped back from the edge, she backed right into Ryan's chest. His hands came to rest on her shoulders, then he pulled her body close to his. She could feel his heart beating behind her.

Calming at his touch, she ventured to look at the scene around them. It was nearly 6 p.m. and though the sun had not yet set, the evening sky was slowly arriving. She could see the path where she and Ryan had walked and the Ferris wheel turning in the distance.

Leaning down, Ryan whispered, "Is it as scary as you thought?"

The fear that if she shifted the slightest bit her weight might cause the car to plummet to the earth, had waned. "It's unforgettable."

He replied, "Like you, Lanie."

Climbing a few moments longer, the car finally stopped. The doors opened to the interior, which was a gift shop. Regaining her composure, she stepped off and perused the displays. Allowing her some time before they ventured on, Ryan followed along.

She noticed a large automated wall map. Beside it photographs of visitors were displayed. Suddenly she was met by an image of Ryan and herself. He noticed her reaction.

"Am I that ugly?" he joked.

She tried for normalcy. "Sorry, I just didn't expect it."

Rebounding, he asked, "Do you want to go outside? I don't want to scare you but the views of the city are out of this world."

Lanie chuckled now, finally releasing some of the tension in her body. "They should be, at this height we are closer to outer space than planet earth."

He liked her sense of humor. "A cheeky one, aren't you?"

She inhaled before agreeing. "Let's go."

Taking her hand, he wove her past the other visitors to the exterior door. Wanting her to be comfortable, he walked along beside her, keeping her closest to the wall. Pointing out landmarks as they went, he could see she was relaxing.

He ventured, "Do you want to look through the telescope?"

That would mean getting close to the edge.

Surprising him, she agreed. "I would."

He inserted the coins and motioned for her to step forward. Squinting one eye, Lanie looked through the tube. It was incredible what you could see. Moving the unit in different directions, she was enjoying the scenery.

131

"Wow." She stepped back, conscious that he might want to look before the time ran out. "Your turn." She motioned for him to take over.

He did as told and looked up once the shutter snapped shut.

"It's an amazing perspective, don't you think?"

She'd stopped thinking the moment she saw him at the train station. "This whole day has been a dream, Ryan."

Peering down at her, a grin on his lips, he agreed. "It certainly has. Unfortunately, if we are going to catch the last train home, it is time to go."

They rode the car down; this time Lanie was less frightened. Holding her hand, he guided her past the other visitors and to the cab line. They arrived at the train station just ten minutes before it was set to depart.

Settling into their seats, Ryan put his arm around her shoulders—a gesture that was beginning to feel familiar. Too tired for the mental anguish, she relaxed into his arms. Before she knew it, a loud voice roused her. She had slept the entire way home. Embarrassed by the realization, she said as much.

"I'm so embarrassed that I fell asleep on you like that."

Standing and helping her to her feet, he smiled in response. "Don't be. It means you are comfortable with me. It felt good holding you close. You're beautiful when you sleep. You're beautiful period."

Exiting the train, Lanie felt a little bit sad that their time had come to an end. The emotions warring inside her would be examined at a later time. They walked wordlessly toward her car.

Once they got there, he turned her to him and said, "Thank you for making this one of the best days I've ever had, Lanie. I want to see you again. Tomorrow?" Before she could answer, Ryan took Lanie's mouth in the softest, most teasing kiss. She responded in kind, their tongues twisted like one of the sculptures they'd seen earlier in the day.

Pulling back, Ryan's expression was impossible to read. "Drive safely, Natalie," he taunted, and she smiled.

12

What next?

The next morning Lanie woke up without the alarm. She looked at the clock on the bedside table and saw it was, once again, before six. Not typically an early riser, she wondered what was happening to her. That question could apply to so many things lately. Instead of ruminating on the subject, she decided to take the morning Vinyasa Flow class. A little Yoga couldn't hurt; besides, that was the one place she could go to blank out all the questions.

With renewed motivation for a little self-care, she made coffee and went about her routine. Taking a quick shower, she snugged on a pair of black Capri-length stretch pants and a pink tank. After slipping on flip-flops and finding her mat, she left the building. The studio was a few blocks away and the morning light was beautiful. Covering the distance quickly, Lanie felt empowered by the simple task of putting one foot in front of the other.

When she arrived, she was greeted by the familiar faces of her fellow practitioners. Monique, her favorite instructor, welcomed her and told her she would need two blocks for today's class. Lanie gathered the props then settled onto her mat. Deciding on the intention, "live in the moment," she closed her eyes until the class began.

At 8 a.m. sharp, Monique called the group to their feet. As instructed, Lanie traveled through the poses. Each time her mind wandered, she brought everything back to her practice. Determination pushed her as she took the poses to heart, contorting herself toward an impossible elegance. She was invigorated, if not angry. Pouring all of her emotion into the moves, she felt liberated.

At the end, Shavasana was the only time where she couldn't stop her mind from racing. Sensing her activity, Monique came to her mat and rubbed lemon essential oil at her temples and down the sides of her neck. Accepting her gentle nudge, she relaxed. If there was one thing that yoga taught Lanie, it was that everything would be all right.

Finally, they were guided to find a comfortable seated position. Lanie placed her hands in prayer at her heart and mentally thanked the instructor for her kindness. She then wished that same kindness on her fellow classmates and finally herself. Slowly people stood, rolled up mats and returned their props.

Monique spoke to Lanie. "How are you doing today? I sensed a little tension?"

"You are so intuitive. I'm working through something. Thank you for the extra care."

Monique had a peaceful beauty that glowed as she said, "Remember, take every moment for what it is. Things have a way of working themselves out."

Feeling transparent, Lanie only managed a non-verbal response. Touching Monique's arm, she nodded her head and went for the exit. After collecting her bag, she checked her phone and noticed she'd missed a call from James. Nervously she redialed the number but got his voicemail. It was just after 9:30 a.m., he was probably out fishing or on a hike. A sense of relief washed over her, and she was thankful she could postpone a conversation a little while longer.

The gallery was closed on Tuesday so she had the day to herself. It would be a good time to visit with Audrey, who was completely unaware of the recent developments. She wondered what she would think if she told her the situation and considered whether she'd share her secret. Her phone buzzed in her purse. She pulled it out and saw it was a message from Ryan.

"Yesterday was like a dream. Have dinner with me tonight so I can prove to myself that you are real?"

Not wanting to keep him waiting, she typed a response. "I'd love to. Where should I meet you?"

She could see the three dots on her display indicating that he was typing as she waited. A bubble of excitement rose from her belly to her chest.

"Meet me at Mississippi Pizza? Is 7 p.m. good?"

She hadn't been there in a long time but remembered it to be a fun and relaxing place. They made good drinks and usually had live music.

"Great," she responded. "I'll see you then."

An instant later his reply read, "Looking forward to pinching myself and who knows, maybe even you."

She couldn't help but smile. Feeling happy, she embraced the day. Finding her contact in the directory, she dialed Audrey.

As she answered, Audrey's voice was overpowered by her young.

"Hold on a second. Let me barricade myself into the bedroom so I can hear you. Lee, put that down right now!" she admonished, and Lanie had to suppress a laugh.

She knew her friend well enough not to tease at a time like this.

Audrey was now decipherable. "Hey there."

Lanie could hear a deep exhalation emanating through the line.

"What are you up to?" she asked.

"The usual hysteria. I was thinking about getting the kids out to the zoo. You game?"

Lanie thought about it for a beat then agreed. "Sure, when should I meet you?"

After a pause, Audrey said, "How is noon? That'll give me time to get them down for a nap. We can feed them lunch at the park."

"Sounds great. I'll see you at the entrance then."

"Okay, I'd better go before something breaks."

Lanie chuckled and said, "See you soon."

AT NOON LANIE stood at the zoo entrance waiting for her best friend's arrival. She was rarely on time these days and had an attitude if people mentioned her tardiness. While waiting, Lanie soaked in the forested surroundings. The zoo was one of several attractions that abutted Forrest Park, which was the country's largest urban park. There were miles of trails, and around every corner were glimpses of the bustling downtown skyline. Unexpectedly on time, Audrey called out as little Lee raced forward. Recognizing Lanie, he ran into her arms. She scooped the little boy up into a tight hug and soared him around like an airplane.

"Hey, kiddo."

He smiled at Lanie then steadied himself as she set him on his feet. Audrey arrived pushing the two-man stroller they'd affectionately named the Mars rover, due to its oversized form. Convenient as it was, one had to wonder why those dimensions were required to carry two tiny people.

Embracing, the two friends said their hellos. Lanie saw that Lily was wide awake and smiling. She bent to kiss her forehead and pretended to steal her nose. The littlest bundle smiled in response.

Impatiently, Lee announced, "Go!"

The friends made eye contact and in unison said, "Yes sir."

This caused the girls to laugh. After supplying their membership cards to the attendant, they entered through the gates. Lee was happily skipping along while Lily studied the activity around her. The day was beautiful and not too warm yet. By four o'clock it would be well over 80 degrees; for now they could enjoy the mid-70s temperature and the beauty of the park in comfort.

Making their way toward the elephant sanctuary, they walked quietly for a while. Audrey's face was relaxed. She was enjoying the outing and the chance to get the kids out of the house. Lanie wanted to know how she was. "Are you doing well, Aud?"

Smiling at the familiar nickname, she answered, "I am. It was a crazy morning after a long night. Lily is breaking her first teeth and she was fussy last night which meant I was fussy last night."

Unable to relate to this scenario, Lanie felt a momentary pang of fear. "How do you do it? You always look beautiful and somehow manage to keep the kids from dying. I am in awe of you." She smirked but was only half joking.

Audrey shook her head and enlightened her friend. "You see what you choose to see, Lanie. That has always been one of your biggest assets, I think."

Confused, her expression belied her thoughts. "How so?" she questioned.

"For example, I do not look beautiful. I am wearing burnt-out shorts and there is dried mac and cheese on my T-shirt. I haven't washed my hair in three days, which is why it is pulled up onto this mess of a bun. You have a point about me not killing the kids, but that's about it."

Lanie thought about what she said and until her friend pointed those things out, she had noticed none of her tells. "Does that mean you don't have it all figured out?"

"Nobody does and anyone who says they do is full of S-H-I-T."

Slightly reassured—though her friend didn't know the depths of her inquiry—she walked silently a bit longer. They arrived at the elephant enclosure and a large lawn area. Audrey pulled a quilted blanket from the bottom of the stroller and smoothed it out. Lanie unbuckled Lily and set the infant on her tummy to explore the patchwork patterns. Looking up, they noticed that Lee had already made friends with a nearby little boy about his same age. Waving to the mother, they said hello.

Audrey called, "Let us know if you need us to take him away."

She smiled in response and said, "No, please, this is the happiest Johnny has been all day."

Reassured, Audrey turned back to her friend. "Do you mind keeping an eye on Lily while I go to the food stand?"

"No, not at all. Are you sure you don't need help?" she offered.

"I've got it. I'll bring you a sandwich back," she said over her shoulder as she made time for the restaurant.

Lanie settled herself beside Lily and watched as she used her tiny fingers to pinch the miniature bunnies that covered the cute blanket. She cooed as if speaking a language all her own. An overwhelming sense of happiness washed over her as she looked on. Suddenly her eyes stung with tears.

Remembering Lee was nearby, she glanced over to find he and the other boy were playing with toy trucks. They were crashing them into each other in a mock head-on collision. Satisfied that she was honoring her duties, Lanie tilted her head back and allowed the warm sunshine to soothe her nerves. She had so much to be grateful for. The looming situation she had created over the past few days seemed less daunting as she basked in the moment.

Just as she began to relax, she felt something near her leg and opened her eyes to see that Lily had rolled onto her back. Holding both feet in happy baby pose, Lanie poked her chubby belly.

Using her best baby talk voice, she teased, "Who has a Buddha belly? Lily, that's who, you little yogi in training." Lily gurgled in response, her mouth open in a full smile.

Lanie realized that motherhood was not just peaceful times like this but also late nights, dirty diapers, and little solitude. When the time came, she would have a lot of adjusting to do. Fortunately, she would have her friend to help her through it. That was when she realized she had to confess everything to Audrey. Just as she concluded this, Audrey returned with a tray heaped full of food. Stopping to speak with the mother at the neighboring blanket, she returned with both boys in tow.

"Lanie, meet Johnny."

"Hello, Johnny."

The young, brown-eyed tike rolled his eyes in silence.

"Typical," Lanie joked.

Audrey settled the little ones with sandwiches, carrots, and milk, then handed Lanie a basket with a sandwich and fries.

"Sorry," she apologized, "they don't have charcuterie platters at the Portland Zoo."

Lanie happily accepted the park fare. "Thank you. This'll do fine."

Situating a blanket across her shoulder, Audrey collected Lily and placed her at her breast so she could eat with the rest of them. Using her free hand, she picked at the French fries and carrot sticks. Sensing that her friend needed to talk, she took the direct route. "What is going on, Lanie? Don't say you're fine when I can see you aren't."

Lanie sucked in a deep breath, the remnants of her French fry dry at the back of her throat, and went for it. She told her about meeting Ryan at the mixer, accepting the date for Sunday and about their day yesterday. Audrey listened in silence and when she spoke Lanie couldn't believe what she homed in on.

"Let me get this straight, this guy got you to go to the top of the Space Needle and you actually walked around the exterior then looked through the telescope?" Her voice and expression were incredulous.

"After everything I've said, that is the one fact you're focused on."

Waiting a second, Audrey confirmed. "It is. I've known you for over ten years now. You have the most irrational fear of heights of any person I've known, yet with this guy you go to the top of a six hundred-foot building and stand near the ledge. That's not a minor detail, Lanie."

Not certain how to respond to her observation, she explained.

"I was scared, of course, but something about being near him made me feel like I could do it, like it would be okay. What are you thinking? Tell me."

Audrey faced her. "I can't tell you what to do, won't tell

you what to do. I will say that you can't make a bad choice. The wrong decision doesn't exist. James is a good guy, a little distant at times which is a contrast to you. I've always admired your passion and openness. Opposites do attract though, and you've invested a lot, but you aren't married yet."

Lanie absorbed her friend's words.

"You owe it to yourself to be as certain as possible before taking the leap. I know you well enough to understand your reservations, but it never made sense that you were willing to wait six years before making a commitment. I also don't understand not wanting to live together and I know you haven't begun marketing your condo yet. Those are pretty glaring facts. Not to mention that you both entered into a gamble so close to the wedding."

Lanie faced her friend with a desperate look on her face. Her tone matched when she said, "Oh my god, I can't imagine calling it off now. We are literally only ten days from the date."

Audrey's expression was calm, giving Lanie a glimpse into what her demeanor might have been like in the corporate world. "Can you imagine living a life that isn't pulling you uncontrollably toward it?"

Her silence gave Audrey the room to carry on.

"This"—she waved her hand demonstrating the toys and food strewn about the lawn—"isn't something you can half-ass. You'll never be one hundred percent certain, but by now you should know that a life with James is what you can pour yourself into. It need not result in a family overnight, but you love kids and it should already have entered your mind you want that with him."

"He's a good man," Lanie hollowly defended.

"The world is full of good men. That doesn't mean you should marry them. If you want my opinion, I say see this

Ryan again tonight and ask yourself how you really feel. When James gets back tomorrow, do the same with him. In the end, you are the one who has to live with this decision."

———

IT WAS NEARLY 7 p.m. as Lanie navigated the ever-busy Mississippi Avenue in search of a parking spot. She was in luck as an SUV was pulling away from the curb ahead. Signaling, she parallel parked in the recently vacated spot. Taking her small bag, she exited the car and was greeted by a whistle. Her eyes moved to the direction of the sound and she found Ryan waiting. As she walked over to him she wondered again if she had chosen the right outfit. Who wears a frilly summer dress to a pizza place? Once she was in front of him, he pulled her in for a hug.

"Not only do you look beautiful, you smell intoxicating and you know how to park. How on earth did you come to be?"

Feeling proud of herself now, she stood a little taller assisted by the cork-heeled sandals she'd chosen. "Why thank you."

He looked and smelled incredible himself. The scent of spice and verbena filled the space between them. Today Ryan was wearing a pair of tan shorts with a green oxford, cuffed to below the elbow.

Placing his arm around her, they walked the short distance to the entrance and waited in line for their turn to order food. Studying the slices of the day, they each selected two. They agreed to get their drinks at the bar since the selection was larger.

Carrying their slices, they made way through the small doorway and to the bar. The area was a throwback to a foregone era with dim lighting, red velvet wallpaper, and dark wooden furniture. Bellying up to the bar, Ryan asked Lanie what she wanted.

"I'd like a Tito's and grapefruit with a splash of soda water." She smiled at Ryan and said, "I love the fact that they squeeze the juice fresh here."

He could barely pull his eyes off of her. He noticed her hair was done differently. Her bangs were pulled atop the center of her head giving her an almost childlike look. The soft tendrils were glowing blonde, highlights that the sun had enhanced.

The bartender got his attention, "What will it be for you?"

Repeating her drink order, he added his, "I'll take the IPA."

Beverages in hand they made their way to a seat in the corner. The dining section was bustling with families but the bar was for adults only. It was more intimate and Ryan wanted to monopolize her attention. After they settled, he asked how her day had been.

"It was pretty nice, I have to admit. I woke up early, probably because of that long nap I took on the train. Sorry again about that."

"Please"—he took a sip of his beer—"I enjoyed every minute of it. You were so soft next to me."

His words gave Lanie a sensation she couldn't quite face yet.

"What happened after you woke up early?" He wanted to know what her daily life was like.

"Well, I took a morning yoga class and after met my best friend Audrey and her two kids at the zoo."

The investigator in him kicked in now. "Hmm. Did you tell her about me?"

She smiled. "I did."

Excruciating, he thought. "Am I going to have to pull every last detail out of you? What did you tell her about me?"

"I told her about the Space Needle and she couldn't believe it."

A little unexpected, he was surprised that was the thing they discussed. His curiosity was piqued. "Would she like me? More importantly, would she like me for you?"

The conversation was becoming more serious than Lanie anticipated, but how could she feel that way? They had spent nearly two full days together, plus the hours they talked on that first night. It was only natural that things would progress. If she weren't engaged, this would all seem normal.

"She would like you and you'd like her. She is beautiful so all men fall for her and she's very smart. These days she spends most of the time taking care of her two little ones. Lee is two and Lily is just six months old. They are super cute."

A serious look crossed his face. "What about you, Lanie. Do you want a family?"

The answer was a no brainer and she responded without hesitation. "Yes, I do, very much."

This obviously made him happy as his smile reflected. "I have to let you know that I'm leaving tomorrow afternoon for a quick trip to New York."

A feeling of disappointment irrationally came over Lanie which she brushed off. If she were honest, the timing was good since James would return tomorrow evening. "Oh?"

"Yes, I'm meeting my agent to discuss the outline for my next book. I'll be back on Saturday morning."

"Sounds fun. What is the title for your next work?"

He looked puzzled. "That's the problem, we are

warring a bit on the subject. I hope to have more clarity after the trip. I'm going to miss you, though."

Feeling the blood rush to her face, a flicker of panic rose.

"Don't panic, after that day on the boat, I got the picture that you like to take things slowly. I'm not pledging my undying love, *yet*," he emphasized. "Can we have dinner on Saturday night?"

Shit, shit, shit! Think fast, Lanie. "I'd love to but I have a girl's night on the books. You wouldn't believe the trouble it is for Audrey to make arrangements for Ron to keep the kids. He's"—she paused, searching for the word and not wanting to paint a negative picture—"at a loss without her."

"I can imagine with two as young as those." Undeterred, he ventured, "Sunday then?"

Lying was not second nature to Lanie. She felt badly for the story about Saturday night, plus her omission of the fact that she was engaged. She had no ready excuse. "Yes, after work? I could meet you around seven o'clock?"

"Great. We have some time to work on the details. The important thing is that there is a next time, Lanie. I'm really excited to see where this goes. You are a very special woman and I'm happy *you* bumped into *me* at the mixer." On that note, he picked up his glass in toast, and she raised hers too.

"Here's to lovetest.love and my editor; both very good matchmakers, I must admit."

Their glasses touched and they sipped before digging into more of the delicious pie. During the rest of the meal they spoke casually, touching often and enjoying each other's company. It all felt so easy. For an instant, Lanie couldn't imagine not knowing him this way.

He stood and bussed their table. When he returned, he

said, "Unfortunately, I still have a few things to prepare before I leave tomorrow."

They walked to her car together. The street was quieter now that it was after nine. Pulling her to face him, he studied her briefly. Lanie could feel her heart pulsing in her chest. They kissed, and for a time, were lost in the pleasure and nearness of being connected.

It must have been a sight to see because they were taunted by a passerby. "Hey, get a room."

The comment caused them to pull back and when they did, both were laughing. It was time to say goodbye.

Ryan spoke first, "Drive safely, Lanie. I'll talk to you tomorrow."

"I will. You have a good trip. Good night."

He waited as she got into her car and started the engine. She lingered at the wheel, holding eye contact with Ryan just a little longer before driving away. From the rearview mirror she could see he was standing in the same place, watching her leave. Suddenly, a flow of tears came and her body shook into a gasping sob. How was she going to let him go? She couldn't fathom hurting him. Instantly she felt remorse. This allegiance was owed to a man whom she'd promised her future to.

13

Surprise me not.

Wednesday arrived and with it came some amount of respite. The gallery was open so Lanie had work to occupy her. With Ryan out of town, it gave her the much-needed time to sort matters out with James. She needed space to sift through all that she was feeling. She knew it was unfair and unkind for her to proceed beyond what she'd already done. This experience was foreign to her and one she had no desire to prolong.

The impending heartbreak ahead was a fact that could no longer be denied. If she told James and called the wedding off, he would be hurt and her family would be devastated. If she broke things off with Ryan, he'd want an explanation. The pain they would both face was unimaginable. Could he forgive her, let alone trust her, after learning the depths of her deceit? Sure, he forgave the pseudonym and her vague personal details as it pertained to her career, but omitting a fiancé was probably more than he could accept.

Arriving at the gallery, she was grateful to see Jay speaking with a couple. They were looking at the colorful abstract in the corner. Feeling more sure of herself in her own stomping grounds, Lanie booted up her computer and reviewed the day's check list. As the couple exited, Jay was quickly by her side. Looking up at him she knew this would be a tough session.

Seeing her pained expression almost made him hold off —almost. "That sappy expression is not getting you off the hook young lady."

As soon as he spoke, the door chimed and much to her shock, panic, and delight, in the doorway stood Ryan. In his hand was the most exotic spray of flowers, including Evening Primrose and the rare White Dove Orchid. She had never seen this varietal in person before. The shocked expression on her face caused Jay to turn toward their guest.

Standing, Lanie covered the distance toward the door and greeted Ryan. "What are you doing here?"

Jay noted her voice was higher than usual.

Gesturing for her to accept the flowers, Ryan wondered if he miscalculated by showing up at her business unannounced. "I didn't want to leave town without seeing you and giving you something to remember me by."

Floored by the gift, she asked, "Where on earth did you find these. Do you know how rare these flowers are?"

Smiling now and feeling more confident, he leaned forward to kiss Lanie on the cheek. "I'm glad you like them. They reminded me of you. Not of this world and impossible to forget."

At that, a sound emanated from Jay. He was chomping at the bit to be introduced. Lanie looked over her shoulder as she made the introductions. "Ryan, I'd like you to meet Jay, my gallery director. Jay, this is my new friend, Ryan."

The two shook hands and sized each other up.

"It's so nice to meet you, Ryan. Lanie has said good things about you, so far."

Catching the undertone, Ryan knew Jay was important to Lanie.

"Good to meet you, Jay. Though I have to admit, I had to do some digging to learn about you. It seems our friend here has a way of keeping secrets."

Nearly choking then, Jay rebounded by turning it into a quick cough. Looking over at the bewildered Lanie, he gave her a break so she could pull herself together.

"Lanie, why don't you put those into that stunning Baccarat vase while I give Ryan the nickel tour?"

Thankful for the exit, Lanie practically ran to the back office. She tried to compose herself before she fainted from hyperventilating. Oh my god, Ryan was here, at her gallery! Holy shit, this was turning into a complete disaster. Get it together, she admonished herself. Knowing this little game of hers would get people hurt, she couldn't allow it to go much further. Damn, why did he have to look so good? The crisp white shirt and jeans he wore looked like they'd be so much fun to toss on the floor. He was so hot. *For certain, you are going insane.* Lanie was convinced she was having some sort of psychotic break. She was literally talking to herself now. Setting the extraordinary blossoms in water, she took a "cleansing breath" before carrying the vase back into the gallery.

When she returned she watched Jay with Ryan. She could tell from his body language he found him attractive. He leaned in giving the appearance that they were conspiring. She noticed he touched his shoulder a couple of times. Clearly Jay had no qualms being in the center, nary the instigator, of her twisted love triangle. Deciding it was time to break up their little bromance, she approached.

"Are you two having fun getting acquainted?"

Jay's eyes danced flirtatiously.

Ryan was the first to speak up. "Lanie, you've done an amazing job curating these extraordinary works. I had no idea how special this place was but I should have known, after all you are the owner."

Embarrassed by his accolades, Lanie tried to change the subject. "Thank you, Ryan. The flowers are incredible."

"Like you, my love." His words hung in the air between them, and even caused Jay to retreat.

Looking at his watch Ryan announced, "Well, I'd better get going. My flight is in less than two hours." Lanie walked him to the door. Once there, he said, "You look so pretty today." Before she could respond, he pulled her into the kind of kiss typically reserved for Hollywood movies. After releasing her, he said, "I can't wait until Sunday." Before exiting the building, he called over his shoulder, "Great to meet you, Jay."

The door closed and Lanie felt as if her feet were glued in place. Jay made his way to her side, took a hold of her shoulders and steered her back to the chair. After a few moments of silence, he'd waited long enough to start the inevitable conversation. "I take it you had a wonderful day yesterday?"

A blank expression belied Lanie's obvious confusion.

"The way he kissed you made me melt, Lanie, and not in the usual way. I melted for you."

Holding her silence, she was still in shock.

"Lanie, you have to work this out. I know you and I'm afraid this isn't going to end well if you don't face the music."

Platitudes were not in order at the moment. "Don't you think I know that, Jay?"

Her raised voice and hardened expression did nothing

to deter him. Pressing her buttons, he asked. "Have you ever looked at James the way you do Ryan?"

What a stupid question, she thought. "How the hell would I know? I can't see how I look when I'm looking at someone else."

She stood and paced like a caged panther. Jay kind of liked this fiery side of his boss and he would not back down.

"Take it from me. I've watched you now with both of them and I've never seen you look so . . . seductive. You are alive, Lanie. It is apparent. He's even had an impact on your work. That piece you just finished is phenomenal. He is a great influence on you."

Soothed by his words and the compliment, she spoke. "Sorry for raising my voice. This is a lot to take in."

"Lanie, don't apologize. I love seeing the passion and light in your eyes. This can't be easy on you. I know I can be a bit of a child at times but I'd never forgive myself if I didn't tell you the truth."

Bracing, she knew that he wouldn't reserve his opinions as Audrey had. "What do you think I should do?"

"It's obvious to me. You can't marry James. You've fallen in love with Ryan Glass and he is head over heels over you. He's taken a genuine interest in you, Lanie. From my vantage point, I can see that Ryan is capable of the kind of intimacy that James can't give. You need that in your life. You aren't a Stepford and I don't think you'll be happy in the long run if you marry James."

Tears filled her eyes and rolled down her cheeks. She knew what he was saying was true in so many ways but the train had left the track. How could she stop the plans at this stage? "What would I tell James and my family?"

"I'm sorry Lanie, but fuck James and your family. Have you and he even spoken since he left?" Not giving her the chance to respond, asked, "Was he here for your big showing last week? For that matter, does he even know which artists you have on display? Did he try to stop you from taking the test or did he encourage it?"

Her face fixated on the floor. He continued in a softer tone.

"As for your parents, have they ever really known or supported you? Can you remember one time when they actually encouraged you to go after your dreams? It's no fault of theirs because they have their own perspectives but Lanie, they don't know what's best for you."

"And you do?" she snapped.

"No, only you know what's best. Look at all you've accomplished and have faith in yourself. You can get through this next phase. If you give it a chance, I have no doubt you'll be able to build the kind of life you deserve. Don't sell yourself short. I love you, Lanie. I want you to be happy."

She was crying now and Jay pulled her into a hug. He held her while she emptied herself on his shirt. Finally, she pulled back and observed the mess she had made. Mascara and pink lip gloss mixed with salty tears, making his shirt look like one of the abstracts on display.

Trying for levity, he teased her. "Now look what you've done." He smiled while handing her a box of Kleenex.

He walked to the other side of the desk and picked up his cell phone. Activating the voice feature, he demanded, "Hey Siri, call Dragontree Spa."

Once connected, he set up an emergency massage for Lanie. A regular at the spa, they always accommodated him. Collecting Lanie's purse, he marched her to the door, then practically shoved her out. "You need to be there in fifteen minutes. After you're done, go home and get some rest."

SHE ARRIVED at the giant set of doors and raised the old-fashioned latch. Entering the space was like being transported to Bali. The walls were dark wood. Oriental rugs rested beneath velvety sofas and the faint aroma of incense filled the air.

She approached the counter and was greeted by a woman with braids.

"Are you Lanie?"

"I am," she confirmed.

"Great, let me take you back." She was escorted up a ramp to a changing area that contained showers and a sauna. The woman handed her key #11, on it was the word Clarity. *How ironic*, Lanie thought. "You'll find a robe and sandals in the locker. Once you're changed, please have a seat in the waiting area. Erica will be with you shortly."

"Thank you," Lanie replied.

Changing into the robe, Lanie was grateful for the simple task. She secured the locker and found a seat on one of the soft, velvet chairs. In no time, Erica arrived.

"Lanie?"

Her expression was so serene. "Yes." She stood and followed Erika into a room with rust-colored walls.

"We understand from your friend that you need some nurturing today. For the next ninety minutes, please feel at ease. I promise to take good care of you."

"Thank you so much." Lanie accepted the woman's kindness.

"I'll be back in just a moment. Please disrobe and start face down on the bed."

Hanging the robe on the hook, Lanie then climbed onto the heated massage table. It was a comfort to be in this darkened room, enveloped by a blanket with nothing to do but lie still. A moment later there was a soft tap at the door and Erica returned.

"How's the temperature, Lanie?"

"Very nice, thank you."

"I'm going to use my special blend of essential oils today. Do you have any allergies or concerns before we get started?"

"No, I don't."

"Great. Let me know if you need the pressure adjusted as we go; otherwise, relax and enjoy."

Erica's strong hands knew just what to do as they stroked Lanie from head to toe. The scent of roses, lavender, and honey filled the air between them. Soon her cares floated away as she succumbed to the decadent treatment. Her mind wandered and she thought of James who would be returning today. A moment later she considered Ryan who was on his way to New York. Sensing her stiffen, Erika spoke.

"Let go for now Lanie. This is your time and those questions will be waiting for you when we are though."

Surprised, if not embarrassed, Lanie wondered if her masseuse was reading her mind. But she saw the wisdom in her words so she let everything go. The soft classical music overhead tangled with the aroma of flora and Lanie breathed deeply. She was finally relaxing. Then she saw James standing in front of her. He was at the end of a path, looking toward her with a blank stare. In his hand he held a velvet box. She was trying to walk toward him but he kept getting further and further away. He was shrinking and suddenly he disappeared. With a start she awakened. Erica felt her warring and soothed her into reality.

"You dozed off, Lanie. You're safe." Placing a warm compress at her neck, she said, "Take your time getting up.

We did some pretty deep work and you might be a little light headed. When you're ready, I'll meet you in the hallway with a cup of Chamomile tea."

Shaken by the vivid dream, Lanie took her time sitting up. Once seated, she stretched and rolled her neck before standing to replace the robe. She felt lighter than when she arrived, but once she opened that door, she knew there was something difficult to face. Pausing, she studied her hand on the knob and contemplated hiding under the table. The childish notion was evidence she was not conducting herself in a way she could be proud of. It was time to face the music.

As she left the cocoon of the spa, Lanie felt odd. The interior had been so dim, it gave her the sense of it being nighttime, yet it was only four o'clock in the afternoon. She walked slower than normal, taking time to enjoy these steps before she had to face the inevitable. The short mile walk ended too quickly for her comfort. If she were honest, a hike up Mt. Everest wouldn't be long enough to prolong this matter. When she got inside the house, she opened her bag and pulled out her phone. She noticed that Ryan's jacket was still there at the bottom snuggled against her unworn silk blouse. Pulling it out, she attempted to straighten the wrinkles and noticed it smelled like him. A guilty pleasure indeed, she put the jacket on and breathed deeply.

Taking her phone in hand, she went to sit on her favorite leather chair. Unlocking it she checked to see if she'd missed any calls. There were no new texts or calls this afternoon. Interesting, she thought. By now she expected James to be back from his trip. Relief washed over her since she could hide just a little while longer.

Hearing a growl that emanated from her stomach, she realized that she hadn't eaten today. Walking into the kitchen, she opened the refrigerator and pulled out a block of Winey Goat cheese. From the pantry, she selected some wafer crackers and a pear from the basket. She put everything on a cutting board and carried it to the living room. She decided a little mindless TV was in order so she flipped on the power. Clicking through channels, she selected a harmless and non-thought-provoking flick, *What Happens in Vegas*. It was nice to be in her own home, snacking and hiding her thoughts behind a slapstick, romantic comedy.

Before she knew it, she had finished nearly the entire block of cheese. The pear was also a thing of the past. Full but thirsty she got herself some water and returned to the final part of the movie. In this scene Ashton Kutcher was in the courtroom, hopeful that Cameron Diaz wouldn't show and, therefore, their divorce wouldn't be granted. Just as the doors swung open announcing her arrival, Lanie's phone rang. Her stomach lurched. It was James. Her heart was literally pounding in her head as she tapped accept.

"Hello," she said.

"Hi, Lanie."

His voice sounded distant to her.

"How are you?" she ventured.

"Good. Just getting back. What about you?"

"I'm doing ok," she replied.

"What are you up to tonight?"

At least she could be honest about this. "At the moment I am watching a pretty dumb movie." Knowing he would hate the chick flick, she downplayed that she actually liked it.

"Good for you." His short reply made Lanie feel like she needed to fill the gap with small talk.

"How was your long weekend?" she asked politely.

"It was . . . long."

"Yeah, I can imagine. Are you tired?"

"Exhausted actually, but that doesn't matter because I have so much work to do before our meeting on Monday."

"I guess you guys didn't accomplish much over the break, huh?"

"Some, but not as much as I would have liked. Would you mind if we got together on Friday? I want to see you but also know I'll be no good if I'm torn between time with you and the details of this project."

Hardly believing her luck, which would really be slow torture, Lanie readily agreed. "No, not at all. I understand what's riding on this deal for you but Friday won't work. The girls are throwing me a little bachelorette party, remember?"

"Oh sure, I totally forgot about that. Why don't we have a nice date on Saturday night then? I'll take you out to a fancy dinner, just you and me. Does that sound good?"

"It sounds great." Relief and the tiniest bit of disappointment washed over Lanie.

"Ok then. I'd better get cracking. I'll call you tomorrow to check in."

"I'll talk to you then, James."

An instant later the line was dead and Lanie couldn't help but burst into tears for the second time that day.

Mopping her face with the towel by the tray, Lanie stood, knowing what she needed to do. She walked the short distance to her studio and took out a fresh canvas. After moving her latest painting aside, she selected a pencil and constructed the outline of the Space Needle. Her pace was feverish as her hands moved rapidly. As if in a race, she outlined the base and top of the monstrosity quickly. Next, she set about creating the surroundings—first the Ferris wheel, then the apartment buildings, and finally the vast sea.

Stepping back, she studied her work. She liked the way it was taking shape. She selected an assortment of hues. Choosing a near-sunset perspective that mirrored her recollection of the day, she started by painting the sky. Hoping to capture the last vestiges of daylight, she used pale yellow, white, and peach to form the backdrop. The ocean was next; slate grey with hundreds of white caps, giving the viewer the impression of movement. The buildings shined as the setting sun reflected off of their mirrored windows and cast their shadows over lush greenery that peeked along the hillsides and between structures.

Finally, she took on the focal point of the piece. The towering building that had once been her nemesis was now the subject of her expression. Mixing white and ice grey she blended the perfect color. In deliberate strokes she followed the outline, then finished by highlighting in the roof. The elevator cab glowed bright orange as the sun beamed against the observers inside. Creating tiny figures at the observation deck, she added the people who made the landmark a destination.

Lost in the piece, Lanie noticed the sky outside her window had grown dark. Looking at the clock behind her, it was after 10 p.m. Exhausted, she dropped her brush, wiped her hands, then shut down the lights before exiting the room. Quickly she washed her hands and face, tossed her clothes to the floor and fell into bed. Spent, she fell into a dreamless sleep.

14

Let's Talk

The gallery was quiet when Lanie arrived. For once, she beat Jay in and was grateful for the solitude. After she made herself a latte, Lanie took some time to study her surroundings. This time, she wasn't critiquing placement nor was she rearranging pieces for optimal exposure. She studied each piece as if seeing it for the first time. Walking clockwise, she started at the north wall then made her way around the space until she'd come full circle. Next, she visited the works at the center of the room, glad once again she had the faux wall constructed a few years back. It increased her capacity, giving her the ability to show even more work.

There was a vacant space where the Hans Martl piece, *Whimsy*, had previously hung. The anchor was still in place, calling for its next guest. Lanie was about to do something she hadn't done in a long while. Setting aside the coffee, she walked toward the desk and unwrapped her painting of the person standing on the bluff. Taking the step stool from its stowed location, she carried it along with the painting to the vacant spot. Without hesitation she stood atop the lift and raised the piece to the wall, adjusting until she could see it was straight. She stepped off of the stool and back a few paces. The morning light highlighted the shards of rock along the cliff, the bright, white clouds, and the impending darkness. She hadn't yet chosen a name for the painting but was considering *Last Chance*.

After waking during the night, Lanie couldn't fall back asleep. Instead, she tossed and turned, her mind unable to stop racing. The misery of it gave her the courage to take this step, and the answer of what to do next. Maybe she didn't have the entire thing worked out, but at least she knew what she needed to accomplish today. Decisive—she didn't want to belabor it further—she walked to the computer and typed the words *Don't Jump*, and beneath she typed her name, Lanie Blackwell. Selecting the print feature, the machine by her side fired up. She took the scissors from the pen cup and cut the paper into a tidy square. Walking to the canvas, she slid the card into the plastic slot. Standing back, she took a final study of *Don't Jump*. It gave her the confidence she was moving in the right direction. Facing the truth would not be easy but she knew it was the only way.

An hour later Jay arrived. He was smiling and humming to himself. When he noticed Lanie at her desk, his expression changed. He became almost somber, concern washed away his joy. The metamorphosis was unmistakable. She felt terrible having taken his good mood away. He cared enough for her that he didn't feel good when she didn't. Lanie acknowledged how blessed she was to be surrounded by such kindness.

Standing, she went for the barista station and brewed a cappuccino, Jay's favorite. She started the dialogue. "Good morning, Jay."

Placing his things down on his desk, he walked her

direction but stopped midway after noticing the new addition on the wall. "Lanie, you decided to show your piece." His face was once again alight.

Bringing the cup of essentially foam to her friend, she spoke. "I did. It looks good there, don't you think?"

Her voice was light and Jay thought maybe the massage worked, or was there something else at play? He inquired.

"How was your night?"

Contemplating the happenings, she recanted the events of the evening. Relaying her conversation with James—more like non-conversation—she opened up about the crying session, painting the Space Needle, and the long sleepless night.

His expression changed with every revelation and it settled on slightly angry. She knew it wasn't directed toward her, but her disconnected intended. He remained still, getting the sense she had more to share.

"I woke up today wanting to accomplish a couple of things."

Waving her hand toward the newly installed art, she continued, "This, for one." She went silent for a moment. "I also decided that I'm going to pay James a visit at the office today. I know he's busy, but if he is to be my husband, part of his job is to know how I'm feeling. I'm going to start that conversation with him. It can't wait until Saturday, at least not for me."

Jay couldn't help but feel a stab of pride and his face showed it. The Lanie he knew and loved had shown up today, and he had been missing her. "Lanie, I'm proud of you. You don't look like you had a sleepless night."

His gaze scrolled up and down her tiny stature. She was wearing a fitted, navy skirt and flowing white blouse that tied near the throat. A pair of simple beige, suede heels finished the classic look. He especially appreciated the blood-red lip rouge she'd selected, the only vestige of cosmetic enhancement to be found.

"You know this piece won't last long, right?" It was a rhetorical question. "As for confronting James, I think you're dead on. Either way, you deserve to see him in person to discuss whatever it is you need to."

"Thank you, Jay. You are a godsend."

He scoffed out loud while feigning fear and ducking slightly. He directed his next comment toward the ceiling. "Oh boy, I sure hope lightning doesn't strike the building."

They laughed together.

LANIE WAS calm as she rode the elevator to James' floor. For once, in recent times, she didn't require a special breathing exercise to soothe her. She was confident this step, be it a minor one, was the right thing for both of them. Once the cab opened, she passed the reception desk as if she belonged. She made her way through the busy cubicles and down the hall toward James' office. When she got there, she saw he was on the phone and Nick was in his chair.

Greeting Lanie in his usual loud fashion, Nick circled the desk to stand by her. "What a pleasant surprise, Lanie, and don't you look sexy today?" His tone was suggestive.

"Good to see you, Nick." She accepted his smashing hug as a deed to get over quickly. "Would you give us a minute, please?"

Her tone was all business, causing Nick to raise his eyebrows.

He responded contritely. "Sure. I need to review something with finance anyway."

"Thanks." As she spoke the word, James set down the receiver and walked toward her.

"Wow, you look great. What brings you in for a visit?" He pulled her into a hug and she let the sensation ruminate in her body and mind.

After a beat he released her and she asked, "Can we sit?"

She started for the round table at the corner and selected a chair. He followed her lead and took the chair across from her. Feeling antsy because of the mound of items on his check list today, this unplanned visit wasn't slated. She could feel his tension but didn't care.

"What's going on Lanie?"

She was quiet for a second; though brief, the pause felt like an eternity. It was time to open up the can of worms. "James, I know how driven and how busy you are. Even as we sit here, and though you haven't seen me in days, I can feel that you want to usher me out so you can get back to your project."

He was silent. No point denying the facts.

She continued, "I've been feeling, for some time now actually, that maybe I'm a line item on your list of things to do."

This was coming out of left field and he was unprepared to respond, but improvised. "I never want you to feel that way. I'm doing all of this for you, for us, so we can be happy and secure."

Not accepting his standard response. Lanie applied the pressure she had been avoiding for some time, years really. "James, you are doing this for you and some deep need to show your dad what you are capable of. I don't blame you and wouldn't want to hold you back, but lately, I've been feeling very distant from you. It's like you're here in body only, and at times it seems like you're going through the motions."

Whoa, he thought, where was this coming from? James wanted to find the right words, wanted to reassure her but didn't know how. "This has been a hectic time for the company, it's true." He threw her a bone then went on, "But Lanie, I am doing this so we can have the kind of future we've both dreamed of."

Not accepting his words and getting pissed by this stereo-typical response, she fired back, "Bullshit. The kind of future I've dreamed of is already here. The gallery is exactly what I've wanted from a work perspective and I'm very proud of it. Do you even know what it looks like in there these days? Do you have any idea how the show went? Do you care?"

Ahh, he thought, that's what this was about. She was still mad because he couldn't make it that night. "I told you how sorry I was that I lost track of time that day. You have to believe me."

"I believe you—at least I want to believe that—but deep down, I don't think you care all that much. I mean, it's a nice fact to share with others that your fiancé has a successful gallery. I think for you it proves you aren't like your father because your woman has a career, unlike your mother, but those are just hash marks."

Suddenly, the intercom on his desk phone chimed. It was Bethany reminding him that his meeting was going to start in ten minutes. Flushed, James turned his attention back to Lanie. His torn expression said it all. "I'm sorry, Lanie. This day has been impossible so far."

Not caring about his meeting schedule, and intending to say what she came to say, she continued as if the inter-ruption never occurred. "You gambled with me James, with us!"

Oh shit, he thought, Nick was right. He would not live that stupid test down. He tried to rationalize. "It was a dumb thing to do, that dating test, but in the end, it was harmless."

"It wasn't harmless to me James. I was having doubts and instead of noticing that, finding a way to make me feel important to you, you acted over-confident, as if a wager would settle my fears."

It was true, in the heat of the moment he hadn't considered the angles, but he made a good living by taking risks when others were afraid. He thought this was a calculated one. "I didn't mean to be casual or insensitive to your feelings. You have to know that I want us to be good together. I'm sorry if you felt that way."

Her blood was boiling now. He was placating her and they both knew it. She repeated his words back to him as if she were a stenographer reading back testimony in court. Her voice was shrill as she responded, "I'm sorry if *you* felt that way?"

The door opened behind her, it was Nick. "Buddy, it's time for our finance session."

Acknowledging his friend by holding up two fingers, the door closed. "I can see that something is really upsetting you. We should have this conversation when I'm not so distracted. Can we please table this until Saturday?"

She stared vacantly ahead as James stood. He walked to her and kissed her forehead before making his way to the desk to undock his laptop. Slowly Lanie rose and watched him go about the task. Knowing she'd get no satisfaction today, she resigned herself to wait until Saturday. She had a lot of thinking to do until then. Without another word she exited his office.

AS SHE WALKED out of the building and traveled down the city streets, Lanie felt a strange vacancy toward James. It was almost like she was having an out-of-body experience. She moved automatically toward the gallery, feeling devoid of emotion. Fortunately, she was not facing a blank canvas in this state of mind. It would sit untouched, a reflection of her numbness.

Her phone buzzed so she took it out. Her immediate thought was that Jay needed something. As she examined the display, she saw the telltale red flag atop the corner of her text icon. Tapping the option, she saw Ryan's number highlighted. Clicking again, it opened to a photo of the Empire State Building. The image, so telling, spoke volumes and was confirmed by his message.

"I saw this and thought of you. Lately, most things remind me of you. Maybe we could travel to all of the tallest buildings in the world together? I could help you conquer your fear of heights and you could keep bumping into my chest."

Her heart skipped and a smile covered her face, emanating from somewhere deep inside her. She wasn't empty now. Certainty wasn't here yet, but it was fast approaching.

Tossing logic out the window, she typed a reply. "I'm thinking of you too, Ryan. Let's discuss our travel plans at a later date." She added a winking smiley face then hit send.

DURING THE MEETING, Nick noticed a few instances when James was not his typical self. He stared off and didn't hear a couple of key questions directed toward him. After it ended, they walked together to their joint space.

Once inside, Nick shut the door and turned to his friend before speaking. "What's going on with you? Does your mindset have anything to do with Lanie's surprise visit today?"

Shuffling things around his desk so he could anchor his computer, James refused to look up.

"Come on, little buddy, tell me what the deal is."

James responded angrily, "I don't have time for your shit today."

"Please tell me you didn't tell her about that mountain chick you went home with on Monday night."

His response matched the furious expression on his red face.

"Shut the fuck up, Nick. You know I want to forget that happened but you keep bringing it the fuck up. Enough."

Undaunted, Nick pushed. "So, I take it you didn't tell her?"

Shaking his head, James confirmed. "I'm not an idiot. Of course not. I still can't believe it happened. I haven't stepped out on her since the beginning and I don't know why it happened now."

"Yeah, she wasn't even hot, dude. No one holds a candle to Lanie's little bod."

Circling around the desk, James practically jumped on Nick. Grabbing his collar, he spoke through gritted teeth. "Don't ever talk about her that way again, got it?"

Understanding his friend meant business, and they were being observed by the office staff, Nick acquiesced. "Okay, I won't bring it up again."

At that James released his strangle hold and Nick went toward the door. Before exiting, he turned and spoke his peace. "You may not want to talk about it but you should think about why it happened. If you don't want to get married, don't do it. Lanie deserves better than a guy that can't make up his mind, and this is your oldest friend talking."

Nick stormed out of the office. The air around James sizzled with his stinging truth.

———

LANIE COULDN'T FACE Jay again today after the non-conversation she just had with James. She opted instead for a hot yoga class. Afterward she went home for a cool shower. Spent and lounging in her robe, she heard the phone ring and limped over to pick it up. It was her mom and she was using the Face Time feature. Great, she thought, then plastered a fake smile on her face before accepting the video call.

"Hi, Mom."

"Hi, baby. Oh, you're home early and wearing a bath robe. Are you sick?"

"No. I'm not sick. I just took off early and got in a workout."

"Well, you shouldn't be cutting out too early since you're the boss and the owner. You don't want people to leave because the shop isn't open."

Frustrated that her mother knew so little of her business, but endeavoring to keep the snarkiness out of her voice, she soothed instead. "Did you forget, I have a manager? You remember Jay, don't you?"

"Oh sure, I do, but no one cares like the boss, Lanie— no one."

Shaking her head in agreement because there was no point in belaboring the point, Lanie tried to change the subject. "How are you and Dad doing?"

"Oh, pretty good. We are just about ready for our big trip next week. Are you getting excited?"

A wave of panic overtook Lanie which she tried to hide before responding. "Excited, yep."

Rani Blackwell could be single minded, and oblivious to subtleties, but not with Lanie. "Are you nervous honey?" Silent a beat too long, Rani continued with the expected worn-out statement. "Everyone gets some form of cold feet before the big day. Remember to enjoy this time. It is the most romantic period of your life. Once you're married and living together, there will be so much more to work through. You'll want these memories to carry you."

Great, Lanie thought, feeling even more deflated; but she responded as expected, by mustering a cheerful tone. "Thanks for the advice Mom. Do you need anything else? If not, I have a few bookkeeping items to take care of before the day is over."

Glad to hear that Lanie was keeping her eye on the ball, she hastened to sign off. "Love you, sweetie. We'll see you next week."

Responding in kind, Lanie said, "Love you too. Say hi to Daddy for me. Bye."

Too exhausted from last night and the conversation with James, Lanie couldn't delve into the psychology of her familial relationships too. Time to order Chinese. This time she'd have it delivered, so she wouldn't have to face any more music today.

15

Party Time, but first a delivery.

After a long, restless night, Lanie awakened to the instant rush of reality. Her first thought was about the conversation with James the day before. A mixture of emotions flooded her. His indifference yesterday—and if she were truthful with herself, often—wasn't something she could pretend about any longer.

From an outside perspective, people thought James doted on Lanie. In some ways he did but that was just James. He was a caretaker and liked doing things for others, but only when it fit into his agenda. His romantic overtures were usually done out of expectation. He never missed a holiday or birthday, but it wasn't often he surprised Lanie. She couldn't recall a day when he randomly called off of work to have an adventure with her. There weren't a lot of spontaneous moments between them.

Glancing at her phone, she noticed a missed call from James that came in after 9:30 last night. Not ready to speak with him, she went about her morning rituals. Once showered, Lanie chose an outfit for the day. She pulled a peach pencil skirt and matching off-the-shoulder, silky blouse from the closet. Moving to the lingerie drawer, she chose matching undergarments. Finishing the outfit, she slipped on a new pair of dark denim-covered pointy heels. Examining herself in the mirror, she applied lip gloss and blush in the same cheery hue. Seeing the final effect, she thought the outfit a good decoy to mask how she was actually feeling. Twisting her hair into a clip behind her head, a wandering curl escaped. Her throat caught, stopping short of a sob. James loved her curls, but did he love her?

Making her way down the hall, the Space Needle painting caught Lanie's eye through the doorway. She paused. Leaning at the door frame she studied the portrayal that summarized her day with Ryan. Her eyes gravitated to the top of the building and focused on the people inside. From this distance the tiny figures had no depth, no emotions, and no fears. They were just people enjoying the view from a monument to the Emerald City. A sense of sadness washed over her, a despair she hadn't experienced before. The world felt heavy today.

SHE ARRIVED at the gallery just before 10 a.m. and remembered Jay would be late this morning. Taking her usual coffee, she sat at her desk and began the routine of opening up her computer. The incredible blue flowers that Ryan delivered two days earlier stood proudly in the clear vase, reminding her that the world was full of miracles. She thought to herself, *I could use one right now.*

Interrupting her thoughts, the door chimed signifying the arrival of a kindly looking older man.

"Good morning." She stood and greeted the gentleman.

"Hello." His voice was soft and serious.

Getting the idea that he may want to browse undisturbed, Lanie made a brief comment before retaking her chair. "Please let me know if you have any questions."

His stern reply confirmed his desire to be left alone. "Thank you, young lady."

She sifted through emails and tackled some of the accounting she'd lied to her mother about the day before. The man was quietly moving through the space, taking his time to study each item as he went. His presence forced her to keep it together. With the man in sight, she could hardly stare off, deep in thought about her wedding plans, and fear it was the wrong thing to do.

She noticed that he was standing in front of her work. A tingle of fresh nerves assaulted her. It was always disconcerting for a stranger to critique her art. He lingered a long while before speaking.

He finally said, "This is remarkable."

Do your job, Lanie, she intoned silently. Standing, she went to his side and opened a dialogue. "Thank you. It's a recent addition to the gallery."

His eyes never left the painting as he spoke. "It reminds me of something, a long time ago."

Naturally, her curiosity was piqued so she inquired. "Would you be interested in sharing?"

The man sighed, a deep sound that came from a place of regret. He finally looked down at Lanie, his crinkled brown eyes combined with a sad smile that barely touched his mouth. "It reminds me of a time when my life went away."

Not anticipating such a deep revelation but wanting to know more, Lanie had to say something. "That's a beautiful connection but it sounds a little sad."

Returning his gaze back to the work, he agreed. "Yes,

and I imagine the artist who painted this was also a little sad."

Feeling as if he could see into her soul, Lanie retreated. "May I offer you some coffee or tea?"

For a long moment, the man didn't speak. After an odd silence he did. "No, thank you. I would like to purchase this painting though."

The shock must have been evident on Lanie's face as the man clarified. "It is for sale?"

Rebounding quickly, she gained her voice. "Yes, of course it is. I just hung it yesterday and expected it to be here a bit longer, that's all. Won't you follow me and we can complete the transaction?"

Complying, the man took a seat in the modern leather chair in front of Lanie's desk. She asked some standard questions.

"We offer installation as a part of delivery. Where should I send the work?"

The man considered her question, which she found odd. The entire exchange was strange, but people who appreciated art were drawn for many reasons. Obviously, something moved this mystery man to procure her piece. "Please send it to Annette Main. This is the address and phone number. Would you call her to make the arrangements?"

"It's a gift, then?" She slid a blank card and envelope to him.

He accepted it and penned something brief before sliding the paper inside the envelope.

As she finished the transaction, Lanie couldn't help but wonder where her work was going. She may just have to complete the delivery herself.

Lanie stood and thanked the man. "I'm so grateful you

found meaning in my work. Please do come back and visit any time, Mr. Main."

He studied her from across the desk before speaking. "Whatever it is you are grappling with young lady, if I may advise, just follow your heart."

Lanie stood and watched as he retreated from the gallery then vanished onto the city streets. Once she regained her composure—she knew it was wrong but didn't care—she took the unsealed envelope and pulled the card out. There were two words scrawled on the sheet.

"Forgive me."

Tears welled up uncontrollably. She fell back into her chair and cried.

———

BY THE TIME JAY ARRIVED, Lanie had collected herself. Entering silently, he walked over to her desk and didn't talk, knowing she would speak her mind eventually. He was right.

"Something strange happened today."

Wondering what had happened, he asked, "Oh, what was that?"

She told him the story of Mr. Main, then showed him the card he had written.

After reading it, Jay said, "That is strange. I can't wait to see what happens next. Around here, lately, every day is like an episode of *As the World Turns*."

Shaking her head but sort of seeing his point, she agreed. "I guess you've got a point there."

"Dare I ask how it went yesterday when you saw James." Lanie's expression flickered to angry making her seem formidable. Jay liked the look on her.

"It went as you'd expect. James was too distracted to

have a meaningful conversation. He had a meeting scheduled and didn't have the flexibility to talk."

Shaking his head now and feeling angry himself, he wondered how this guy had occupied so many years of Lanie's life. He wouldn't hold his sentiments back, not at this critical juncture. "I don't want to make things worse for you, but Lanie, if he couldn't tell how upset you were yesterday, if his work couldn't wait long enough to give you some attention, and obviously needed reassurance—"

Holding up her hand to stop him, she agreed. "Trust me, I didn't miss it, Jay."

The air buzzed silently around them. He knew enough to stop while he was ahead and chose a softer tack next. "I'm here for you. Whatever it is you need, say the word and I will do it."

Their eyes connected and she nodded almost unperceptively.

The rest of the day was a blur. Lanie left a message for Annette Main and was eager to hear back. She and Jay decided they would deliver the piece together. The little distraction and unknown saga was a nice diversion from the gravity of the real trouble brewing for Lanie.

The phone rang and Jay answered.

"Yes, Ms. Main, so glad you got back to us. Someone came into the gallery today and purchased a painting for you. He asked that we deliver it, today, if possible."

There was silence and Lanie paced in front of Jay's desk anxiously waiting for the call to end.

"I have the address, will six o'clock work for you?"

After a moment, he agreed.

"Perfect, we will see you this evening. Goodbye."

THEY CLOSED the gallery and loaded the covered painting into the back of Lanie's SUV. After getting into the passenger seat, Jay plugged the address into the navigation system. Annette Main lived in the West Hills, not far from the gallery. As the car indicated, they followed the directions. Soon they arrived in front of a virtual monument.

The mansion stood on an enormous lot surrounded by manicured grounds. Mature Oregon white oaks stood proudly at the start of the long path that led to the front door. The home was obviously well maintained and appeared to be freshly painted. The gleaming white walls and black lacquered shutters established a simple elegance, leaving the mind to wonder what was inside. As they followed the path to the front door, the air was filled with the glorious aroma of roses. Dozens of established bushes burst in a rainbow of colors. Perhaps this was actually the rose garden? Looking at each other one last time before ringing the bell, Jay mouthed, "Wow."

The chimes seemed to rouse more than the recipient as it intermixed with the boisterous sounds of barking dogs. When the door swung open, a tiny, grey-haired woman smiled sweetly as the pack of dogs ran circles around her feet. There were four furry beasts, of different sizes and mixes. The diminutive woman spoke, in a voice that didn't seem to fit.

"Ausfahrt," she commanded, and the dogs ran one by one out the door.

"Please, come in." She gestured and they did.

"Hello Ms. Main, I am Lanie and this is Jay. We're glad to have caught you this afternoon."

"Yes, thank you. I am confused about your delivery though."

Lanie took the lead and explained while handing her

the card. "A gentleman visited the gallery today and purchased this painting for you. He asked that we deliver and install it."

Without speaking, she turned and walked through the home. They followed behind and found it impossible not to drool. The parquet floors gleamed and highlighted antique Persian rugs. A dining table that could accommodate twenty held an ornate silver candelabra, and the formal living room was decorated with contemporary furnishings. Mrs. Main directed them to have a seat on the overstuffed sofa while she took a position on one of the chairs.

All business, she asked, "What do you have for me?"

Jay stood holding the painting as Lanie hesitantly unfolded the fabric they'd covered it with for transport. Her hands were sweating, concerned this woman of obvious discerning taste would not appreciate her work. Insecurity was the artist's bane, understandably in this moment. Once the piece was uncovered, Lanie stood back giving Mrs. Main an unobstructed purview.

Standing, Mrs. Main was silent for what felt an eternity. Noting the question in Lanie's eyes, she sensed the artist in her midst.

"Is this your work, young lady?" Her tone, once again, was stern.

"It is," Lanie ventured softly in response.

"Remarkable. Follow me."

The woman seemed to power walk everywhere. Jay and Lanie were practically jogging to keep up. They arrived at a wide set of stairs. The curved black handrail gleamed, while the white marble stairs gave the impression they were walking on piano keys. Ms. Main covered the distance to the top and they followed.

Gesturing toward the blank wall, Mrs. Main instructed. "Place it there."

Jay pulled the necessary objects from the tool belt he'd brought.

Mrs. Main said to Lanie, "This appears to be a one-person job. Will you follow me?"

"Of course."

Lanie walked beside Mrs. Main and back to the first floor. They entered a light-flooded kitchen flanked by a wall of gleaming windows. In the distance Lanie could see the smattering of dogs sniffing and running to and fro. Her hostess walked silently to the refrigerator, pulling a pitcher of lemonade almost as big as she from inside. Taking three glasses from a cupboard, she filled them and carried two to a circular table that overlooked the garden.

"Please, sit."

Lanie settled into a chair across from Mrs. Main and watched silently as the woman slid the card from its sleeve. She stared at the messy writing before looking out the window. There was a long silence before she spoke. Turning her attention back to Lanie, she confessed.

"I love him still. It's been twenty years since we lost our only child, and since I lost him."

Knowing there was a story and sensing the woman needed to speak, she felt it wise to remain silent.

"Our boy, Christopher, arrived some ten years after we were married. The doctors said it was a miracle I conceived at all. He was our treasure and the most delightful young man you would ever hope to know. When he died in a routine flying exercise, we were devastated. He was a fighter pilot, a Blue Angel."

The woman's face wrinkled into a melancholy smile. "I found solace in the church but Thomas, he cursed God. It was an awful time for us both. When he started drinking heavily, I was helpless. Nothing I said worked. He would drink from the time he woke up each day until he passed out at night.

"One day I woke up and found a note. It said he was leaving and that he loved me, but knew he was not the man I needed. It broke my heart to face each day alone. Somehow, I managed. At first, I just went through the motions."

As if on que, one of the dogs, a wire-haired mutt, bounded through a doggie door and made his way to her side. Smiling down, her gaze was met by huge brown eyes. She ran her hand over the dog's head. "These creatures helped me get through the loneliness but I've never been the same. You see, Thomas was the love of my life. He and I were one, before we had Christopher. A mother's love for her child is remarkable, overpowering in some ways, but that man . . ." She paused, staring out the window before going on. "He was my universe. This is the first time I've heard from him since he left me that day."

Shocked by her tale, Lanie was at a loss. Powerful emotions tugged at her. She was grateful that Mrs. Main shared her story and that her painting had found its rightful home. She reached over to touch the woman's arm and was taken aback by the strength she felt beneath the thin white blouse. "Thank you for sharing your story with me. It means more to me than you know."

The woman studied Lanie's face before speaking again. "Whatever it is you are facing, follow your heart. We are given a certain a number of days on this planet, use them wisely."

There was no time for Lanie to respond; just as she finished that statement, Jay found them. "The painting is mounted and looks perfect in its new home."

"Thank you." Mrs. Main smiled. "Please take some lemonade and join us. We are discussing the decision that Lanie is about to make."

Eyes bugging out of her head, Lanie couldn't believe what she was hearing. Jay was ecstatic. Collecting the glass from the counter, he practically ran to join them at the table.

Noting the expression on Lanie's face but not caring, for an old woman was entitled to her eccentricities, she addressed her question to Jay. "I guess you are very good friends."

"We are," he agreed, and a mischievous look crossed his face.

"Spill the beans, young man. What is happening with this lovely woman?"

Jay started from the beginning as Lanie listened to her life through the narration of her friend and confidant. Another out-of-body experience was to be. The woman appeared riveted by the tale. As he arrived to the current date, Mrs. Main pulled her attention from Jay and looked toward Lanie.

"There is only one answer. Remember what I said earlier."

At that, the woman stood and collected their glasses, signaling it was time for them to leave.

After saying their goodbyes, Lanie and Jay drove silently for a few minutes. Once they composed themselves from the unexpected experience, Lanie shared the story of Mr. and Mrs. Main with him. It was a moving epic. One that neither would soon forget.

Looking at the time on the dash, she realized it was almost 7:30 p.m. She was meeting her girlfriends for dinner then a night on the town. "Jay, would you mind dropping me at the restaurant? You can keep the car tonight if that's ok."

"No, not at all," he agreed.

They arrived in front of Little Bird, the restaurant

where the girls were meeting, and Jay broke the silence. "Have fun tonight. Don't think about any of this for the evening. Get drunk and party like a rock star. I've got the gallery tomorrow, so don't you dare come in. Are we clear?"

Knowing he was right because she felt like an overinflated balloon about to pop from the pressure of the day, she agreed. "Yes, sir. Thank you, Jay." She said the words and meant them.

Taking the key, Jay emulated air kisses toward Lanie as he circled around to the driver's side.

WHEN LANIE CHECKED in with the hostess, the young lady smiled knowingly. "We were expecting you. Please follow me." They ascended the stairs and Lanie was greeted by six of her closest girlfriends. There were several old friends from college, her first gallery assistant, Olivia, and Audrey.

The chairs were adorned with floating white balloons secured by blush-colored ribbons. The hostess motioned for Lanie to sit at the head of the table. In front of her was a lovely tiara with a smooth white veil attached. The sight of it assaulted Lanie with an undeniable truth. They were there to celebrate her upcoming wedding. This was her bachelorette party and next week she was expected to marry James.

Audrey not only sensed her best friend's apprehension, but the little heads-up text Jay sent her indicated that Lanie needed some fun. Standing, she pulled her friend into a tight squeeze, then whispered in her ear. "Don't worry, just have fun tonight. I've already cleared it with Rob, I'm staying with you afterwards."

Reassured and wanting the company, she pulled back from her friend in time to be passed around by the rest of the girls. Lanie thought they each looked so beautiful and different. Her guests could have come straight out of the Disneyland's It's a Small World ride. She thought it a lovely scene to capture on canvas then morbidly realized the title might be *Last Meal*. Settling down in her seat, Lanie picked up a sparkly flute of pink bubbles and called a toast. "Here's to nights we won't remember with friends we can't forget."

Glasses clinked and everyone cheered.

"To Lanie," Audrey chimed, and the group joined the choir, "To Lanie."

They ordered appetizers, entrées, and dessert and as the meal progressed, Lanie felt at ease for the first time in weeks. She loved these girls and was overjoyed by their company. Her face was flushed, assisted by the seemingly bottomless glass of champagne.

Audrey could see that Lanie was having a good time and asked the server for a group picture. One day, she would look back on this evening with fresh eyes and maybe even a little smile. They all fussed to arrange themselves just so. "Don't get my arms," one girl called. "Take it from this angle," another requested.

Their server prompted, "Okay, on the count of three, say cheers. One, two, three—"

They chimed at once, "Vain Girls!"

He chuckled before saying, "I think it is a good one. Let me know if you ladies need anything else."

Her most amorous friend flirted not entirely under her breath. "Oh, I can think of something I want from you."

He laughed and retreated. "I'm afraid I'm not off duty for some time still. Enjoy the show girls."

They all laughed and ribbed Olivia for her failed attempt.

Audrey took control of their agenda. "Ok girlies, time for our show at Lips!"

Next on the list, they were going to the well-known female impersonator musical a few blocks down the road. As they made their way, Lanie realized she was feeling hopeful. The events of the past week had taken a toll but tonight proved there would always be light at the end of the tunnel.

As they entered the building, Audrey took the lead and announced their reservation. Immediately they were guided to a table right in front of the stage. When they were settled, a drop-dead gorgeous blonde woman came to take their drink order. Olivia spoke for everyone as she addressed the Amazonian beauty.

"We'll have six jello shooters and six cosmopolitans!"

Tomorrow they would pay for this, but tonight, nobody cared.

The show was unbelievable. One had to marvel at the transformation these entertainers went through to put this on. Assembling the costumes alone must have been an enormous undertaking. Lanie couldn't remember the last time she laughed so hard. Her face was aching from smiling that much. When the last performer finished, the entire cast returned to the stage for one last bow. It was standing room only as everyone cheered and some even threw roses toward the stage.

Afterwards, the group filed outside and stood waiting for Audrey's next directive.

"Listen up everyone, Jones is our next and final stop. I'll only say this once so pay attention—first round is on me!"

Oh crap, Lanie thought, tomorrow would suck but

tonight she would dance "like it's 1999." Feeling silly and near drunk, she did not want to think about tomorrow.

They arrived at the club and waited as Audrey spoke to the bouncer. Removing the velvet rope from its clip, he motioned for the women to enter. Wow, Lanie thought, Audrey still had it. Once inside, they were assaulted by flashing lights and booming hip hop. Shuffling through the crowds, they made their way over to the bar and waited as their decisive friend ordered a round of cosmos. In a flash, a row of drinks were ready. They quickly sucked down strong pink elixir, leaving their empty glasses behind.

Forming a chain by holding hands, Audrey led them toward the fun. "Onward," she forced, and the women followed her to the center of the dance floor. Forming a circle, they all took turns getting in the middle. When men tried to enter, they squeezed them back out again. This was girls' night and they weren't sharing their time with anyone.

More than a few side aches later, the night was winding down. They exited the club and everyone stood outside exchanging goodbyes. Only Lanie and Audrey remained. Yet again taking the lead, Audrey hailed a cab. In no time, they were spirited away and shortly after, arrived at Lanie's apartment. Paying the driver, Audrey approached as Lanie was fumbling with the code to release the door. Noticing her struggle, she had to tease but slurred, unwittingly.

"You, my friend is dunk, drunk."

Laughing, Lanie had to agree. After another attempt, she got the door opened. They both leaned on the wall as they rode the elevator to the top. When they entered her condo, Lanie missed the hook and instead dropped her bag on the floor. The contents strewn about everywhere went unattended. Audrey snickered then stumbled herself. Tossing their shoes aside, the girls headed to the kitchen.

Lanie took two glasses from the cupboard and filled them with water while Audrey rooted around the pantry for a midnight, nay, 2 a.m. snack. Finding the chips, she was satisfied. As she tore open the bag, half of its contents flew onto the counter and floor below. They laughed like kids. Lanie reached her hand inside the bag and grabbed a handful of the greasy treats. She chomped and dropped several on the ground. Realizing they were fucked up, she managed a bit of logic. "We should get some sleep."

"Uh-huh," Audrey agreed as she clutched the bag of chips and followed her friend to the bedroom.

Lanie set a water glass on the side of the bed that Audrey was already settled into and staggered to her side. Before falling in herself, she tossed her skirt to the floor and guzzled half the glass of water. Pressing the remote, she turned off the lights.

"Good night, Aud." She looked over to find that her friend was already sound asleep.

16

Is this really happening?

The next morning came with a screaming beam of light. Lanie felt like her head would explode. Her neck ached horribly and her stomach was rolling. She stirred and recalled that her friend had stayed over. Looking to her right, she saw that Audrey was just showing signs of life, herself. As she tentatively opened one eye, she winced visibly.

"Mornin'," Lanie said, while trying to bite back the bile and sickening desire to vomit.

"Ugh. How much did we drink last night?" Audrey questioned.

Shuttering, Lanie did not want to think about that. She said, "Way, way, too much."

Standing, Lanie went to the restroom and splashed cold water on her face. Morning light illuminated the dark circles under her eyes, a telltale sign of her overindulgence. Returning to the bedroom where Audrey still lay, she tossed a terry cloth robe in her direction.

"I'll start some coffee."

Audrey merely growled in response.

Entering the living room and kitchen was like walking into a teenager's bedroom. Ignoring that the items from her purse were spilled all over the floor, she advanced to the kitchen. As she did, she stepped on shards of Kettle chips. The feeling on her bare feet was unwelcome. This, she could not ignore. Using a small broom, she swept up the chips then dusted the crumbs from the counter before starting the coffee. Today, she would use the traditional pot. It was easier and she needed that.

Thankful there was a French baguette on the counter, Lanie warmed the oven to 375 degrees and placed the bread inside. From the refrigerator, she pulled a wedge of Brie and pot of Marion berry jam. Setting them on the table, she set two plates, napkins and knives down to join them. After pouring the coffee, she placed them in front of each plate. As she brought the cream and warm bread to the table, Audrey grumbled into the room. Staggered slightly, she fell into a chair. Lanie joined her at the table. They sat silently at first, forcing down the first bites of warm bread.

A few sips of hot coffee later, Audrey was the first to speak.

"Some night, huh?"

Head swimming, Lanie had to agree.

"Yeah."

Realizing she hadn't taken the time to properly thank her friend, she said, "Audrey, thank you for going to all that trouble. It was really a fun time. Once my head stops pounding, I'm sure I'll laugh."

Feeling green herself and out of party practice, Audrey reassured her, "Me too, sister."

They ate silently for a little longer, enjoying the simple act of taking sips and bites then Audrey spoke. "Other than the hangover, how are you feeling?"

Contemplating the question she knew was coming, Lanie was honest with her response. "I'm feeling like this is more than cold feet."

Audrey could only imagine the strength it took to utter those words. She knew her friend would not make such a statement unless she were serious. She had to ask the next question. "What are you going to do?"

Lanie still didn't have the answer, which was the most debilitating part. "I don't know. I tried talking to James on Thursday. I surprised him at the office and that didn't go well."

Unaware, Audrey wanted details. "What did you say to him?"

Lanie shared the highlights.

"I told him that I sometimes feel like a hash mark on his check list. I let him know how bad it made me feel he was so into the test, and risking us so close to our wedding."

Audrey knew this took a lot of bravery on Lanie's part. She breathed her next question. "How did he respond?"

"He told me that it was a harmless bet and then he asked me if we could table the conversation until dinner tonight. He was really busy at work and I did show up unannounced."

Typical James, Audrey thought. She chose her next words carefully and spoke out of love for the friend who was more like a sister to her. "There will be a lot of times in the future when things come up and they won't fit into a schedule. If I didn't have Ron's support, there would be no way for me to take care of everything. There are things I take for granted. For example, when Lee got sick last month, he took off of work without me even asking. He knew how full my hands already were with Lily and that I wouldn't easily be able to take care of them both alone. Every day I fall more in love with him. He and I are one hundred percent in it together. I want that for you."

Lanie's lips were in a straight line, her fingers stroked a drop of coffee that slid over the side and down the cup. She responded simply, "I know."

Before she could say anything else, the intercom buzzed and she could hear Ron's voice coming through. She looked at Audrey with a quizzical expression and watched as she crossed the room to buzz him in. "He's come to save us. Thanks for the toast and all, but today I needed an iced tea and a greasy breakfast burrito, otherwise known as a gut bomb."

They laughed together as the rambunctious crew spilled into Lanie's apartment. It was a noisy and welcome scene, as she enjoyed spicy Mexican food while watching her best friend's family interact. She was in love with them all and they were in love with her.

———

AS PLANNED, Jay opened the gallery that morning. He had a renewed sense of purpose after their fateful encounter with Mrs. Main the previous day. Decisively, he picked up the phone and dialed the digits, calling Mr. Main.

When he answered, Jay made it quick. "Hello, Mr. Main?" When he received affirmation, he continued, "This is Jay from the gallery where you purchased the painting yesterday." His statement was met by silence so Jay took the liberty and carried on. "We wanted you to know that the work was delivered to Mrs. Main yesterday." Still there was silence. Undeterred, Jay went on. "She loved it and wanted you to know, she'd like to see you." Did the man have no voice? Jay wondered. Then, finally, a response came through the line.

"She said that?"

Jay improvised. "She did indeed."

The man's voice was gravelly in response. "Thank you."

Before Jay could respond, the call was disconnected. He sat for a moment wondering what would happen next. What a saga the entire tale had become. He didn't have time to ponder the matter for long before the door chimed, signifying a customer. Looking up, Jay was shocked to see Ryan Glass standing in the doorway. He surveyed the space, clearly looking for Lanie. His face showed a flash of disappointment as he crossed the room, meeting Jay halfway.

To take sting out of the situation, Jay spoke up first. "Well hello there, Ryan. What brings you in today?"

"I just got back from New York and I know Lanie has plans with her friends tonight, but I couldn't wait until dinner tomorrow. Is she here by chance?"

Quick on his feet and getting good at games of the heart, he lied. "I'm so sorry, you missed her. She had a delivery and some business to attend to today. Can I get a message to her?"

Ryan's face showed obvious disappointment. As he spoke, he reached into his pocket and extracted something. He handed the item to Jay. It was a miniature figurine of the Empire State Building.

"Would you please leave this for her and tell her I am looking forward to dinner tomorrow?"

Jay's heart leapt in his chest. If Lanie didn't fall for this guy he would do everything in his power to convert him. Plastering his best poker face on, he agreed, "Of course, I'll get it to her."

Pausing a moment longer, as if he thought Lanie may still arrive, he eventually turned and said, "Thank you, Jay."

Wanting to give him something and feeling as though the spirit of Cupid had possessed him, Jay said, "Ryan."

He turned around. "Yes."

Jay covered the distance and stood close as he spoke the next words. "She is incredible and the most ethical and dedicated person I know. Don't give up on her."

Confused by his words and sensing there was more to the statement, he knew it would be pointless to question. Ryan decided not to press. He replied with the kind of conviction that Jay wanted for his close friend. "I won't." At that he turned and left the gallery.

For a long while Jay stared at the door, shocked by the events of the day, and hoping for the best. He walked to Lanie's desk and placed the figure next to the exotic vase of flowers that were as fresh as the day they arrived.

———

TO EXORCISE the last vestiges of her hangover and burn off the double breakfast, Lanie took a walk. As she left her building and traveled along the city streets, she knew where she was going. She would walk to Washington Park and visit the Rose Garden. It was a special place to her and one where she always found inspiration.

Traveling along the residential area of NW Portland, she enjoyed the community. Each house had its own distinct style and all were lovingly cared for. The architecture, sizes, and colors of each home stood on their own. Nothing cookie-cutter or uniform was found here. With its proximity to downtown and amazing restaurants, surrounded by the sprawling urban park that showcased the city from every vantage point, the neighborhood was a gem. It took just over thirty minutes to reach the top of the park. Standing at the long staircase that led to the lush garden, she soaked it all in.

In the distance, she could see a range of buildings—most prominent of them was "Big Pink." The 42-story building housed the famous Portland City Grill on the 28th floor; from its towering heights, diners could see for miles. The views changed as you moved inside the enormous restaurant. Gleaming windows provided an uncompromising vantage point, framing the many bridges, the Willamette River, and the green hillsides covered by evergreen trees.

Bringing her attention back to the park, she studied the foreground below. There were throngs of visitors walking the aisles of flowers, careful not to touch, but enveloped by the sweetest fragrance that permeated the air. Descending the stairway, Lanie joined the crowds. As she walked, she stopped to smell the orange, then lavender roses. She made her way down several rows, then found herself at the entrance to the Shakespeare Garden. It was a lovely area with a fountain, but the wisteria covered trellis was the focal point of this little carve-out in the garden. She took a seat on a vacant bench and let the sun's rays shine down on her. It felt incredible to be surrounded by such beauty and happiness. Her mind was clear and her heart full; inspired by the sensations, she decided this would be her next painting.

As that thought entered her mind, she felt a buzz from the phone in her pocket. It was a message from James that made her stomach lurch. It read, "Angel, I'm sorry for the way our conversation went the other day. I am looking forward to making it up to you at dinner tonight. Meet me at Departure at 8?"

Setting the phone down, Lanie surveyed her surroundings. Birds flitted about, children ran and laughed together, couples strolled hand in hand, and here she was observing it all. Her mind wandered back to the breakfast scene with Audrey's family, then to their conversation. She knew Audrey could do anything she set her mind to. Knowing her friend as she did, it was amazing to see that she let her guard down with Ron. Her admission of how much she depended on him, and feeling like she couldn't do it without him, was mind blowing. Decisively, Lanie opened her phone and keyed a succinct reply. "I'll see you at 8."

Looking at the time, she noticed it was after four o'clock. It was time to make her way back.

WHEN SHE GOT HOME, Lanie drew a hot bath then added peppermint oil. The bathroom mirrors steamed up from the heat. It was warm for a bath but she had the time and wanted to relax the last of her hangover away. Settling into the balmy water, she concentrated on only her breath, the way it sounded, felt, and the fact that it was a constant. Luscious mint permeated the air and opened her sinuses. The water grew tepid and it was time to get out.

Reluctantly, she removed the plug then stood and pulled a towel from the shelf. Wrapping herself, she made her way toward the fogged vanity. Wiping the mirror with her hand, she applied moisturizer and let it absorb while she selected an outfit. From the closet, she chose a black halter dress that clung at the waist while the skirt flowed scarf-like to just above the knee. Since it would be a warm out, she finished the outfit with strappy black sandals.

A flash of nerves came over her as she tormented herself with a fast forward to this evening with James.

Earlier in the day she committed to taking in each moment until it was time to face her fiancé. Instead of fretting the minutes, she wanted to be present. She knew the best thing she could do to quiet her mind and find the answer was to set the puzzle down.

Regrouping, she picked black panties and a strapless bra from the drawer, and got dressed. Walking back to the vanity, she smoothed and styled her hair into a high pony-tail. Next, she applied makeup. She chose black eyeliner, penning a slash above each eye, and added black mascara to open her eyes further. For the final touch, she outlined her full lips with a dark liner and filled them in with a frosted peach lipstick. She looked at her reflection and willed her mind to emulate her exterior. It was time to leave.

Breath, she coaxed herself. From the closet, she selected a small black evening bag and a thin white shawl. Carrying both, along with her shoes, she went to the living room and put them on. It was 7:40 p.m. and time to go. Rising deliberately and walking through the door, Lanie knew she was moving toward her destiny. Her stomach lurched and this time, she couldn't breathe her way out of it.

DEPARTURE WAS a trendy Portland hot spot and styled more like a restaurant you might find in Los Angeles. At the top of The Nines hotel, it boasted stunning views from the oversized decks that were always busy during the dry summer months. Exiting the elevator, she walked along the darkened pathways, lit only by the strange, neon lights. The design gave the impression one was traveling in the Starship Enterprise.

Her actions of forward movement starkly contrasted with her thoughts. She considered fleeing the building but knew that wasn't the right thing to do. She approached the hostess stand and was greeted by a slender brunette with a stark ponytail and black lipstick.

Her monochromatic tone stated unconvincingly, "Welcome to Departure."

Nervously she replied, "Thanks, I'm meeting James Roberts."

The robot-like voice directed, "Please follow me."

Lanie trailed behind the hostess, passing a long bar and rows of bench seating on the way. They arrived at the patio doors and her guide held the door, allowing Lanie to pass. With a hand gesture, she waved in James' direction. His back was to her. She could still run. Squelching the thought, she thanked the hostess who had already turned and was heading back to where they started. She steeled herself before walking to the table where her fiancé was waiting.

Sensing her presence, James turned and stood as she approached. A genuine smile on his face, he pulled her into a hug and brief kiss before speaking. "You look amazing." He said, admiring her dress.

"Thank you, so do you."

He wore an untucked, crisp, black button-up shirt, with smooth silver cufflinks to accent the look. Taking her seat across the table, there was a moment of silence before their server arrived.

"Good evening, my name is Shane and I'll be serving you tonight."

His tone and demeanor were a stark contrast to the hostess who had seated Lanie. The hangover was finally gone and Lanie had considered avoiding alcohol this evening, but knew she'd need something to settle her nerves. Taking the one-and-done route, she ordered. "I'll have a Belvedere Martini, a little dirty, please."

"Thank you, and sir, would you like another manhattan as well?"

"Sure, thanks," James replied.

Noting his drink was drained, Lanie wondered if he had been waiting long and asked, "Am I late?"

"No," he assured. "I made it a little ahead of time and the table was ready so I had a seat."

He seemed edgy to her, but they hadn't seen one another in over a week unless you counted that awful conversation two days before.

He spoke softly. "You look gorgeous, angel." Did she detect a hint of sorrow?

"Thanks. I had the time since I didn't go to the gallery today."

"Oh, why not?" he asked.

"Well, Jay forbade it actually."

"Huh, why would he do that?"

She wondered if he had forgotten her "bachelorette night."

"He assumed I'd be in no condition after a night on the town with the girls."

James rebounded, "Of course, how nice of him. What did you ladies get up to last night?"

She gave him the highlights and noticed his attention was wavering. Time to change the subject.

"How's the project coming?"

"Good, actually got a lot of ground covered the past few days." He looked anything but pleased.

Timing was good as their drinks arrived. After setting them down, Shane went through the specials of the day. "Today we have fresh Sturgeon served with black caviar lentils. The soup is a pepper and citrus gazpacho. Have you had time to consider the menu?"

James looked over at Lanie and she deferred. "Please, you order for us both. We can share like we usually do."

James ordered two sushi items, the fish special, and two of the soups to begin.

Their server left and they sat in silence for a time. The setting sun faded the towering buildings to black, contrasting against the pink and orange evening sky.

Simultaneously, they spoke. An awkward chuckle arose and Lanie paused, waiting for James to continue. As he was about to begin, Shane returned with their gazpacho.

Smiling politely, they each tried a few bites.

"Hmm, it's really flavorful," she said, a harmless truth. That had her mind racing; not all truths were harmless.

"Yeah, it really is," he agreed, though he didn't give a flying fuck about the soup. Nerves were pricking his skin. He'd had an ominous feeling all day.

Lanie ate the soup not tasting it over the salty reflux that kept creeping up from the pit of her stomach. She was grateful for the diversion when their server arrived with a range of other dishes for them to nibble on. The options included eel in chocolate sauce, spicy tuna rolls, and the Sturgeon dish. They ate politely; James placed items on her plate as they shared the meal in near silence.

When it was obvious they were winding down, Shane returned with an assistant to clear their plates. He asked if they would like to order another drink. James did while Lanie opted to stick with water.

Once his drink arrived, James finally had the courage to move forward with his plan. Until then, he hadn't noticed that Lanie wasn't wearing her engagement ring. "Hey, where's your ring?"

Looking down at her hand, she recounted the

events of the past week, and realized she hadn't worn it since the night of the mixer. "It's in the safe at work. Jay reminded me to take it off before the mixer, and I didn't notice it was missing until just now." That realization brought a whole new clarity of thought forward.

As if reading her mind, James spoke rapidly and reached into his pocket. From it he pulled a rectangular shaped velvet box that he placed on the table between them. "Forgetfulness, as I'm told, is a bad trait and hopefully not one that our children will inherit." He lifted the lid and Lanie saw the most stunning, jeweled bracelet nestled inside.

She couldn't let him continue and reached to place her hand on his. Just as she was about to speak, a familiar voice called her name. She looked over and was sickened to see Ryan making his way toward their table. He arrived by her side and she was at a loss.

Noticing the frozen expression on her face, James tensed and stood. On wobbly legs, Lanie joined the men, standing between them.

Ryan surveyed the table and saw the jeweled cuff gleaming in the candlelight. A look of confusion was overtaken by one of disgust. "Some girls' night," he said.

James was feeling very territorial and wanted to make certain to piss on the bushes. He sneered a response, "I'm no girl. I'm her fiancé. Who are you?"

At that, Ryan looked Lanie dead in the eye. His response was a whisper, "I'm no one."

Before Lanie could speak a word, he turned on his heel, vanishing into the building and out of sight. Seeing her expression, and the attention they were receiving from other diners, James took her arm, and pulled her to sit. Her mind was racing. This was not how she wanted Ryan to learn of her situation, nor how she'd expected the night with James to turn out.

His voice was cold now and he demanded an explanation. "Who the fuck was that, Lanie?"

Too tired from the mounting stress of the past weeks, she resigned to tell him what happened. "We met at the mixer. It was an accident at first and then," she hesitated, "we struck up a sort of friendship."

"Bullshit," his voice cut, "that didn't look like a friend and why did you have to lie to him if that were the case? He seemed to think you were at a girls' night."

Decisive now and angry herself, Lanie chose her next words from a less than Zen place. There was no stopping what she was about to vocalize, what she knew deep down inside, what she had come to say. "James, I can't marry you."

His face turned red. Leaning closer, he spoke in the harshest whisper. "Why not, that little fuck had his way with you, and now you're throwing away six years—six good years?"

"It has nothing to do with him and everything to do with us."

His silence egged her on.

"I want you to know, I didn't sleep with him, but we did start a relationship."

He stared down at the table, unresponsive.

"The fact that I could enjoy spending time with another man, that I was open to it, even though I knew it was wrong . . . it showed me that we aren't right for each other. There's something missing between us"—she reached for his arm—"and we both know it."

Tears welled in his eyes; there was wisdom in her words and truth but he panicked at the realization. If he couldn't make it with her, he couldn't make it with anyone. "How can you say this to me? We are supposed to be getting married next week."

Sitting up straight, she closed the velvet box and slid it to his side of the table. "That is exactly why I'm saying it to you, now. I love you, but I'm not in love with you, and you aren't in love with me. I cannot marry you, James."

When she spoke the words, final as they were, she knew without a shadow of doubt they were true. Standing, she leaned over and kissed him on the temple before walking away.

17

The Aftermath

The room was dark, all except a pink light. Moving forward she followed the path. At the end of the walkway, there, in the darkness, was an unlikely door. Hesitant, but needing to see what was behind it, she turned the knob. A flood of light blinded her as the door swung wide, into a dimly lit bedroom. She peered in, and saw a bed. On it, was James. He was being straddled by a naked woman. He didn't notice her standing there. She could hear him. He spoke gruffly, "That's it baby, keep going, don't stop, don't stop." Suddenly he cried out in ecstasy as the woman looked over her shoulder toward Lanie, a sly smile curved at her lips.

She awakened with a start; sweat poured down her spine and between her breasts. She was home, alone. It was a dream but that was no assurance after last night's reality. Funny she would turn the tables and make James the adulterer in her dream.

A shiver ran up her spine as she considered how much she had to face. She'd cope by going into the gallery where she could bury herself in something normal for the day.

Tomorrow would be soon enough to tell her family what they, nay, what she decided.

Not having the strength, nor caring to pull herself together, she dressed quickly in a pair of jeans and flowing black blouse. After slipping into flats, she pulled her hair up and into a bun, splashed water on her face, dabbed on some concealer and finished with red lipstick.

As she left her bedroom, she got a glimpse of her most recent painting of the Space Needle. Decisive, she walked to the easel, removed the picture and carried it with her out the door. It would be best to bury it in the back office at the gallery. She wanted no more painful reminders slapping her in the face. She left the apartment without coffee or a backwards glance.

She opened the gallery, and went about getting ready for the day. As she flipped on lights and straightened paintings, she couldn't avoid the ever-persistent finality of what happened the night before. She and James had been a big part of each other's lives for so long. It was hard to imagine what things would be like without him in the background. They were friends and he supported her in ways that no one else had. He wasn't always emotionally available, but there was something about him she trusted. Sadness overtook her and everything felt heavy today.

The door chimed at her back, announcing Jay's arrival. From her position at the coffee station, she looked his direction. Their eyes locked, but both were silent as he set his bag on the desk. Walking to Lanie, Jay studied her face. Devoid of cosmetics, she looked like a child.

The espresso machine made noise and he said, "Sit, I'll finish this."

She walked to her desk and sat. It was then that she found the tiny figure of the Empire State Building. She reached for the little statue and looked questioningly in Jay's direction.

Carrying the coffee to her, he said, "Ryan dropped it by for you yesterday. He said he hoped to see you, couldn't wait until Sunday. The young suitor was quite disappointed to find you weren't in."

Tears filled Lanie's eyes and rolled down her face.

Seeing this, Jay assumed the wedding was still moving forward. Resolved to support his friend, no matter the decision, he spoke up. "You'll be happy with James. You will make a life together and everything will be great, just wait."

Shaking her head, she could barely fathom what she was about to say. "I called it off."

Hallelujah, he thought to himself, but responded appropriately. "That must have been so hard, Lanie. I can only imagine what you are going through but you never would have done it if it wasn't the right thing. Ever since I've known you, you've always done what's right."

Her tearful eyes looked pained as she replied, "You don't understand. Ryan saw us. He was at the restaurant. He and James had words. Well, James mostly told him he was my fiancé and Ryan left. I haven't spoken to Ryan since."

Jay was in shock. Good lord—this woman, who avoided drama, and always walked the straight line, had managed her share over the past weeks. "Oh my god."

As she looked at him, a vacant expression washed over her. "I told James how we met. At first, he was so angry, then he looked heartbroken. I told him I wasn't in love with him anymore and I couldn't marry him."

What did one say in response to a tale like this? "Lanie, how are *you* feeling?"

"Shocked . . . empty. I haven't told Audrey or my parents yet. You are the first to know."

Taking charge now, Jay decided it was the least he could do.

"Well, I can't be the one to tell your parents but I can undo the arrangements, and send out an announcement to the guests. Let me do that for you, but first, you need to speak with your folks."

"I know I do. I'll call them right now."

As she uttered the words, the door chimed and in walked James. Jay thought he looked like hell and had a pang of empathy for the man. Rising, he acknowledged him with the briefest nod before exiting to the back-storage room.

Lanie stood and walked around the desk to face him. He hugged her and pulled back, keeping a hold of her arms. As he stared into those sad green eyes, the ones he had fallen for all those years ago, James was filled with remorse. He couldn't help but wish he'd done many things differently. His regret was evident in his tone.

"I owe you an apology, for so many things, especially for not being the kind of man you deserve. I know I haven't been perfect, far from it in some cases. You were right to have doubts. There is something inside me that I haven't worked out yet. I can't explain why I've handled certain things as I have, but I want you to know, I never meant to hurt you. Never. I'm sorry for what I've done."

Lanie sensed this was his roundabout way of making a confession without actually stating the sin, but she didn't care. He had been such a big part of her life and she would miss many things about him. "Don't be sorry," she said. "I wouldn't have changed it, any of it. Without you"—she waved her hands around the gallery—"this may never have happened. I'm so grateful for our time together and sorry that it came down to this."

"Me, too. I called my parents this morning. My mother is beside herself, Dad is too. They love you."

"I haven't made the call yet." She looked down. "I'll do it tonight. Don't worry about cancelling anything else, I've got it handled."

"Are you sure?" he said, then stopped himself as if remembering something. "Come to think of it, you handled most of the arrangements, I guess I wouldn't know what to do to help." His expression was even more glum. "Sorry about that too. I'm a real jerk."

His sadness was palatable and for a fleeting moment, she questioned their decision to end it. Knowing what she must do next, she said, "Wait here, will you?"

"Sure," he replied, rooted to the spot.

She went to the back and as she entered, Jay was standing there holding her engagement ring. Blinking away the tears, she accepted it and returned to the place where James was standing. "This belongs to you." She handed him the ring.

He studied it in his hand for a long while before sliding it into his pocket. Their relationship concluded with his final words. "Take care, Lanie." No longer did he call her angel, his former term of endearment. "I'll miss you."

Tears streamed down her face as he turned and walked out of the gallery, out of her life.

HEARING THE DOOR CHIME, Jay returned to the front and to Lanie's side. Having first-row seats of their final conversation gave him no thrill. Even he and his restless soul had a moment of hesitation, wondering if they should try to work it out. Knowing that his uncertainty was the absolute last thing she needed, he spoke in such a way to hide his question. "That was clearly difficult for you both. Sometimes doing the right thing hurts for a short time, but it's better than living with what's wrong for a lifetime."

She knew he was right, and this would be the worst day of several. Resolved to get the thing she was dreading most behind, she walked to the desk, got her cell phone, then went to the back. It was time to call her parents.

As the phone rang, her anxiety heightened until finally, her mother's voice answered.

"Hi, Lanie." She sounded subdued.

Fresh tears exploded as she struggled to speak. "Mmm, Mom, I have to tell you something."

Concern showed by Rani's pitch as she responded, "What is it honey? Are you hurt?"

There was silence for a beat, then she uttered the words in a rush. "James and I are calling it off."

The air between the miles sizzled as they each processed what was just said. Finally, Rani broke the quiet. "I'm sorry, Lanie. Knowing you, this wasn't a decision you took lightly. Are you all right?"

Thankful for her soft response and kind words, Lanie wanted to ease her mother's concern. "I will be. We both will. Jay is going to help with the cancellations, thank goodness."

Relieved to hear this, but still wondering how her daughter would hold up over the next several days, Rani wanted to help. "Why don't I come out this week and spend some time with my little girl?"

Knowing she couldn't manage her own emotions along with her mom's, Lanie politely refused. "It's okay Mom. I've decided to take a little trip on my own, to clear my head. Don't worry, please."

Rani would worry but she wanted to respect her daughter's wishes. "I understand. Please call me and let me know you're okay. I'm so sorry, sweetheart."

"Thanks Mom. Tell Dad I love him."

"We love you too, honey."

WHEN SHE RETURNED from the back, Jay couldn't miss how fragile she looked. He hated to see her in pain and wanted to do what he could to help get her through the day. Taking matters into his own hands, he had called Audrey. "How did it go, kiddo?" he asked.

"Okay, I guess."

She looked like she was barely holding on. "I hope you're not upset, but I called Audrey."

Lanie looked up.

"She'll be here shortly."

Taking a deep breath , she asked, "Can you hold things down here for the next few days? I need to get away."

Without a second's hesitation, he agreed. "Of course, take all the time you need." A little concerned, he did want to keep tabs on her. After noticing the painting she'd brought in, he suspected he already knew the answer but wanted to be sure.

"Where are you headed, Lanie?"

"Seattle."

As she spoke the words, the door chimed. To their shock, in walked Mr. and Mrs. Main.

With the events of the day, Jay hadn't filled Lanie in on his little matchmaking scheme. A trickle of panic raced through him, knowing they couldn't handle another blow today. His salesmanship kicked into action as he put on a brave face and greeted the two. "Good day Mr. and Mrs. Main. What brings you in for a visit?

They walked resolutely to face him and Lanie. Mrs. Main broke the silence. "Young man, am I to understand you put words in my mouth?"

Shit, this day kept doling it out. He grappled for a response as Lanie's focus also trained in on him. "I may have improvised a little." Jay shifted his weight from foot to foot, obviously uncomfortable with the confrontation.

Mr. Main placed his arm possessively around his estranged wife. His stern face cracked open in a happy smile while his dark eyes crinkled at the corners. "I cannot tell you how grateful we both are. You forced my hand, young man. It was exactly what I needed to get my courage back."

Finally, the air let out of the balloon and it flew through the room. The happy couple laughed, Jay followed, and a few seconds later Lanie's sweet voice joined the mix. Audrey arrived in time to witness the unexpected scene.

AFTER JAY'S FRANTIC CALL, Audrey hardly expected to arrive at the gallery to find Lanie laughing. Noticing her friend enter, Lanie gestured for her to join them.

"Mr. and Mrs. Main, this is my best friend, Audrey."

Her corporate manners automatically kicked in and she extended her hand to shake theirs. Mr. Main commented, "That's quite a grip, young lady. In my past business dealings, I found a number of men with weak handshakes. I believe that to be a sign of weak character as well."

Smiling, Audrey agreed. "It seems you and I have had similar experiences, Mr. Main."

Jay was relieved to see his plan had worked and wanted the details of their reunion. It was also a wonderful distraction for his boss. "Shall we have a seat? I know this may be indelicate of me but I can't help it. I want to hear more of your romance."

Mrs. Main responded now, alight with joy, her demeanor so different from two days prior. "We would love to share. Our story has had a couple of twists along the way yet here we are, together again, at long last." Her eyes shone as she looked up at her husband.

"Please, this way." Jay directed and they all walked to the long table situated on one side of the gallery. "Take a seat. Would either of you like a cup of tea or coffee? We also have sparkling water."

"No, thank you." They spoke in time and it was as though not a single day of absence had passed between them.

Jay, Audrey, and Lanie, sat opposite the reunited pair, looking on expectedly. Clearly the story teller of the two, Mrs. Main began.

"In 1954, when I was just nineteen years old, well . . ." she paused as if envisioning the period, "things were different back then. You obeyed your parents in a way that doesn't exist today. My parents had a dairy farm in Eugene, which I worked every day before and after school. My father, the descendant of German immigrants, had long expected I marry the son of the cattle farmer whose property abutted ours.

"Dad was a very practical man. Though I had a younger brother, who would carry on the family business, he was in no position to double our land mass through such a union. The boy next door, Bobby Smith, was a nice young man but not very sophisticated. We had known each other most of our lives. The marriage seemed logical to my folks because we were close in age and it made sound business sense."

She paused, glancing over at her husband. "Ever the dreamer, I dreaded the idea of a lifetime on that farm. There were good things about it as it instilled a strong work ethic. I did love the animals and it was a peaceful existence, but I couldn't imagine spending the entirety of my life there.

"My mother understood what so many women, particularly of that era, didn't. She advocated on my behalf with Father and pressed for me to attend college at University of Oregon. She told him it would help me sow my wild oats, arguing that the rigor of academia would cure my wanderlust. He agreed but only if I promised I'd marry Bobby when I graduated. I agreed."

The young people were silent, fascinated by her tale. Mrs. Main saw a light enter Lanie's eyes, intuitively sensing their meeting had more than one reason.

Jay couldn't stand it any longer. He prodded, "What happened when you went to college?"

Mrs. Main shut her eyes for a moment. Her face rewound to a much earlier time, and she continued, "It was incredible. The instruction was nothing like I had experienced in my formative years. The professors were all so exotic to me. Some had traveled or mastered subjects well beyond my young imagination. Keeping up with my scholastics and responsibilities at home was trying, but I never faltered. I had something to prove to my father and more important, myself.

"There were many practical items I learned at school that helped with the dairy business. For example, the accounting courses I took allowed me to establish better costing metrics. With a stronger balance sheet, we found more favorable terms and a larger credit line from the bank. This allowed us to increase our herd, thus growing our volume of milk production. Business was thriving, and even my once reluctant father came around."

She smiled in remembrance.

Mr. Main spoke then, knowing the sadness she still felt when thinking of her departed parents. "He adored you, Annette. You were the apple of his eye."

Patting his hand, a gentle smile played on her mouth as she continued, "It was there at school where Thomas and I met. He was working on his engineering degree and three years my senior. We met at a study group we were both a part of. When our eyes locked across the table, I felt something I had never experienced before. My reaction to him confused and excited me. Between group meetings, I'd find myself counting the days until our next Wednesday afternoon session." She looked toward her husband—the memories had an impact.

Seeking to create some levity, Mr. Main joked, "It was my wavy hair that won her over."

They all laughed.

"Yes," she agreed, "and your dreamy eyes; but his intelligence had everyone enamored. He was a straight-A student and always the first to raise his hand with the correct answer.

"After a few weeks of study group, he invited me to join him for lunch the following day. Sheltered as I was, I had never been on a date before. I remember how nervous I was. He doesn't know this," she said with her head tilted toward her husband, "but I actually vomited a few minutes before we met."

Mr. Main looked surprised. "I certainly did not know that."

Turning his face to speak to his wife, he spoke earnestly, "Darling, it was I who was nervous. You were the prettiest girl in school, and I knew from the kids around that your father was an important land owner in the area. It mattered so much that I make a good impression, but I fumbled terribly on that first date."

Chuckling together, an inside joke passed between them. Mrs. Main picked up.

"He certainly did. We agreed to meet at the cafeteria on campus. We met at the entrance and walked the buffet line together. Pushing our trays along, we selected food items that would remain untouched. Who could eat at a time like that?"

Mr. Main chimed in now, wanting to share his perspective of the day. "As we arrived at the counter, the worst thing imaginable happened."

The young people leaned forward in anticipation, awaiting Mr. Main's next words.

"I reached into my pocket and realized that I had forgotten my wallet."

They all gasped.

After a beat, Mrs. Main went ahead with the tale. "It was an awkward moment for Thomas, but his faux pas helped assuage my nerves. There was nothing left to do so I paid for our meal. This turned the tables in my favor and I relaxed; a new-found confidence had taken over."

Mr. Main flushed at the recollection and said, "To this day she teases me about the fact that *she* paid on our first date. It was and still may be, the most embarrassing moment of my life."

At that, Mrs. Main resumed the story. "The next few years went by in a blur. Thomas was ahead of me in grade so he graduated well before I did. After college, he accepted a position at Tektronix, learning everything imaginable about oscilloscopes. The trouble was we weren't able to see one another as much. There was quite a distance between us so we had to concentrate our visits. At times we would speak on the phone, but we had to do a lot of planning in order to talk when my father wasn't around. We had a secret romance for over two years."

Mr. Main added, "Our separation was torture but I needed to make something of myself before asking for her hand. Annette had explained the commitment she made to her father but I knew she did not love that boy.

"I knew Bobby had eyes for another girl, Becky, who worked at The Coffee Cup on Willamette Street. I'd seen him in there a few times and could tell there was something between them."

Mrs. Main picked up and resumed the telling.

"One weekend in May, when Daddy was away on a buying trip, Thomas and I met at the school. He picked me up in his new Buick sedan and drove me to the coast. We spent the day in Florence and had a lovely time. The sun came out and, as you know, that isn't always the case during the month of May. We walked along the sand for hours and had a long lunch. Any awkwardness between us was long since forgotten. We fell deeply in love."

The look that passed between them was unmistakable. Lanie marveled how they had endured so much and still had that spark these years later. "Wow," she said. "You two were a 1950s version of Romeo and Juliet."

"Young lady, you have no idea," agreed Mr. Main.

Unable to stop herself, Mrs. Main had to complete the story. "That evening when Thomas dropped me off, he pulled to the end of the driveway. I hadn't expected my father to return until the following day but he had concluded his business early. He saw me arrive and knew the car didn't belong to Bobby or anyone he knew."

Mrs. Main went silent. The three outsiders wanted her to go on, but they realized her age and respected the need for a break.

Jay stood and spoke. "I insist on bringing some refreshments. Please don't resume until I return."

He is such a smart man, Lanie thought. Audrey stood to join him. The two were back quickly with glasses, a bottle of water, and chocolate-covered cookies. Placing the items down, they retook their seats across from the older couple.

Mrs. Main took a sip of the bubbly water and began with a renewed voice. "That evening was terrible," she recalled. "My parents were waiting in the doorway as I walked in. I was told to sit in the chair. I can still remember staring at that old carpet, my father's voice booming down at me. He demanded to know who dropped me off. Mom tried to calm him but there was no stopping his anger.

"So many emotions were brewing inside of me. I hated disappointing my parents but my love for Thomas was undeniable. How could I marry a stranger out of obligation, when this man"—she tapped Mr. Main's arm—"had my heart? I told them as much and my father became even more furious."

She hesitated, taking a sip of the water. The room was silent awaiting her next words. "He gave me an order, I was to marry Bobby by the end of that summer. I sobbed and tried to convince him that Thomas was a good match. His voice went to the bottom then; he said I had betrayed my word and told me to get out of his sight."

Taking a deep breath, her face belied the deep emotions that must have been in that room all of those nights ago. "I could hear my parents arguing for a long while after I left them. Nothing made me feel worse than hearing my mother spoken to so harshly. My father blamed her for the entire 'sordid', as he called it, affair. It was awful. I couldn't stand how I'd failed them both. My heart was breaking and I knew what I needed to do."

Unwittingly, the three young ones had locked hands on the table before them. It was obvious they were dying to know what happened next.

Mr. Main took over, "She wrote me a Dear John letter. Told me that her heart would always be mine, but her obligation to her family would have to come first. I still have the letter. I can't tell you how many times over these past twenty years I've re-read those words."

Looking over to his wife, a look of remorse was on his face. "I'm so sorry, Annie. You are such a better person than I."

Mrs. Main gave a little tsk-tsk, then closed her eyes as if reliving long-ago events. She continued, "He tried calling but my mother intervened. She knew I was devastated but she wouldn't betray her husband nor did she want to see her only daughter disowned. It was an awful time.

The wedding plans were set by the fathers. We were to be married at our farm on Labor Day weekend. The week before the wedding my mother took me for my final dress fitting. Afterwards, she walked me to the local jewelry store and told me to select a groom's gift for my fiancé. As I went about the task, my heart was heavier than you could imagine. I surveyed the cases with disinterest until finally, Mom stepped in. She asked the clerk to see one watch. It had a black leather band and the label was Tissot. The clerk handed it to her then she passed it over to me. I studied it and listlessly agreed to the purchase.

The clerk asked if I'd like it engraved but I couldn't fathom what to say to a man who was almost a stranger. Once again, my mother assisted." She took the pen and notepad from the clerk and wrote a phrase. It said, "Thank you for your patience. 9.1.58"

Lanie gasped. They all stared as she leapt from the table and exclaimed, "Wait right here! I have something to show you."

Exchanging glances around the table, Jay whispered under his breath. "She and her fiancé called their wedding off last night."

"Oh dear," said Mrs. Main. "I hope we haven't upset her."

Audrey reassured. "No, your story is beautiful. She loves it. We all do."

Lanie returned, and she carried a worn leather box. Too excited to sit, she snapped the lid open and removed its contents. In her trembling hand was a watch, with a black leather band. She handed it to Mrs. Main before speaking.

"Was this the watch you gave to your intended?"

An old woman could only take so many shocks and now she had seen everything. Her breath caught. When she spoke, the air pressed from her in a near wheeze. "It found you." Examining the watch, Mrs. Main turned it over and saw the inscription that confirmed it was her watch.

Jay and Audrey were still in the dark. Never shy, Jay spoke up. "Do you mind letting the rest of us in on your little secret?"

Mrs. Main finally spoke. "On the eve of our wedding, after the rehearsal dinner, I gave Bobby this very watch. In exchange, he gave me a stunning emerald bracelet. I never wore the piece and after many years, I finally decided to let it go to that charming shop on NW 23rd. So many young folks these days like vintage jewelry, I thought it might finally find its rightful home."

Lanie could not believe what she was hearing. Nothing could ever have prepared her for the events of these past few weeks. Shocked beyond imagination, she croaked, "Last night, before we called it off, James tried to give me an emerald bracelet, like the one you described. I bought this watch for him. I didn't accept the bracelet nor did I get around to giving him the watch. This is unbelievable."

Lanie sat with a thud while Audrey and Jay looked at each other in total amazement.

Knowing his wife had had a lot of excitement for one day, but aware they all needed closure, he cleared his throat and said, "On the day of the wedding, I knew I couldn't let her go without a fight. The devil had possessed me as I sped down the highway toward my Annette. When I arrived, the guests were all seated. I could hear the wedding march playing. In the distance, I saw my love in white, approaching her would-be husband. I've never run faster, never."

He looked down at his wife and they all got a glimpse of the younger man he must have been.

"There was dust flying behind me and that big yellow dog—what was his name?" He shot a questioning look toward Mrs. Main.

She smiled. "Tiger; his name was Tiger."

"Yes, Tiger, how appropriate." He chuckled. "That dog was barking up a storm and chasing me as I sprinted to the aisle. The ruckus we made caused everyone to turn. I had to swallow a lump in my throat, but the barking dog at my heels and my love for this woman"—he squeezed his wife's shoulder—"motivated me."

Collected now, Mrs. Main picked up the tale. "He could barely speak, so out of breath from the run but once he did, he said . . ."

Mr. Main had to say the words he spoke those many years ago.

"She belongs with me. I love her with all of my heart."

The room was silent. So much had happened of late and this story was something out of a motion picture. Audrey pushed this time. "What happened next?"

Mrs. Main spoke, "Bobby had said aloud, 'Oh thank the Lord.' Our parents demanded that Thomas and I join them, and Bobby, in the barn. It was an awful scene as our dads inevitably concluded that the union was not to be.

"Bobby, Thomas, and I listened while they discussed our fates. After a time, my father made his way to Thomas.

"Not backing down, my strong husband stood to face him.

"He said, 'Mr. Zollner, sir, I apologize for the trouble I've caused you, but you must understand that I love your daughter. Though it won't stop me, I'd like your permission to marry her.' "

For a long while, no one spoke. Each was absorbing the fate of this moment. The events that led to this day and how each situation intertwined was unfathomable.

Mr. Main took command. Standing, he placed his hand on the shoulder of his once estranged wife and she joined him. Jay, Audrey, and Lanie stood and followed them as they walked toward the door. Once there, they exchanged hugs with a promise.

"You young people will join us for Sunday supper next weekend," Mrs. Main commanded. They all agreed.

"Young lady"—Mrs. Main called Lanie to the side —"something incredible is waiting for you. I expect to be apprised of the developments. Perhaps you can bring him along to dinner on Sunday?"

Lanie shook her head, doubtful. "I'm not sure that will happen, but I promise to be there."

"Good day," called Mr. Main, and he spirited his bride through the door.

AFTER THEY LEFT, Jay, Audrey, and Lanie were in total disbelief. Jay could only imagine the range of emotions that Lanie was experiencing. He himself could not believe the twists of fate that brought them all together. He smiled to as he considered his part in the chain of events.

Audrey spoke first, looking at her friend—she knew it was time to get her home. "What do you say we take off, Lanie?"

Nodding, she went to collect her bag. A moment later she returned and with a final hug, she said to Jay, "I can't thank you enough. I'll check on things later this week."

"Please, don't worry," he replied. "Take some time and clear your head. You've been through a lot and I'm so proud of you."

BACK AT HER APARTMENT, Lanie packed while Audrey booked her a hotel room and a seat on the last train to Seattle. "I'm glad you're taking some time away, Lanie. I know it'll do you good."

Lanie was flooded by a well of emotions, stemming from the events of the past couple of weeks. She couldn't imagine how two articles of jewelry crossed paths, apparently for the same purpose, but some fifty years apart. She puzzled that Mr. Main's random visit to the gallery was only two days before. The events culminated into a saga, connecting strangers and changing their futures.

Zipping her suit case closed, she stood and Audrey joined her. They left the condo and walked silently to the car. When they pulled up to the station, they looked at one another. Audrey spoke from her heart. "You deserve the kind of love that will endure, Lanie. Trust the Universe and try to have a good time this week. I'll check on you tomorrow."

Lanie looked at her best friend, then opened the door and walked away.

18

What happens in Seattle stays
in you.

Riding the train northward, Lanie's thoughts were unstoppable. The range of emotions and confusion she was experiencing were all over the place. It was difficult to settle on any one event from the past couple of weeks.

The happenings of today, alone, were so much to absorb. Meeting the Mains, as happenstance as the encounter initially seemed, was an unbelievable twist of fate. The watch she'd purchased for James turned out to be a powerful artifact, one that put the nail into the coffin of two prospective marriages, and over a span of fifty years. She couldn't help but wonder if the bracelet was the same one Bobby presented to Annette so many years ago. Before today, although she believed in the energy and even magic of art, Lanie couldn't conceive such a thing were possible. As the train sped along the track with darkness impending, she felt as if she were free-falling.

Her last conversation with James was today, yet it seemed like an eternity ago. She recalled the moment when their eyes met, possibly for the last time. It broke her heart to say goodbye to him and the ideas she had for their life together. They had many memories as a couple and had made plans, plans that were now irrelevant. The finality of last night and closure of today created a fresh wave of panic. Her vision for tomorrow was now a blank canvas. Although there was a part of her that knew things weren't perfect between them, he had been her man during a crucial time in her life. Inspiring her to do more, he pushed her as only he could. Things would be different now.

Thinking back to the night before, to that fateful rooftop exchange, she felt a fresh wave of heartbreak. Although they'd only been acquainted a short time, there was something special about him. She'd never dream of hurting him and knew that what he saw, couldn't be explained. She'd save the memories of their time together in a place of hope, a shining beacon of light in a world that was sometimes dark. His kiss, the one that stole the breath from her lungs, would remain locked deep in her heart. Maybe, one day, she could replay their times, like watching an old movie. Maybe, one day, it wouldn't cause a crushing hurt to watch. Today wasn't that day.

Thankful for her friends, she was relieved that they would handle the cancellations. Switching off her phone, a shiver ran down her spine as she wondered what the aftermath would be like. So many guests, people they had known as a couple and long before, would be dying to know what happened. There would be no running from their inquisitions. People had morbid curiosities for gossip, particularly the kind that led to broken engagements. *Don't think of that now*, she incanted mentally. *Face that when the time comes.* She agreed with herself to keep her phone off until she returned to Portland on Thursday. That was soon enough to face the music.

She arrived at King Street Station, pulled her bag from

the shelf, and exited with the others. Odd, she was retracing the steps she and Ryan had taken only a week before. She felt different this time around. The butterflies she'd so recently experienced were a part of some other life, or a dream. The gravity of her actions, her deceit, would be with her for a long time.

After hailing a cab, she instructed the driver to take her to the Pineapple Hotel. They drove a short distance, and found it. After paying him, she made her way to the check-in area. She'd never visited this hotel, but Ryan mentioned it during their day here. Wanting any last bit of insight and connection to their brief romance, she asked Audrey to book it for her.

The lobby was wide and lovely. The floors were tiled in marble with a giant mosaic Pineapple at the center. Floor-to-ceiling windows flanked the space, and a colorful array of furnishings were set against the brightly wallpapered backdrop. In the corner was a small bar. Tall white stools snugged against the gleaming counter and faced a mirrored wall. She might just get a glass of wine before heading to her room for the night.

The host, Greg, greeted Lanie cheerfully. "Welcome to Pineapple."

His tone was more than Lanie could handle; not wanting to seem rude, she struggled to bring a smile to her face. "Thank you. I have a reservation under Blackwell, Lanie Blackwell."

Greg typed a few strokes on his keyboard and said, "Yes, I have it right here. You are reserved in a view, king suite for four nights. It looks like this is your first stay with us. Please let us know if you need anything while you are here."

"Thank you," she replied, wanting the exchange to end quickly.

"Would you like two keys or one, Miss Blackwell?"

His cheerful tone was grating—the question a slap in the face, given all that had happened lately. "One, please. Thank you."

Greg inserted a colorful access card into the slot of a machine, and once it turned green, he said, "You're all set. I have you in room 411. Take those elevators," he pointed to the side, "to the top floor. There will be signs directing you to your room."

She was relieved the process was complete and followed his instructions. After using her access card to move the elevator cab, the doors opened to her floor. Following the signs to her room, Lanie noticed the décor along the way. Ever the artist, these color combinations were difficult to miss. There were floral-patterned carpets, brightly painted walls, and a range of print art paying tribute to jazz musicians. It was funky and cheerful, the antithesis of how she was feeling at the moment.

Arriving at her door, Lanie inserted the card into the slot and entered, flipping the light switch on the way. A small foyer led to an ornate mirror and shelf; beneath was a luggage rack. She slid her bag there and placed her purse on the shelf before continuing into the space. As she turned the corner, there was only one item in focus. Beyond the sheer curtains, she could see the outline of the Space Needle. She moved toward it just as she moved toward Ryan. Unable to stop herself, she pulled back the drapes and gazed upon the monument that had changed her life. It was bathed in bright light, a beacon against the night sky. A lone tear ran down her cheek as she pondered the structure. "Was this really a good idea?" she questioned herself aloud before pulling away from the scene.

Replacing the sheers, then dragging the heavy drapes along the wall of windows, she turned from the sight. The suite was large. Even the king-size bed was dwarfed compared to the square footage of the space. Gleaming wood floors were adorned by a few decorative rugs. There were two leather chairs, upholstered in orange and situated around a glass coffee table. Through the double door was a jetted tub and separate tiled shower, large enough to fit two. That realization stung.

"Move forward," she chanted, "one foot in front of the other." She unpacked since she would be here for several days. Once the task was complete, she decided it was time for a glass of wine. Grabbing her room key, she made her way downstairs and to the bar.

She was greeted by a cheerful young woman with spiked blonde hair. "Hi there. How are you tonight?"

"I'm well thank you."

"What can I get you?"

"May I have a glass of pinot noir?"

"Sure thing." The bartender selected a bottle and poured a generous serving into a wide-mouthed glass.

She placed the glass in front of Lanie and asked, "Would you like to start a tab?"

Wanting solitude after the grueling past few days, Lanie declined. "No, thank you. I'll be heading back to my room. It's 411. Can you add this to my room charges?"

"I certainly can." As she keyed the order into her system, she made small talk. "You staying with us for a while?"

Lanie politely responded, "I'll be here for a few days."

"Glad to have you. I'm Elizabeth. We're open until midnight, every night. Come visit me."

The girl was sweet and Lanie didn't want to be rude. "Thank you, Elizabeth. You can count on it."

After signing the ticket, Lanie walked the short distance back to the elevator. Using her access card, she was spirited up to the fourth floor and her hideaway for the next several days.

In for the night, she set the wine at the bedside table and changed into pajamas. After putting on a pair of silk shorts and matching button-up top, she climbed into the oversized bed. Snugged under the comforter, she grabbed the remote and turned the TV on. Wanting to escape from the mind-boggling events that overpowered her lately, she zoned out to Jimmy Kimmel while getting a nice buzz from the over-pour her new friend, Elizabeth, extended. She hadn't eaten all day, and therefore the wine had no obstruction as it entered her blood stream. In no time, she was fast asleep.

———

THE FOLLOWING MORNING Lanie awoke to the sound of the TV. The background noise, coupled with the large glass of wine, helped lull her into a long sleep. Sitting up, she looked at the clock beside the bed and found it was already 7:30. Recalling the events of the past few days, she wondered if she should bury her head under a pillow and stay there. Avoiding things wasn't her way so she stood and made coffee using the little machine near the mini-bar. It smelled wonderful and she was grateful to find fresh creamer in the tiny refrigerator. Waiting for the coffee to brew, she walked to the curtains. Quickly, as if pulling a band aid from a wound, she yanked them back. The room was flooded by brilliant light.

Bracing herself, she studied the towering Space Needle. It wasn't as menacing in the morning light. There was nothing ominous about the structure. Now that she had ridden to the top, only admiration remained. The sound of the coffee maker stopped; Lanie filled the cup she took from the shelf, and added cream before settling into one of the chairs. She had absolutely no plans today. No one was expecting her and there was no gallery to run to. She would drink her coffee slowly, then have a bath in that oversized tub. Later she'd take a walk and find somewhere to eat. After yesterday, she knew she needed the sustenance, even if her heart wasn't in it. Standing, she walked to the bathroom and drew a bath.

⸻

THOUGH IT WAS CLOSED, Jay arrived at the gallery by 9 a.m. on Monday. He went to the back and wrapped a painting that needed to be delivered and made an important phone call. Once he confirmed the recipient was there, he took the painting and walked outside, locking the door behind him.

As he drove the short distance to meet the beneficiary, he smiled to himself. Finding a parking space in the busy downtown structure took longer than expected. He found a spot on the end of a row, just wide enough so he could slide the piece out. Painting in tow, he walked the short distance to the elevator and exited at the lobby. He made his way to the second bank of elevators that led to the office suites above. A kindly woman noticed his hands were full so she asked what floor.

"Six, please. Thanks for your help."

"But of course," she said in a grandmotherly voice.

After waiting on a few other floors, he arrived at his destination. Jay walked up to the reception counter. The gleaming *Oregonian* logo in the backdrop confirmed he was in the right place. Approaching the desk, he plastered a smile on his face and ignored the tiny ball of nerves at the pit of his stomach. He greeted the hipster-looking receptionist, "Hello, I have a delivery for Ryan Glass. It is a surprise from a close friend of his."

The woman behind the counter had jet black hair. Her bangs were cut into a severe line and she wore angel's wing glasses in bright fuchsia. He hoped her attire matched her spirit. Perhaps she was the playful type and would let him pass without announcing him.

She smiled and obliged. "I should announce you but I do love surprises. I saw him earlier and he wasn't as friendly as usual. Seems like he could use some cheering up. His office is along the left wall, toward the back. Do I get to see what you have?"

Jay smiled and responded, "Absolutely; as soon as he sees it, I'll send you back on my way out."

A little disappointed she didn't get a sneak peek, yet understanding the equity in his logic, she called, "Good luck."

The office was abuzz with activity. As one would expect, there were cubicles with low walls at the center. Printers busily shuffled papers as people tapped on keyboards. The room was surrounded by television screens showing news feeds from all over the world. Along the wall were private offices, each with a placard indicating the owner. As he passed, Jay saw several names he was familiar with prominently displayed. Acting as if he belonged, he continued to the left corner until he arrived at the office that belonged to Ryan Glass.

Before entering, he peered inside and saw the figure of a man sitting in a chair, his back to the door. He was looking out the window toward the streets below. Jay couldn't see his face. He tapped at the door frame to announce himself. Ryan turned around. The blank expression quickly turned to one of skepticism. Jay couldn't miss the transition and decided he'd better start talking.

"Hi, Ryan. It's Jay from the gallery, Lanie's assistant—well, friend and assistant."

His response was tepid. "I remember. Why are you here?"

He took a deep breath and started. "Could I sit?"

Showing good manners, Ryan agreed. "Yes, but I don't have much time. There's a staff meeting at ten."

"I understand." He paused, then explained the reason for his visit. "Look, I know what happened the other night. Lanie told me how you saw her at Departure. She was very upset. You can't imagine how upset she was."

Ryan was silent, and his face flashed melancholy then back to stoic in a matter of seconds.

"What you don't know is that she *was* engaged."

Ryan stood and paced to the window. Once again, his back was to Jay. When he spoke, his tone was ice. "I can't imagine what this has to do with me."

Understandably, this would be a battle. "I can only imagine how you are feeling at this point."

He turned then, eyebrows raised and with a red face, he spoke.

"I feel like an idiot. Hearing that she was engaged to that guy, well, I guess she was taking me for some kind of joy ride. Was I a last fling before she tied the knot? Did she use the mixer as an easy way to meet someone?"

Jay walked toward Ryan. Remaining calm, he said, "You were anything but a joy ride. Lanie is one of the most honest and kind-hearted people I know. She was about to marry the wrong person, then she bumped into you."

Ryan's face softened at the reference, realizing she must confide in Jay. He didn't know what was coming next.

"Her fiancé wasn't right for her. The whole thing, going to that event, it started as a test. He actually egged it on."

Ryan was quiet for longer and Jay continued, "Did she act like a woman after a last fling?" Jay paused, wanting to find the right words. "They never kissed the way you and she did."

Ryan's expression was sullen and his words matched. "It was just a kiss. A few dates, a few kisses, no big deal. Obviously, she didn't think much of it since she's not the one standing here. You are."

Acknowledging his truth, Jay agreed. "You're right. I am the one standing here. There's a good chance she'll never contact you again, but not because it isn't what she wants. That girl fell all the way for you. She hasn't ever done that before. You were the first person who made her throw caution to the wind. I saw the way she looked at you and how her face glowed after your day in Seattle."

Ryan eyes were affixed to his feet as he listened to Jay's speech. When he looked up, there was a small change in his expression. His voice was resigned when he spoke. "It doesn't matter now, none of it does."

Not afraid to use old fashioned guilt, Jay retorted, "Maybe it doesn't, but I wanted you to know that I believed you that day when you told me you wouldn't give up."

He scoffed at this. "She belongs to someone else."

Jay lowered his voice before speaking. "She belongs to you, Ryan. That night, what you saw, was Lanie breaking it off. They were supposed to get married this Saturday. A week before her wedding and only a week after meeting you, she knew about *you* what she had never been certain of after six years with James."

Ryan's shock at this revelation was written on his face.

Stop while you're ahead, Jay thought. "She painted this after her day with you. Seems to me, you are the rightful owner." He placed the painting on a bookshelf near the wall, and in closing said, "I'll leave you to your staff meeting." He walked out of the office leaving Ryan in awe.

━━━

THROUGHOUT THE MEETING, Ryan was in a daze. As if the past couple of days hadn't been enough to swallow, Jay's revelation was yet another twist. He couldn't imagine calling a wedding off a week before the date. Though he had more questions than answers and was still upset by her deception, he couldn't help but wonder how Lanie was doing.

Finally, the meeting concluded and when it did his boss called him over. He liked Erve and had learned a lot from him over the years. His slight stature and salt-and-pepper hair could fool people—Ryan knew he had a black belt in Taekwondo and a long military career. All that and he was a damn fine reporter.

As a supervisor, he brought many characteristics one would expect of a person with his background, leadership among them. One unexpected component of Erve's personality—he was a softy. Even after all he'd seen in his life, he still led with empathy. It showed in all he did for his family, the community and the *Oregonian* staff.

"Walk with me." Erve's comment was a command.

Knowing his boss, Ryan realized he was in for a talking-to. Side by side they covered the distance toward Ryan's office and when they arrived, Erve shut the door. Ryan spoke first. It was best to steer the conversation. "What's on your mind, Erve?"

Erve's eyes homed in and he replied, "Funny, I was about to ask you that same question."

"All good here." Ryan tried to brush his attention away.

"I've known you a long time, kid; seems to me you've

got something weighing on you. Care to let an old friend in on it?"

Ryan plastered a fake smile on his face, confirming Erve's suspicion that things were not fine. "Nothing to concern yourself over. I've got some research to get to today."

Erve knew Ryan well enough to understand he wouldn't be sharing any time soon. Still, he didn't like the glum expression and distant look in his eyes. Wanting to help, he offered the best option he could think of. "Why don't we get a workout in this afternoon? I could use a sparring partner."

Realizing the ploy but hard pressed to resist the strenuous activity a match with Erve presented, he agreed. "You're on."

Erve squelched a sinister grin before speaking. "Meet you at the elevators, say five thirty?"

Not missing a thing and knowing he was in for an ass-kicking, Ryan agreed. "Yup, see ya then boss."

Smirking now as he walked to the door. Erve had to toss an early jab in Ryan's direction. "And no whining to HR when I level you, kid."

"Whatever you say, sir." Ryan's smart-ass reply gave him hope that the kid would snap out of whatever was bothering him.

After he left, Ryan walked to the door and closed it. Throughout the meeting, his brain was working overtime as he tried to process what Jay told him. The missing link —whatever was behind the fabric that covered the painting he'd left, seemingly without permission.

Closing the distance to the shelf where it stood, Ryan studied it a bit longer. Then he noticed a card attached to the front. Pulling it off, he saw it was Jay's business card. When he turned it over, he saw a note that read:

"Climbing to the top can be quite scary, especially when you've been taught to fear the view."

Setting the card aside, Ryan could wait no longer. He moved the canvas forward and unwrapped it from the back. As he let the fabric fall from the top, what he saw took his breath away.

———

AT 5:30 ON THE DOT, Ryan met Erve at the elevator. Already dressed in his shorts and T-shirt, Ryan was ready to go. Today, of all days, he needed to sweat it out. The two waited silently for the elevator to reach them. When it did, Erve pressed the button that lead to the 18th-floor gymnasium.

The door opened and they crossed the hall to the entrance. They entered into the state-of-the-art facility that only the tenants of Fox Tower could access. The gym offered an unobstructed view of the city that most would find inspiring. Ryan noticed none of it today.

Swiftly putting on gloves, they went for a quick warm-up at the speed-bags. Once their hasty warm-up was finished, they were ready to face off. As they arrived at the ring, the silence between them was deafening. It was a tactic for certain and one that Ryan relished in today.

Lou, their sometimes coach and referee, saw them enter and made his way to the ring. As he addressed the two, his tone was challenging. "A little game of cat and mouse today?"

Their grunts in response confirmed that it was going down. Lou knew he was in for a treat. He stood on the sidelines as the two opponents sized each other up. They danced around the mat without breaking eye contact. Their silence was finally interrupted by Erve.

As he skipped in rhythm with Ryan he challenged him to a bet.

"After I kick your ass, you're going to tell me what's bothering you."

Sniffing then finding a parallel retort, Ryan teased, "And after I level you, ol' man, you will buy me a dinner."

Lou chuckled, thriving in the scene.

As the words exited Ryan's mouth, Erve lunged forward and sent a well-placed jab to the side of his face.

Shaking it off, Ryan responded in kind, connecting solidly with Erve's jaw.

They stepped back to size each other up and strategize how best to dominate their opponent.

In time, the two lunged forward and began administering a series of blows. Solar plexus, check; jaw, check; and let's not overlook a solid smash or two to the eye socket. They were crushing it up today and Lou was in heaven as he stood on the sidelines.

The kid looked pissed and Lou sensed it concerned whatever Erve wanted him to spill. The old man was in his usual form, giving Ryan a run for his money. If he were a betting man— and Lou was not—his money would be on the kid. Anger was propelling him today.

As the thought entered his mind, he watched an unbelievable series of hits. Ryan administered a gut shot, then a right followed by a left hook, and Erve was on his back. It was time for Lou to become ref, even though he would love to see the finale. "Time," he called, though no clock was running.

Erve tried to blow it off as he stood. He huffed as he spoke his next words, "I let him win. The kid looks a little thin—someone's gotta feed him."

Lou chuckled as Ryan folded in half, resting his hands on his knees. He strained to catch his breath.

"Nice match, you two. A little longer on the warm up next time and maybe an Epsom soak tonight." He left them and moved on to a group of ladies who had come in for their training session.

Tossing a towel in Ryan's direction, Erve said, "Hit the showers kid, we're headed to Higgins for dinner."

Standing to his full height, Ryan walked slowly to the locker room. He needed the shower, and dinner couldn't hurt.

———

THEY CHOSE a booth at the bar and were promptly greeted by a jolly server.

"Good evening gentlemen, I'm Paulie. Can I bring you some drinks while you look at the menu?"

Erve chimed in, "Yeah, I'll have an IPA."

Ryan agreed; the carbs would be well received after their sweat session. "Make that two."

"Coming right up. Today's specials are on the board." Paulie gestured to the wall.

Once he was gone, the men studied the menu. After a quick perusal, they set them aside.

Within no time Paulie returned, beers in hand. After setting them down, he asked, "Have you decided what you'll have?"

Erve answered first, "Yeah, I'll have the burger, medium rare, with the beet salad to start."

Ryan was next and couldn't resist getting in one more jab, "Since he's buying, bring me the steak, medium-rare, and a salad."

"You've got it guys. Enjoy the beers while I put your order in." Paulie left them to their drinks.

Erve had waited long enough, and this little counseling

session was costing him so he got to the point. "I'm buying —start talking, kid."

Ryan took a sip of his beer and returned it to the table. Looking at his friend, a man he had known for over fifteen years, there was no doubt he could trust him with the matter.

"Remember the girl I met when you forced me to cover for Jane at that singles thing?"

"Yeah, how could I forget? You were on cloud nine after the fateful night. Seems to me, you should be the one buying me dinner after that."

He sneered the next words. "Not so fast. Turns out she's engaged or was engaged."

"Shit." Erve's response mirrored Ryan's thoughts.

"Yeah. My sentiments exactly."

Not missing the semantics, Erve spoke. "Was engaged or is engaged?"

"Was, apparently. If I can believe her friend, I guess she broke it off."

"Was or is really doesn't matter, does it?" Erve's logic was not always in line with Ryan's.

"I'm no home wrecker. It's pretty low to take another guys woman, don't you think?"

"First of all," Erve said, his voice showing obvious frustration, "no one can take anyone who doesn't want to be taken."

Ryan was silent and took another slug of his beer.

"Second, this isn't the turn of the century. I'm pretty sure the woman has a mind of her own. She's not the guy's property or anything, so what's the problem?"

Erve always had a way of calling him out. Still, the deceit was bothering him. "She wasn't honest about it, Erve."

Erve was hard pressed to rebut his statement. "I can

understand how that would be an issue, but it's only been a couple of weeks since that event even happened. Maybe she was going to tell you but was waiting for the right time. What did she say when you asked her about it?"

Here it comes, Ryan thought, the fatherly version of Erve was about to show up. "I haven't talked to her, not since I saw her having dinner with the guy."

Erve's eyes were bulging, his words like rapid fire. "So, let me get this straight, you saw her having dinner and gave up?"

Ryan's silence gave Erve pause, then he questioned him further.

"I'm confused, if you didn't speak, how do you know about the engagement?"

Taking a breath, Ryan responded. "Her friend; he came into the office today and told me the whole story. I guess she had been with the guy for over six years. They were supposed to get married next weekend, and she called it off. He said I walked into the middle of her breaking up with him."

Old softy was combining with the drill sergeant to form a response. "Just so we're clear—you met a girl who you were crazy about, happiest I've ever seen you; the two of you went out on a few dates and you had the time of your lives; she was so enamored by you that she cancelled her wedding, and now you're sitting across from me sulking?"

"Why do I tell you anything?" Ryan breathed the words.

"Because you know I'll give it to you straight. You're fucking up, kid. What's more, this sounds like a great story for the romance section."

"Great," Ryan said. "My love life is your next headline."

"I'm only going to say this once, so listen carefully. Life

is too God-damned short to be wasting chances. You walked into each other's lives for a reason. You don't look fate in the eye and say no thank you. Seems to me you're a scared little boy. After all that you've done in life, I can't believe you are too chicken shit to see this one through."

A tentative Paulie arrived in time to place their meals in front of them. Slow to speak, but a consummate professional, he did. "Can I bring you anything else, a couple of shots maybe?"

They had a chuckle and Paulie took his leave while the friends ate dinner in amicable silence.

19

Going the distance.

Lanie spent her first day in Seattle holed up in the hotel room. She had every intention of getting out but found she had little inclination. Instead, she ordered room service and spent the day crying while watching daytime TV. In the evening she managed to make it downstairs for a visit with her new friend, Elizabeth, the bartender. The first night's pour was no fluke. She carried the glass back to the cocoon of her suite, and sipped the night away while eating microwaved popcorn.

Today, she resolved to leave the hotel. Dressed in a white smock dress, she slipped on her beige flats and added a dotted scarf to cover her shoulders. Finding sunglasses, she left the safety of her hideout and ventured outdoors.

Walking along the quiet Queen Anne streets, she had no destination in mind as she put one foot in front of the other. It felt good to move, to obey the street signs while blending in anonymously with other pedestrians. Lanie traveled for some time before arriving at the center of downtown Seattle. The monorail track ran overhead and she heard a range of street performers along the way.

Arriving at the mall, she thought about doing some shopping but had no desire. She wanted to find gifts for Jay and Audrey, to thank them for all they had taken care of, but tomorrow would be soon enough.

Her stomach grumbled and she realized she hadn't eaten yet. Seeing a nice-looking café called Fare Start, she walked to the front and pushed open the glass doors. When she entered a cheerful young man greeted her.

"Hi, are you here for lunch?"

"I am, thank you."

"Sure, right this way."

He indicated a seat near the window where she could people-watch as she ate. Once seated, he handed her the menu. Quickly, a server arrived. "Hello, I'm John. Can I bring you something to drink while you decide?"

After looking over the selection, she had to try their specialty. "I'll have the lavender lemonade please."

"Great choice. Before I leave, I want to let you know we have a terrific smoked trout board on special today, and the soup is a crab bisque."

"Thank you," she replied.

When John left, Lanie set the menu down and looked outside. It was a busy Tuesday afternoon, and though she had no watch on, she'd guessed it was around 1 p.m. The streets were active with professionals heading to and from lunch. She could pick out several tourists enjoying the Pacific Northwest's largest city. She had to admit, Seattle always had a special place in her heart, and more so after that day with Ryan. The thought made her sad and immediately guilty. She should be more depressed by the conclusion of her engagement to James.

Absently, Lanie picked up the menu and noticed an "about us" section on the front. She was surprised to learn that the restaurant was run by ex-convicts who'd been taught the culinary arts to help them find new prospects after incarceration. What a great idea, she thought, and immediately felt remorse for own self-indulgence. Her problems were small compared to some. Saving her from further self-condemnation, John returned with the fresh lemonade.

"Have you decided what you'd like for lunch today?"

She hadn't even considered it. She didn't feel hungry at all. "The specials you mentioned—the trout and soup—that sounds terrific."

"Great choices. I'll bring the soup out first."

"Thank you," she replied, and he removed the menu.

Taking of sip of the lemonade, Lanie was in heaven. She hadn't realized how thirsty she was and this hit the spot. The juice wasn't overly sweet and had the perfect lavender essence.

With nothing to occupy her but this moment of solitude among the crowd, her mind wandered to James. After so many years together, it was odd to know he was no longer her concern. Life would move on and he would become a part of the past. The idea raised a combination of emotions, loss being at the top, but also relief. The anxiety and cold feet she had been feeling as their wedding date loomed closer were a lot to manage. The nagging doubts she experienced were greater than her excitement at the prospect of starting a life with him. Even she knew there was something off about the fact that they'd never chosen to live together.

Saving her from another round of mental circles, John arrived with the crab bisque. "Here you are," he said as he placed the bowl in front of Lanie. "This," he added, then settled a tiny pitcher beside the bowl, "is Sherry. It can be a delicious compliment to the soup. I'll leave it here so you can add it yourself. I recommend starting with a few drops until the flavor is to your liking."

Lanie smiled politely as he departed.

Picking up the little pitcher, she added a few drops as instructed. Stirring gently, she tasted the broth. Flavors of smoked paprika and the sea melded into a wonderful combination. Still salty, she added a little more of the Sherry and stirred. Savoring the next spoonful, the flavor was to her liking. The extra bite that the liquor gave the buttery soup awakened her depressed taste buds. Her stomach juices thanked her for waiting until such a feast was available.

John's return was well timed and his face showed delight when he saw the empty bowl. He placed a wooden board with smoked trout, pickled egg, marinated onions, horseradish cream, and sprigs of asparagus in front of her. "I hope you like the trout as much as the soup. Do you need anything else before I leave?"

Surveying the platter, she said, "I think this will do it, and please send my compliments to the chef. That soup was incredible."

"I'm glad you liked it. Enjoy."

Lanie was thrilled with her selection. Everything was so fresh and the combination of items blended delightfully. Before she knew it, the last morsels had vanished. She was embarrassed when John returned. There was nothing lady-like about the way she leveled that platter of food.

"I see you enjoyed the trout," he said with a smile.

For once, in the past weeks, Lanie was without an ounce of shame. "I did. Everything was divine."

"Well then, might I interest you in dessert?"

She paused, considering, but wanted to save something for later. She had all the time in the world and no agenda.

"Thank you; I'll pass, but you can count on me coming back."

"I understand. I'll leave this with you. Please take your time."

Lanie pulled bills from her purse to cover the check and tip. Standing, she was ready to take a stroll back toward the hotel.

⸻

RYAN HAD A LESS than fitful night's sleep because of his visit from Jay and the sparring session with Erve. His ribs felt tender and he had a mild headache from the aftermath of Erve's mean left hook. As the morning light shined into his bedroom, he remembered the words of his old friend. He was right; she wasn't married yet and there hadn't been a lot of time for her to open up. Remembering her face as they sat on the train, she was trying to tell him something but he cut her off. Since he'd already learned her true identity and profession, his interruption may have taken her off course. Maybe.

He thought of the painting Lanie made and the words Jay penned on the back of his business card. Recalling their conversations about her family, he imagined she was under a great deal of pressure. Did their expectations have something to do with her becoming engaged in the first place? He cared for her, was even falling for the woman, and he worried it must be a rough time for her.

He decided a run would clear his head. He quickly got into shorts, a fresh T-shirt, and tennis shoes then headed for the door. His floating home was at the edge of slab town, closer to the industrial section of town. As he set out, he chose the challenge of the hills and ran in the general direction of Washington Park. There he could get lost in the trails that led to the top of the reserve. Though it wasn't even 8 a.m., it was already a warm day and soon his shirt was drenched.

Navigating the city streets, he was oblivious to the happenings around him. He couldn't care less about the charming homes he was surrounded by. He wanted to feel the burn and hoped this action would drive the questions from his mind. Pushing himself to go faster, he finally reached one entrance to the park. There were stairs, which he took two at a time until he arrived at the landing in front of a large fountain. He was winded from the exertion of his pace. His legs were screaming for a rest and he finally obliged. He stood, hands on his hips, and surveyed the view.

His thoughts wandered back to Lanie and he knew what he would do. She was worth pursuing. If calling off her engagement had anything to do with their time, they owed it to each other to see it through.

Taking a deep breath, he set out again and made his way back home. Running at an even pace, he made it in under thirty minutes. *Good time*, he acknowledged mentally as he collapsed through the front door.

He tossed his soiled clothes and entered the large glass shower. The hot water soothed his tender muscles. Shutting the tap off, he took a towel from the bar and raked it over his body then his hair. After applying a dab of hair goop and a few splashes of after-shave, he then went for the dresser. Pulling on a clean T-shirt, boxer briefs and jeans, he was ready to make the call.

A fresh wave of nerves tugged at him as he took the phone in hand. Finding her contact, he paused for a beat before tapping the number. The phone didn't ring but went straight into voicemail. Great, he thought, it was hard enough to dial her the first time and now he'd have to do it twice. She was probably on the other line or receiving a call simultaneous to his. He pushed the number again but the same thing happened. His call went straight to voicemail. He was now a little bit worried. Talking himself down from the ledge, he gave it a few more minutes. While he waited, he collected a pair of socks from the drawer and put them on, then found a pair of black converse. After lacing them up, he tried her number again. The immediate response of her voicemail set him off.

He paced, not sure if he should be concerned or feel dissed. What could he do? He didn't know where she lived and the gallery was closed on Tuesdays. Then he remembered he had Jay's card. Heading to the kitchen, he opened his wallet and pulled it out. Yes, printed on the front was his cell number. Making quick time of the action, he dialed the digits and waited for what seemed an eternity.

Jay answered on the third ring. "Hello?"

"Jay, yes, this is Ryan, Ryan Glass."

"Oh, hello, Ryan. What can I do for you?"

Taking a deep breath, Ryan wasn't sure if his actions were, stalkerish but went for it anyway. "I thought about what you said yesterday, and well, I want to talk to Lanie. Thing is, she's not answering her phone. Actually, it isn't even ringing. It just goes straight to voicemail."

There was a brief hesitation on the line. Then Jay responded.

"I'm not surprised. She mentioned she would be turning it off while she was away."

"Away?" Ryan's voice showed he was disappointed to learn that.

"Yes, she left on Sunday night. Took the train up to Seattle."

Ryan smiled to himself. She wouldn't go there if she

wasn't thinking about him. Their day in Seattle had been perfect. "Do you know when she's coming back?"

"Not until Thursday."

"Oh, that's too bad," he replied. His disappointment was evident.

Jay reveled in his matchmaking abilities, and played Cupid a little while longer. "I can find out where she's staying. Our friend Audrey booked the room for her."

Decisive now, Ryan knew what to do. "Would you? I'm heading out the door in fifteen minutes, on my way there. Could you text me the hotel information?"

Jumping for joy through the line but straining to keep his voice calm, Jay assured. "I will. Stand by and I'll send you the details shortly."

"Thank you, Jay, and thank you for bringing the painting."

"You're more than welcome. Take good care of her, or else."

Ryan chuckled but agreed. "I will."

"And Ryan—good luck!"

After ending the call, Ryan grabbed his overnight bag and tossed in a change of clothes. He went to the kitchen to get water and snacks for the drive and slid his wallet in his pocket. He managed to leave the house in under 20 minutes. As he walked to the parking garage, he wondered if this was a crazy idea. Oh well, he would do it anyway. If she could cancel an engagement soon after meeting him, he could show up unannounced during her vacation. Turnabout was fair play. He got to his Silver Range Rover, clicked the unlock button, and tossed the bag into the passenger seat. Shaking his head, he fired up the engine. He was going for it.

THE MOMENT RYAN and Jay disconnected, he dialed Audrey's number. As she answered he could hear the rambunctious sounds of her family in the background. This terrified and also made him a little sad, for he knew a life such as this would not be in the cards for him. As a loud scream erupted, blighting Audrey's hello, he thought, maybe it was for the better.

"Lee, settle down!" she yelled in response to his obvious glee. "Mommy is on the phone. Jay?" she managed.

"Yes. Audrey, you'll never guess who I just spoke to."

"No time for a guessing game here, Jay. Who was it?"

"Ryan Glass."

Her silence through the line allowed even more of the background excitement to make its way into Jay's ear. He could hear squeals of delight coupled with the sounds of Disney songs. It made him smile, and a feeling of joy washed over him. Time to snap out of it—he had a duty to fulfill.

"What did he say and why did he call you?"

Certain there was no way to explain the story to Audrey in her surroundings, he summarized. "Apparently he has been trying to call Lanie but her phone is off. When I told him that she was in Seattle, he said he was going to meet her."

"Woah. That is crazy, but also damn romantic."

"I agree. Only problem is, he doesn't know where she's staying. I told him you made the reservations and that I'd find out and get back to him."

Audrey was quiet for a minute. This was a big deal. What if Lanie didn't want to see Ryan? That's illogical, she reasoned. The girl called off her wedding after a few inno-cent dates with the man. Hoping for the best, she blurted, "The Pineapple. It's in Queen Anne."

Too excited for his own skin, Jay squealed. "Thank

you. I'm calling him with the details now. If only we could be a fly on the wall to witness that reunion."

Audrey couldn't help herself. This was a wonderful development for her best friend. She wanted this love for her. "Jay, I don't know what you've been up to and I do expect you to tell me every last detail when I can actually hear the story. Good work. I hope—"

He cut her off. "Me too. Bye."

As soon as they disconnected, Jay texted the information to Ryan's number. He breathed deeply, knowing that a certain angel in heaven was guiding his actions.

—————

RYAN HEARD the phone buzz beside him. Removing it from the center console, he glanced at the incoming text. It was from Jay.

"She's staying at the Pineapple Hotel in Queen Anne."

After seeing those words, Ryan had to remind himself of the speed limit. It was almost impossible to ease off the gas. He was overjoyed by the message and knew she wouldn't be staying at his favorite Seattle hotel if she thought nothing of their time. A sense of certainty took over.

20

Collision of Souls

Taking her time on the walk back to the hotel, Lanie went through the park that surrounded the Space Needle. It was cutting to seek nearness to the time she and Ryan shared, but she couldn't stop. Her eyes rose to its towering height. Held in a virtual trance, her feet were the only functioning part of her body. Unable to pull her attention from the enormous structure, she acknowledged that her day with Ryan was little more than a fleeting fancy.

Suddenly, she was halted by an obstacle and lost her balance. A hand on her elbow caused her to look up and when she did, the man for whom she'd been longing was setting her straight. It was impossible to comprehend. Once again, Lanie had walked into the chest of Adonis. Time stopped as she tried to process what was right in front of her. She was mute.

"Ms. Blackwell, it seems we have a problem."

Awe and disbelief swept over her. Grappling for a response, after what seemed an eternity she managed, "A problem?"

"Yes, it seems you need someone to keep an eye on you, since you are often looking in the wrong direction."

She needed to say something clever, for the man was in her path and it wasn't a mistake. "Are you that someone?"

His eyes penetrated hers and when he spoke, there was sheer determination in his tone. "I'd like to find out."

The world around them disappeared. Before she could respond, Ryan kissed Lanie and a small sound escaped her throat. The marriage of tenderness and possession intertwined and everything came into focus. She had taken her last chance and it led her to the place where she belonged.

21

Sunday Dinner

The day was mild thanks to the light breeze that balanced the sunshine and warm temperatures. Mrs. Main stood in the kitchen with Ryan by her side. Looking down at the lawn below, they could see Lanie chasing Lee while carrying baby Lily on her hip. The dogs were jumping for joy, ecstatic with the company. Thomas watched from his seat on the lawn.

Mrs. Main turned to Ryan and said, "The magic of that watch sure gave you a chance at happiness. Now, what do you intend to do with it, young man?"

Ryan was humored, but kept a straight face, for his companion was a tad intimidating. "I can't believe I'm saying this aloud but from the first time I saw her, I wanted to keep her. Next month I need to visit my agent in New York. October is the most stunning time of year there and I'd like to bring Lanie along. She and I had a special history with the Space Needle in Seattle. I was thinking we should maybe visit the Empire State building while we're there."

Her smile created a softness, explaining her former

youth. She said, "It is never too soon to start the rest of your life with the person you are meant to be with. I can see it in her eyes, she is in love with you. I have one request, though—actually, a demand."

Not sure what was coming next, Ryan was succinct. "Oh?"

"You must marry here. This home was made for loving memories and we've spent far too many years without the sound of laughter. Do we have an arrangement?"

The woman spoke with such certainty and a lifetime of experience he could not deny. His thoughts had been on marrying Lanie since their first date. "Of course, I would have to consult my future wife." He grinned, nervous at the serious conversation. After all, he'd only known her for a few weeks, but he'd seen enough of the world to know love like theirs didn't come around often. When you find something great, you have to embrace it with everything you have. "I was thinking we might take our honeymoon in France. The Eiffel Tower could be our next conquest together."

Patting his hand, a knowing look on her face, she agreed. "I can think of nothing more romantic."

As she spoke the words, a man's voice came from behind. "I thought you and Thomas had reconciled and here you are flirting with this young buck. I'm confused."

Ryan turned to see a strong-looking man. His complexion was weathered from age and time in the elements. A sweet-faced, mature woman stood by his side.

Mrs. Main hastened to introduce them. "Bobby and Becky Smith, meet Ryan Glass."

They shook hands, then Ryan remembered something. "Wait a minute, *the* Bobby? The cancelled wedding Bobby?"

His deep voice responded with laughter, "None other.

Am I to understand that watch struck again? Are you not the young man who won his future bride after she made that fateful purchase?"

Shaking his head and in awe of the events of the past, Ryan agreed. "Let's hope I'm that lucky."

"Young man, there's no such thing as luck. Follow your heart and the world will open the path."

⸻

OCTOBER 30TH, 2019

The tireless New York City lights flickered around them as they stood at the top of the Empire State building. Lanie perched near the edge, unafraid of the height. Ryan tapped her shoulder from behind. She turned and saw he was kneeling. In his hand was a miniature figurine of the Eiffel Tower. Around it hung a sparkling diamond ring. Confused, then elated, tears welled in her eyes.

"Lanie, meeting you was the most magical thing that ever happened to me. You inspire me, and make me feel at home. I want to build a life with you. Be mine? Marry me?"

For a moment, she couldn't speak. She never imagined feeling this way and she knew he was her destiny. The love she felt for him had grown. She never wanted to let him go. Independence be damned, he was her man and she would belong to him in every possible way.

"I will marry you."

⸻

JUNE 23RD, 2020

Lanie stood at the observation deck, taking in the view from the top of the Eiffel Tower. It was the highest structure she and Ryan had taken on yet. His hand held hers, and with a pang of excitement she noticed their wedding bands. He was hers, and she had the best wedding gift possible to give him.

She leaned back slightly to whisper in his ear.

"I have a surprise for you."

As he spoke, his voice was muffled by the wind and proximity. "My darling wife, I need no more than you."

"Are you sure there isn't a little something else you'd like?"

Pulling back to study her face, Ryan couldn't help but think she looked more radiant than ever. Married life was agreeing with her. "I have more than any man could hope to. I have you all to myself."

"For now," she said. The words hung in the air.

"What do you mean, for now?" He spoke with a tinge of panic. She didn't look like she was having cold feet. Anyway, didn't that generally happen before the wedding?

"I mean, we have about eight months of this until . . ."

His eyes bulged—was she saying what he thought she was? His voice hitched as he asked, "Until?"

"Until the baby arrives." She smiled, overjoyed and a little concerned about his reaction. This was definitely not what they'd planned, but nothing had gone according to plan from the moment they first bumped into one another.

Ryan's face was a range of emotions and when he spoke, his soft words assured. "You are the most precious creature. How did I ever get this lucky?"

Her cheeky reply brought him back to the stranger-than-fiction reality that had encircled them from the start. "Young man, there is no such thing as luck."

Made in the USA
San Bernardino, CA
29 April 2019